West Texas Dead

A Kailey and Shinto Mystery

FRANCES HIGHT

For permissions contact: frances@franceshight.com

Cover by Bavarart

This book is dedicated to Midland, Texas
where a piece of my heart is buried.

FRANCES HIGHT

Chapter One

Kailey and Shinto

The heavy gray metal stairway door opened reluctantly and inched closed. I took the stairs two at a time. No sense being late. I slid my key card in and waited for the beep to enter the squad room. Fresh out of FBI forensics classes in Dallas, it was time to prove my department's sending me there hadn't been a waste of my time and their money. I adjusted my belt, and felt for my gun and handcuffs, ready for the next chapter. The keylock clicked and I pushed. Kailey Carmichael, brand new crime scene analyst, top of her class, and back on the job.

I heard Shinto before I saw her. My head abuzz with forensics notes and lectures and case examples, I can be excused for not recognizing my BFF from before there were BFF's. I expected my first day back to the squad after forensics school to have a little drama. Trust Shinto Elliot to add her delicate spin to the concept.

I came in the back of the squad room in time to see a rookie I didn't recognize slap Shinto Elliot on her ass as she walked between the row of desks. All chatter died down. Even the phones cooperated and quit ringing.

I stopped and crossed my arms. This was going to be good.

Two, make it three seconds later, Shinto had the hapless rookie on the floor, arm bent backwards and up in a wrist lock, her foot pressed onto the back of his neck. Not a man in the room moved to help the guy. They knew better.

"Good to see you haven't changed, girl," I said.

"Kailey?" Shinto switched hands and used the free one to tuck a strand of hair behind her ear. "Holy frijoles. They told me you belonged here. I looked for you, but I missed you by a few weeks. Big D get tired of you showing off that big brain of yours?"

"Got back yesterday. On the job today."

"We need to catch up," Shinto cranked the arm in her grasp a little higher. The guy squirmed and grunted.

"Right? When you get off?"

"Six-ish. You?"

"Same."

"Owww. Owww. All right. I'm sorry. Ahhhhh!" Today's unfortunate object lesson squealed, his face smashed into the tile floor. Every man in the squad winced for him, and stifled grins at the same time. Apparently, my best friend had made quite an impression in her short time on the job.

"Hell, Shinto, let the poor dude up. Your ass is fine, I grant you, but is it worth all this?"

She chuffed and said, "Every bit of it, girl."

"Glad to see your time in Afghanistan put to good use. MP a tough gig over there?"

Shinto let go and dusted her hands off before helping the guy up. "Tough? Nah. Different? Yes. They tell me I don't get to blow stuff up here in Midland."

"They do frown on that," I said. "But we can always find something to amuse you, like teaching manners to rookies maybe?"

Shinto laughed and clapped her pupil on the back. "No hard feelings, man? Just a reaction, you know? PTSD and all."

Dispatch over the squad room speakers cut short our reunion.

"MVA downtown. Injuries. MFD called to the scene. Buses rolling."

"Shinto, you and Allen take that," the Captain called. "Kailey, welcome back. Your old partner's around. Go find Mike and earn your pay."

Chapter Two

Junior

I pulled the crumpled business card from my front pocket and checked the address: 1500 Midland Court Drive, Office 333.

Today is the day I, Junior Alvarez, Number D723497, meet my PO Mr. Robert Miller. Parole officer is a fancy term for leash, and the system loves its leashes.

I looked above the entrance of a ten-story building and saw the numerals etched in gold—1500—over a bank of revolving doors. I heard the whoosh as people pushed through them, felt the cool puffs of A/C scooped out from the lobby with every turn. The street scene behind me reflected in its glass doors. The shabby dude in the center of the scene clearly did not belong. Dressed like an ex-con. Posture like an ex-con. Haircut like an ex-con. Even a low-rent downtown like Midland, Texas has its standards, and I didn't measure up.

I hesitated, deciding if I really wanted to go inside. The screech of tires yanked my head from my ass, and I squinted at the reflection in front of me to see a black jacked-up dually Ford pickup jump the curb, clip a blue U.S. mailbox, and send it flying. People dove to the right and left to get out of its path. I saw the driver through the windshield slumped over the wheel, head bobbing like a crazy, out-of-control doll.

The hot breath of the Ford blew past me, and I glanced over at a car stopped in the exit driveway. The truck bore down on the little red sedan, and the wide-eyed woman inside traded looks with me as the front of the pickup buried the hapless vehicle under three-quarters of a ton of Detroit steel.

The whole thing took less than a few seconds and played out in my head for what seemed like hours.

The crash of crumpling metal, the squeal of tires and shrieks of women faded as I ran for the wreck. I heard nothing but my own breathing and the thud of my heart when I rounded the front of the Ford and saw the damage.

The jacked-up truck with its oversized tires rested on top of the little car like a mastiff dominating a poodle. The driver of the truck slumped against his door, unconscious. I didn't worry about him. I still envisioned the wide eyes of the woman staring back at me the instant before the crash. Where the hell was she?

The icy tang of gasoline cleared my head and added urgency to my movements. I had seconds, maybe, before this beauty ignited and ruined my whole afternoon.

On the far side of the wreck, the door to the tiny sedan accordioned down to half its height; a fabric of shattered glass hung down like a sparkling tongue. I ran to it and pulled the glass free to get a better look inside, scared shitless of what I might see.

The still body of the woman formed itself around a crumpled steering column. The impact had shoved her sideways and pinned her. I saw her eyes blink, and she licked her lips. Those big blue eyes met mine, and she smiled as if to say, "Some mess I made, huh?"

"Don't you worry," I said. "We got this. Piece of cake."

Someone yelled, "Fire!" What happened after that comes in flashes. My hands yanking on the door, trying to leverage it open. Hunks of doorframe coming away in my fists; pulling bits of car and tossing them behind me. Clawing my way toward the poor woman, all the while smelling gas and waiting for the explosion to come.

I touched her arm, and she closed her eyes. Did she faint? Die? Give up? I didn't know and didn't really care. No way I could leave her to be incinerated.

I had leverage, and I've been told I'm pretty strong. I hooked my hands under her arms and pulled and pulled, fully expecting her to slide from the car. She wouldn't budge.

Far as I could tell, she should have moved a little. Dash held up pretty good. No collapse of the car frame on her legs. The steering wheel bent and pushed into her waist, but this woman seemed to be in decent shape. What the hell?

I tried again, pulling hard, with people yelling all around us. "Get out!" "It's going up!" "Save yourself!"

I wrestled and twisted to pull her to me with no friggin' luck, until I noticed the wide strap across her torso. The seatbelt she'd dutifully clicked into place before starting on this epic disaster held on tight like a champ.

I backed out of the car to get a better angle, reached down into to my right boot, and pulled my knife, my daddy's KA-BAR from his Marine years. I don't always carry it. Only those times when I'm going places that make me nervous, like the downtown streets of a new city and going to meet my parole officer. God bless Texas.

I clamped the well-balanced blade in my teeth and snaked back into the car, crawling on my elbows, pulling on anything I could grab to propel myself forward. She hadn't moved, showed no signs of life. No matter. I sawed at the nylon seatbelt, flipped the frayed ends out of the way, and yanked once more.

This time she slithered forward as I inched back. For a little woman, she weighed like someone three times her size, but as I backed from the ruined car on my knees, she came with me. Her limp form folded out of the misshapen window, and several pairs of hands appeared, helping me, supporting her as I stood.

They say people cheered. I never heard it. I did hear the EMTs barking orders as they took over. The folding stretcher clanked as they popped it up. They wheeled her, running, for the back of an ambulance parked a good way down the street. People ran after it, pulling me along, still screaming about the fire that appeared a half second later. The fireball lit the afternoon sky behind me and singed the hairs on the back of my neck.

EMT's roused me, and I came to sitting on a curb, breathing bottled oxygen through a mask. I'm not sure how long I'd been out. I tried to stand. A little wobbly at first, shook off the EMT team's concerns. I pointed at the building across the street and told them I had a date with my parole officer. They shrugged their shoulders and let me go. Minutes later I inhaled the cold air of a mac daddy air conditioner inside the entrance of the building that started this whole dang mess.

Chapter Three

Kailey and Shinto

I killed the siren as Mike pulled us up beside one of the two ambulances at the scene. He took care not to block them from making a fast getaway.

"You ready for this?" My old partner, Sergeant Mike Sorenson, turned to me with a serious look in his eye.

"Hell, yeah, partner. You know me." I loved this guy more than people who've never shared a squad car with someone could know. I'd never let him know that of course. "What are you asking?"

"Wondering if all that time in Dallas might have softened you up a tad." His barely contained grin gave him away and I socked him on the shoulder.

"Not too soft to kick your ass, old man."

He unbuckled his seatbelt, "Let's not keep our fans waiting, sweet pea."

We popped our doors and got out. The smells of gasoline and burnt metal hit me first. Blistered asphalt and the body odors of people in a crowd came second. I inhaled like a swimmer needing oxygen. I was home.

Shinto and Allen parked tight behind us. They joined Mike and I and the four of us took quick stock of the situation. A jacked-up Ford dually, black, teetered atop a tiny red car. The little car could have been anything, its crushed metal and squashed windows an all too effective disguise. Steam escaped from beneath patches of MFD's foam fire retardant and I could still hear steam hissing from shattered radiators and the crack of cooling metal.

Mike and Allen grabbed rolls of yellow crime scene tape and headed off to secure the mangled automobiles for the traffic investigators. Shinto and I made stops at both rescue buses. The first held a silent man with a bloody lip and strips of white adhesive tape on a cheek and forehead. He rocked side-to-side and looked pissed.

Shinto sniffed and grinned at me. "I got this," she said. "Check out the other bus." I heard her say, "How many Lone Stars you slam this morning cowboy?" as I made my way to the second ambulance.

An older woman lay strapped to a backboard inside with two EMTs attending to her.

"Make it fast, officer," the female EMT said. "We just got her stable and we're heading for home."

"Ma'am?" I said softly. "These fine folks will take great care of you. We'll talk later when you're stronger."

"He saved me," the woman whispered.

"I'm sorry? What did you—"

"The nice young man saved me. He's a hero. I need to thank him."

"Sorry, officer" said the first EMT. "Time's up. We're out of here."

I looked at her with pen poised over my pad and nothing written.

"She's talking about the man who pulled her from the burning car, said he had to see his parole officer in that building." She pointed. "You'll have plenty witnesses out there to get your story straight. Right now, we gotta roll." She slammed a fist on the side of the truck and yanked the rear doors shut. The siren lit up and the ambulance pulled away with its engine roaring.

We finished working the scene. Gawkers crowded as close to the wreckage as Mike and Allen would allow. Shinto and I had our trusty notepads at the ready and canvassed the crowd. The EMT was right. We found no lack of witnesses. Though many became uninterested and a bit deflated when they learned there'd be no TV today.

Chapter Four

Junior

I wondered, looking around the high-ceilinged lobby, if the building architects were told to design something that kept close to the penitentiary theme. Don't want the criminals getting ideas when they're summoned to appear. Keep the windows tinted dark and the concrete gray.

A bored security guard barely noticed me. Brown linoleum stretched in every direction like a shiny dirt floor. Brass doors circa 1950 on the elevator across way gleamed. A round information kiosk squatted in the middle of the room listing names and businesses.

I confirmed R. Miller in 333 and felt validated in a weird way. I took the nearest elevator to the third floor. Frigging thing rocked and creaked every foot along its journey. I pitied the poor fools forced to take the thing to the top floor. You'd need a lunch for the trip.

The name stenciled on the dimpled glass door matched my card and the info kiosk. I knocked and a gruff voice yelled, "It's open."

Mr. Robert Miller in his sandals and Hawaiian shirt, looked unlike any P.O. I'd ever known, and I've known my share.

"You Mr. uh, R. Miller?" I made a show of consulting the card in my hand.

"You must be Mr. uh, J. Alvarez. J for—Jesus! What the hell happened to you?"

"No, sir. Not Jesus. The J's for Junior."

He narrowed his eyes, like he couldn't tell if I was messing with him or not, which I was. His smile told me he got it when he stood to shake my hand. "Have a seat, Junior. May I call you Junior?"

"That's what they call me." I sat in one of two gray metal chairs in front of his desk.

He jerked a thumb at the windows on the side of his office. "Something you want to tell me?"

I shook my head.

"Maybe explain the blood on your shirt, the scratches on your hands, and your gasoline cologne?"

"Nope. I'm good."

He sat back in his chair and thought a moment. "Right. If that's how you want it."

I nodded.

"Then let's begin like this is your average first meeting and this is your average starting-off-on-a-new-life kind of day."

"I'd like that fine, sir," I said.

"Oh, and about that." He drummed his fingers. "I appreciate the sir. It's not necessary. Sounds like coerced respect. I don't need it nor do I want it. Call me Robert, Rob, Mr. Miller, if you like. We don't stand on a lot of formality around here. No one likes it, and I find it counterproductive. You don't want to be here; I get that, and I don't want to waste my time on lost causes. Are you a lost cause, Mr. Alvarez?"

How am I supposed to answer that? "I guess we'll have to wait and see, sir—I mean, Mr. Miller."

Miller smiled. "Good answer, Junior." He sat back down. "I have only two rules, really."

I must have frowned, because he held up a hand.

"I know, I know, but they're simple. I tell all my folks the same thing. One, be on time." He counted on his fingers. "Two, be honest. That's it. I'm here to help you, not check boxes on a form. If we do this right," he pointed from me to him and back, "you'll have a smooth transition back to the world. Buy a home, marry a girl, have babies, get a dog, whatever fevered your dreams while you were incarcerated. I'm here to help you get the whole mai tai. Dig?"

I had no idea what a mai tai was. I nodded anyway.

"All right." He rubbed his palms together. "Let's begin."

Miller made quick work of my interview from then on. Probably gave the same speech ten times a day. He explained about the small stipend I'd receive from the state until I got on my feet. He handed me a key with Apartment 211 on a plastic fob, a pamphlet for Chaparral Apartments, and a bus schedule for Midland Transit, with vouchers I could use to buy food at the market.

"That's my spiel, Junior. You have any questions, my number's on my card."

On my way out he said, "Hey, hold up, Junior. One more thing." He opened a bottom drawer on his desk and pulled something from it. "Check this out. We'll talk about it next month."

"What's that?"

He sailed a thin book across the room at me. I caught it and read the cover. "Midland Community College?"

He winked at me. "You're a college man now, Mr. Alvarez. You and I are going to be planning your life together. I suggest you study up."

"College? No, no, Mr. Miller. I'm not what you call college material." I stepped back into his office, holding the catalog straight-armed like I'd grabbed a venomous snake ready to bite.

He waved me off. "You leave that to me, Junior. I've read your records. You don't give yourself enough credit. We're about to change all that. See you in a month."

He resumed his seat and picked up the phone, a clear sign that my time in the box was over.

I turned back for the door and saw shadows move through the frosted glass. A sharp rap rattled the old door in its hinges.

"Midland PD."

I looked at my P.O.

He raised his eyebrows at me. "Already Alverez?"

I got a familiar sinking feeling in my gut.

"He's in here," he yelled.

The door swung open to reveal two, female uniforms standing at polite attention. Each had that standard-issue flat expression that marks a cop from a hundred yards off.

"This have to do with the mess outside?" my P.O. said.

The two cops entered the office. One, not bad looking and the other with an exotic, Indian-in-the-family-tree look. The pretty one spoke. "It does. I'm officer Kailey Carmichael. This is Officer Shinto Elliot. We have a few questions for this man here."

Miller looked at his watch and grinned. "Ten minutes," he said. "That is a new record Mr. Alvarez, even for a jaded old kahuna like me. Officers, may I introduce Mr. Junior Alvarez. Junior, this is Midland P.D. Though somehow, I suspect you've already met them."

Chapter Five

Kailey and Shinto

We'd been back barely long enough for me to find my old desk, the stink of the accident scene still fresh in my nostrils. I rummaged around for a report form and uncapped a pen about the time Shinto strode up and flopped into my other chair.

I shoved the form back and replaced the pen cap. "Long time no see," I said.

"What'd you think?" Shinto said.

"About what?"

"The price of condoms on Main Street. What do you mean about what? Our ex-con's story."

"I believed him."

"Kailey, dude. We interviewed him in his P.O.'s office."

"That P.O. seemed a little strange in a beach boy kind of way. But Junior Alvarez, I don't know. I liked him."

"You remember his name."

I tapped the open pad on my desk. "So does my notepad. What's your point?"

"Something about your Junior. I dunno, I get a weird vibe."

"Testosterone," I said. "You probably don't recognize it up close."

"Oh, that's funny." Shinto sniffed like a dog testing the breeze. "No, it's not that. Plenty of hormones in here. No, biggie. I'll figure it out. Hey, what's this?" Shinto picked up a brown-paper wrapped package from my desk.

"Nothing," I said and grabbed for it.

Shinto yanked it out of reach and held it over her head. "Is it personal? Tell me it's personal."

"Yes. Give it."

She squeezed the package and shook it. "Feels hard, like wood. It's definitely wood."

"Shinto, it's stupid. I wasn't even going to bring it."

"Personal and stupid. Now I have to open it."

"I'll kill you for this."

"Oh, goodie." Shinto tore off the brown wrapping paper. "I was right, it is wood. A plaque kind of wood." Her lips moved as she read: Crime Scene Analyst Accreditation.

Shinto stood and announced to the uniforms still lurking in the squad room. "Hey, everybody, listen up."

"I will *definitely* kill you for this," I hissed.

All talk ceased in the room and my best friend in the world cleared her throat dramatically and commenced to embarrassing me:

This is to certify that Officer Kailey Carmichael of the Midland Police Department has successfully completed the FBI School of Crime Scene Analysis. As a graduate of this intense course of study, the above-mentioned officer has been given the specialized tools to be of valuable service to crime scene analysis and forensic investigation.

She showed me the bottom of the plaque. "Who's that?"

"Read it. You read everything else."

"This is signed personally, by FBI Deputy Director Edgar Flynn," She announced. "You can see it right there. Blue ink on the bottom."

Silence.

"What the hell are you goofballs waiting for? Give our girl a hand. And make it loud." Shinto bowed in my direction and began clapping like an idiot. The rest of the squad joined in and a few even whistled.

"Way to go, Kailey."

"Knew you could do it."

"Don't get a big head." The Captain had come in to see what the noise was all about. He added his congratulations to the rest of them as he came over to see what Shinto had been reading. Shinto handed him the plaque and he looked at it like it was a Tiffany bracelet. "Damn proud of you, Carmichael. This is going up on the wall in the front lobby."

"No, Captain—"

"Good P.R. for the department. You can thank me later, Kailey," he turned and waved a hand over his shoulder. "I meant that about the big head."

"Now I am definitely going to kill you," I said.

Shinto stood there beaming. "Nice, right? That was so nice."

"I need a drink," I said. "La Bodega? After shift?"

"It's a date, gorgeous."

Chapter Six

Kailey and Shinto

Half past 6:00 P.M. the pink and green neon in La Bodega's front window slid its way up my hood as I pulled into one of a few remaining spots. They served better than decent Tex-Mex and generous pours, especially anything with tequila in it. Which made La Bodega the after work go-to bar in town.

I should know. I learned from the best. My daddy worked in the oil fields and loved to hang out at any old bar after the whistle blew. If I wanted to see him, I trucked to his bar de jour and sat while he drank. Fun times. The oil boom in the doo-dah days of the late eighties brought in a lot of guys like my dad to Midland, some wanting to work and others wanting to take their hard-earned money from them.

Rough crowd for rough times, and my daddy loved it. Most memories I have of my dad are either him drunk, heading to work with his hard hat and lunch pail, or getting the shit kicked out of him in a bar. My daddy had a real smart mouth and stupid hands.

I pushed through La Bodega's double doors and up a flight of stairs to the second floor. The smell of corn tortillas and beer made me realize how much I'd missed this place. Dallas had its contenders, but even their dives were too refined. This cinder block cop hangout on the edge of a residential neighborhood would have made my daddy smile.

"Kailey! Hey, girl, where you been?" Shinto Elliot yelled across the crowded bar room. She was easy to spot, holding court mid-bar surrounded by cops and civilians in equal measure. The girl had style and felt more at home in her own skin than anyone I'd ever met. She always had.

Shinto and I have been friends since first grade and became inseparable when Billy Martin lured us into the bushes and pulled our pants down. Between the two of us, we gave poor Billy a bloody nose and a healthy respect for women. Later, Shinto's older brother taught us how to hit him where it hurts. Billy let it be known not to mess with us, and we enjoyed a drama-free childhood thanks to that one encounter. Last I heard he'd married and been blessed with three daughters. Karma is awesome.

I watched Shinto snap her fingers and a Lone Star magically appear in her fist. She waved it at me and started across the bar room. I met her halfway, and she spun me in a gigantic hug. "Good to see you, girl. This is for you."

The icy beer went down like glacier water and half the bottle disappeared before I stopped for breath. "Tastes of heaven," I said.

"I know, right?" Shinto smiled that lopsided grin I remember and we clinked bottles.

I noticed several guys turn and nudge each other. Let them think what they want. Only one of us is gay, and it's not me.

"Let's find a quiet place in here and catch up. Before it gets crazy," I said. "I want to know about Afghanistan, the Army, your love life. All of it."

She let out a low, gassy burp. "Back at you Kailey. Dallas, forensics for shit's sake, your mom—and your love life. I don't see a wedding ring on your finger."

A quiet place in La Bodega was purely a foreign concept, but it didn't matter. We wormed our way into a place at the end of the bar and started yelling at one another over the piped-in mariachi music and the well-oiled crowd.

"Tell me about your mom, first," Shinto said. "How's my favorite lady doing?"

My mother and Shinto had a relationship stronger than most real mothers and daughters. My mom filled in some of the gaps in Shinto's crappy childhood and got a second daughter in the bargain.

"Mom's aging, Shinto. It really hit me when I got back from Dallas. I was only gone six months, but she aged a couple years in that time."

"Not easy living in a chair, Kailey, I was in-country when I heard about the accident. Didn't get any details." Shinto said.

"One night, driving home from their typical date night of momma watching daddy drink, he missed a curve and drove smack into the Scarborough Draw off Big Spring Drive. He drowned. Momma got thrown from the car and broke her back. Police said Daddy's blood alcohol came in at twice the legal limit. Shocker. I came home on compassionate leave and moved in with momma to keep an eye on her. I gradually returned to the force and settled into a life of crime fighting and kicking the occasional badass. Until I got sent off to Dallas for the FBI Crime Analysis gig."

I drained my beer. "Your turn. Tell me about life in the service. How was Afghanistan?"

Shinto's eyes went flat and she took a long pull of Lone Star before answering. "Afghanistan was mountains. Cold. Locals who hate America and love our money. Army, Marines and Guard units performing above and beyond. And me and my MPs walking a line you don't learn about 'til you get there."

"Different from here," I said. More a statement than a question.

"In every way," Shinto said. "Main difference is the intensity. The level of hate is higher and comes at you from all sides. The uniform makes enemies everywhere you go. That MP brassard even makes enemies out of your friends."

"Jesus."

"Here, all we worry about are the occasional crazies, domestics, drunks, drugs and the cartel." She shook her head and flashed two fingers for another round. "There was this one family. Two

22

daughters, who reminded me of us when we were younger. A son. Father in and out and sketchy as hell. But I liked them."

"And you had to leave them there," I prodded.

She thought a few seconds. "No. They left me. Apparently, the father didn't like me hanging around so much. Came down from the mountains one night and slit all their throats. Both little girls, his 12-year-old son, and his wife. Lined all four bodies up on the floor of their tiny home. A message for me, I think."

The bartender placed two more beers in front of us. Shinto drew her finger around the label, her nail found where it pulled away from the damp bottle and scraped it off.

"I spent the rest of my tour hunting the bastard. Never found him. I hope there is some kind of hell for people like him."

"My god, Shinto. I am so sorry."

Shinto rummaged around her purse and pulled out her cell phone. She fiddled with some buttons and handed it to me. "This is them," she said. "I keep them close to remind myself of what I did with candy and kindness."

I looked at a short woman in a hijab, a sullen boy and two little girls eating candy bars. I handed back the phone. "You didn't do anything."

"Just got a family killed." She shrugged and drank. "No biggie."

Chapter Seven

Junior

"Daddy, please, don't make me go with him." I pulled with all the might a skinny eight-year-old boy could muster. The old man's grip tightened.

Dad frowned, and I could see he might be changing his mind. Mommy stood silent, shaking and sweating.

"Please, daddy, I'll be good, promise." I sagged and pried at his fingers.

"Luke, the devil has this boy in his grip." The pastor shook his head and closed his eyes as if the thought were too horrible to contemplate. "I will personally drive Satan out of Junior. It will not be easy."

I kept struggling. His iron grip cinched harder and he wouldn't let go. He laid his other hand on Dad's bowed head. "Pray with me, for your son's soul."

I kicked the pastor and he glanced down at me. His white, cadaverous face and shadowed eyes showed no emotion until he licked fat red lips that creased into a smile. Pastor Hess murmured, "Praise his name" and handed Daddy an envelope.

Daddy grabbed it. Mommy tugged on Daddy's arm and sobbed.

"No, please, Daddy, please." My protests collapsed to a whisper as I sagged in the grip of my tormentor and peed myself. The scald on my leg and smell of urine added shame to my misery. "Daddy, don't leave me. Mommy, please. I promise when you take your medicine and sleep all the time I'll be quiet." I begged. My father and mother's silent retreating backs were my answers.

I awoke drenched in sweat, rolled over, and glanced at the chipped plastic clock on the nightstand. Noon. My stomach growled and my throat felt like baked dry river bed. Rise and shine. That familiar nightmare, burned into me at eight, followed me into my new life. Will I ever shake it?

Midland, Texas is where I landed. Out of jail and into Section Eight housing. My apartment complex is on Garfield across from the Community College. The college with lots of green rolling grass in front, courtesy of the taxpayers. How in the hell did I manage to get here? Surrounded by oil well-studded desert and the only grass for miles is across the street.

I made my way to the kitchen naked and held my mouth under the faucet. I plopped a couple pieces of stale bread into the toaster. Next to it, the list of available jobs from the Midland fish wrapper classifieds

beckoned. Yeah, yeah. I moved to the faded yellow Formica table, sat with a grunt, and spread my future in front of me. Dishwasher, carwash attendant, window washer. I sensed a theme here.

I dabbed the Bic pen on my tongue and got creative, writing down a list of job applications I supposedly sent out this week. A small price to pay for high-class government housing. I live two floors up in a three-story apartment complex. My toilet leaks, the front door leans on one and a half hinges. Not its fault; I came home drunk a couple of nights ago and slammed it. Paradise.

I fingered the fifty-buck food stamp credit card. Have to make it last 'til the end of the month. Ten more days. I folded the job application into a tiny square by the time my toast popped up.

A tub of fake butter and a jar of strawberry jam were all I could find after a search through the fridge. Why the hell did I go shopping loaded? I wiped a semi-clean plastic knife on my thigh, pulled a paper plate from a new package, and grabbed a banana to go with the toast. Damn, I'm hungry.

Munching, I gazed out the large window in front of my table. I caught a glimpse of an older woman in the building across the walkway on the first floor. My being on the second floor had its advantages. I'd seen her around, I couldn't place where.

I stroked myself. She could use some of this.

Too much testosterone, too little self-control, they told me at every mandated therapy session at every lockup I'd been in since I was fourteen. *Junior, you need to control your urges or you will find your way back to jail.* I squeezed myself erect with one hand and held my toast with the other. Multitasking. None of them knew what I'd suffered as a child. I didn't know how to tell them and figured they wouldn't believe me if I did. I concentrated, stroked harder. Been a long time since I slid into a woman, but prison makes you real good with fantasies.

Jesus, it's hot.

I tossed my toast on the table and switched on the fan next to me. I needed both hands for this fantasy. She appeared again at her kitchen window. Like an angel and right on time. I felt the surge tighten my balls, and I squeezed and pumped. She never looked up. I didn't think she could see me if she did. I licked my lips, forgot about breakfast, and stared at her. A little voice behind the heat in my brain whispered insistently. I ignored it and watched her open the window wide. Her red-going-gray hair plastered to her head in the heat. She fanned her blouse, and I could see the swell of her breasts; nice.

The voice in my head got louder when she turned away from the window and I lost sight of her.

There's something about her, it said. You know, something familiar.

The whispers shut down when she returned a few seconds later with a couple of tomatoes. She rinsed them and placed each one on her windowsill and then started doing her dishes. Her breasts jiggled every time she rubbed a plate. Yes, baby, yes. Do it like that. Ahhh.

You Know Her. The frigging voice gave up the whispers and went to full-on shout.

Ah.

You Know This Woman. Hello?

Ah.

Car Wreck? Crashing Glass?

Ah. Ah—Shit!

26

My hot neighbor with the nice ta-ta's is the very same woman I pulled from the car wreck earlier in the week.

Damn it. I picked up my toast, ripped off a bite, and chomped furiously.

So much for my one-man sex show.

Angry and frustrated, I reached behind me and yanked open my kitchen junk drawer. I felt around until I found my father's KA-BAR, the only thing he ever gave me I could actually use. Seven inches of carbon steel, a knife sharp enough to shave with. I kept it with me always, from stint to stint. Joint to joint. First item I search for when I retrieve my personals on checkout. I feel better having it with me. I don't know why, exactly. Protection? Maybe. Shit happens—life inside teaches that lesson on your first day, and I studied at the feet of masters. Besides, here on the outside, guns weren't an option. Not a legal one, anyway. Not for an ex-con. So I've got the next best thing. A big, badass piece of steel with an edge. Like me.

Chapter Eight

Kailey and Shinto

By now we had a respectable lineup of empty Lone Stars in front of us. Shinto rapped on the bar and called out. "Dos mas, señor. Por favor."

"I don't know, Shinto."

"Ah, ah. Your turn, Kailey girl. Last I heard, you were married, pregnant, and living the good life in Houston."

I said. "You're part right. Eighteen and pregnant. Wahoo. I married Michael. We had Emma. Michael snagged a decent job making sixty grand a year. Life seemed pretty good." I shook my head, took a long draw on my drink.

"Pictures. I need pictures."

I dug out photos of my girl.

"God, Kailey. She looks like you, that curly blond hair."

"Cute, always laughing." I continued the script I could now recite aloud without emotion.

"Then the economy hit a wall. Michael got let go and couldn't find work that suited his view of himself. I got a job at a hamburger joint to make ends meet until he could figure out how to land the next big job he felt fit his talents. Which really meant he sat home, watched TV, drank, and smoked pot. Spent our money on any drug he could find."

"Michael? Geez, girl. I never would have thought that of him. He seemed too, I don't know, preppy?" Shinto toyed with a tortilla chip.

"I tried to prop him up, tell him how I believed in him, that this was a blip in our journey. I'd come home and Emma would be dirty and hungry, wearing the same diaper I put on her when I left for work. I couldn't take it."

"That's not right."

"I told him to get a job. I didn't care what; delivering papers or pizza. Anything. Stop the drugs, or I'd leave. I worked twelve-hour shifts and we were still behind. Our house slipped into foreclosure and our cars hung on the edge of being repossessed." I shuddered. "We argued every day. I told him I was leaving after I ended my shift and got paid."

Shinto nodded.

I stopped, took a deep breath, and then continued. "I came home that night to my house lit by klieg lights, police and yellow tape everywhere. Michael shot my beautiful two-year-old baby Emma, then turned the gun on himself. The coroner said later the amount of drugs in his system would have killed him if he hadn't shot himself." I ripped shreds of napkin from under my beer turned up the new bottle. Shinto stayed quiet.

"I stood by her little white casket alone. Just my baby and me. I'd carried that precious child inside me, her every kick a promise." The pain broke my calm recitation. I felt raw hatred curl my lip. "I should have been there to protect her. It's been seven years, and I still want to kill him again and again. Probably will 'til the day comes and I join my baby." I pounded the bar, drank a gulp. "The police were kind to me." I felt the tickle of tears, amazed I could still summon them. "After I fell apart, waded through grief therapy, I enrolled in the academy and moved back in with Momma. I wanted to be the kind of cop that helped me in Houston. My life in a nutshell."

She reached down and squeezed my knee. "I'm so sorry, Kailey. I didn't know. We lived two separate lives for a while. Me with the MPs in Afghanistan. You trying to keep it together on the home front. But we're back, okay? Kind of funny how we ended up though, don't you think?"

"How so?"

"I get back and head straight for Fort Worth PD who took me right in. Guess they figured MP overseas counted as academy enough for me. You come at law enforcement from a different angle. Then I transfer to Midland while you were in Dallas filling up your brain. And voila, here we are. The old team back together again, a little battered—"

"A little bent," I added.

"But damn sure not broken."

We clinked glasses.

"Here's to us, two of Midland's finest." I raised my beer and drained it.

"I kind of pity Midland, you know? They have no idea what they're in for." Shinto laughed.

"Amen to that, sister."

Chapter Nine

Junior

Bored as crap, I felt like flinging a shoe at the TV. Only so much a guy can stomach sober. I pulled on a shirt I picked off the floor next to my bed, slipped into the canvas shoes they issued me in the joint, and headed out. I needed to score some smoke, something, anything to make the day interesting.

The sun cast a red tint over the horizon, and I stopped to admire it. Colorful sunsets are rare in Midland. Something about not enough moisture in the air. Maybe it's an omen. Maybe I'll find some action in this dead-end town.

Across the street from my apartment complex and down a ways an expanse of park more brown dirt than green grass did its job, made some city planner somewhere feel like he'd contributed to the happiness of the populace. The only populace I saw at the moment was a gang of guys and a few chicks lounging around a couple of picnic tables and benches stuck in the middle of nothing. No trees around. Not a single bush. They made their own shade. I headed straight for them. Time to make some contacts.

Two of the girls nudged one another as I approached. Several of the guys stood and puffed out their chests. One made no move other than rest his elbows on the table and watch. He smiled like he couldn't wait to make my acquaintance. The slightest twitch of his eyebrows said different. A welcoming committee like every other one you'd run into in prison, on the street, anywhere. Establish turf. Claim dominance. Mess with the new guy. Always the same. The soldiers do the dance while Jefe watches, amused.

So, let's dance.

"I'm Junior Alvarez. I heard this town had some righteous people in it. I'm looking to find them."

"Where'd you hear that?" said one of the bigger kids. He sported a black tattoo on his forehead, Fuck You, written in script.

"Midland Correctional." I may as well have waved a red flag in Fuck You's face.

"Ooo, manos. We got us a genuine prison issue in our midst."

I remained silent and resisted the urge to tear his throat out.

"So whatta ya want?" a skinny kid with a white bandana tied around his head asked. They all wore wife-beater T-shirts, baggy khaki pants, and white bandanas tied around some part of their body.

Jefe watching on the bench seemed about my age with shoulder-length jet-black hair. A scar ran from his eyebrow to his lip in the shape of a C to meet a mustache draped around his mouth. His eyes glinted dark and cold. He seemed to be enjoying the show.

I shouldered past his boys to stand in front of him. "I need a job. You have any work that needs to be done?"

His gang laughed and punched each other.

"We got all the help we need, puta madre." I knew Fuck You forehead kid would be first to comment. Gotta pay if you want to play, right? I shrugged and turned away. The minute he mugged for his homies yanking on his crotch, I turned and punched him hard in the stomach. He went down gasping and pulling up fistfuls of dirt.

He got up. I had to admire that. I swear my fist felt his backbone. He staggered toward me.

Jefe yelled, "Calmate. Relax." He made a motion like washing his hands. "No need for violence, man." He pointed to the seat next to him. "Como se llama, vato? What's your name?"

"They call me Junior."

"I like a guy who gets to the point." He smirked at his much less merry little band. "Take a lesson, putos. I'm Miguel, by the way." He extended a hand, and we shook. "How long were you in and why?"

I stared at him for a beat to let him know I thought his questions were getting personal. "Stuck a knife in a child molester. Did a couple years."

"Shit, man. You did the world a favor, hombre."

"Took the system a while to come around to that point of view." I spread my hands. "There's worse places than prison. I been to those too."

"So you heard from some vatos in our farm team—my term for Midland Correctional—that Los Demonios was good people?"

"I did."

Miguel smiled and took a swig of a Dos Equis. "Got to speak with our publicist. Los Demonios is bad people all the way, hey, Freddie?"

"Damn straight." Fuck You scowled. Apparently his parents named him Fred.

"Tell you what, Junior. You got a style that appeals to me. Come back tomorrow, and I may have some work for you."

"But, boss—" Freddie complained.

"No, no," Miguel held up his hand. "I know you and Junior got off to a rocky start but Freddie, I think you and him got a future together. I really do."

Fuck You looked down and kicked at a piece of dirt.

Miguel fixed his attention on me. "Freddie's been my boy since grade school. He's ornery, but he's loyal. So, mañana." He held out his hand, and I shook it. "Here's a little something to be friendly, a taste. See you tomorrow."

"Hasta mañana," I said. I smiled and palmed the bag he slipped me. The walk back to my apartment was slow and pure attitude.

Once inside I shut and locked the door—like that piece of shit lock would stop a ten-year-old with a kitchen knife. I unfurled the baggie of dope and stuck my nose in it. Smelled like green hay, good shit. A pack of papers at the bottom made me smile. I could get to like this Miguel dude.

I rolled a tiny one and sparked it off the burner on the stove. A couple good hits and I copped a little buzz. Ten, fifteen minutes later

I sat at my table grinning like an idiot, watching my sexy old lady neighbor through the window once more.

I grabbed the pad I used to make my shopping lists and began doodling. The subject matter stared me in the face. The two globes swaying back and forth on my neighbor's chest filled me with inspiration and lots more. I let my pencil do its thing and got creative. I ended up with two pendulous breasts topped by large, pointy nipples.

I unzipped my Levi's and went on my second date with the swinging tata's.

Chapter Ten

Kailey and Shinto

Shinto's place is a cute two-bedroom red brick home on Boyd Avenue. I wheeled Mom in through the front door. Johnny Cash sang about prison from a pair of speakers in the front room while people milled around everywhere. Most stayed inside the house, moving room to room. The 103-degree temperature made it way too hot to stand around outside.

"Hey, girl. Wondering when you'd show up." Shinto greeted us with a beer in each hand. "It's good to see you, Momma C." She bent down and gave momma a big hug.

Most of the guests were guys—and a few women—from the department and their spouses. Spouses and I infrequently got along. The thought of a woman cop never quite computed with most of them. Like they were worried I'd snag their civil servant hubbies and give them blow jobs in the backseat while we were on stakeout. Which is such bullshit. I almost never go on stakeouts.

After introductions and so many names I would never remember, I followed Shinto into the kitchen. "I'm bored. Let's bust some balls."

"Get a grip, girl." Shinto laughed.

Some of the wives turned to me and frowned. I smiled back and waved.

Shinto pulled a tinfoil-covered platter from the fridge and handed it to me.

"Here," she said. "Quit giving the wives heartburn and go make yourself useful. Slap the meat on the grill. Get all hot and sweaty. Thin some of your venom out." Shinto peeled the foil off a load of steaks, hot dogs, and hamburgers, handed me another ice-cold Lone Star, and shoved me out the back door.

The heat hit me hard. Midland's dry desert will vaporize the piss right out of you. Shinto was right. I relished the heat and the diversion with the grill. By the time I got all the meat cooked, I felt dehydrated and calm. Another cerveza and air conditioning were calling my name.

"Meat's ready. Anybody hungry?" I yelled as I kicked open the back door. That got people's attention, and they moved en masse to grab a seat at the long picnic table Shinto set up in her living room. Kids stopped running and yelling to grab plates and begin whining instead. The radio kept playing country music, which I could hear, now that conversation took a back seat to food.

Shinto sat Momma at one end of the table at the seat of honor. I could have kissed her for that. Momma sat in her wheelchair, smiling at the chaos. I danced a little two-step over to the table and filled a plate with a burger and a dog, beans, and potato salad.

I carried my meal into the kitchen and ate standing up at the counter. It worked for me. No way I could sit in there and make small talk. Plus, I got a chance to watch momma enjoy herself. Enjoy being a part of a family again. Even if it was my loud, raucous work family.

That's all I have now that Emma—

Jesus, Kailey. Do not frigging go there. You're at a party. Enjoy it if it kills you.

Chapter Eleven

Junior

"Junior, I've been checking over your files." Mr. Miller moistened his finger and flipped through a tattered manila folder stuffed with my old files.

"Sir, I thought this city got the Internet years ago. What are those? Dinosaur crap? Looks about the same color." I flopped down in the old wooden chair next to his gunmetal gray desk.

"These are your files from Social Services and Juvenile Hall days," he said.

"Why you wasting time on that shit?" I leaned back and crossed my new black Doc Martins. New to me, anyway. The Salvation Army on Baird Street had smokin' deals.

"You've been tested and you are very smart, very smart indeed. What are you doing with your life? Why are you wasting it on being bored?"

"How could I be bored in this awesome city?" I gave him my most charming smile. Women melt and men usually change their persuasion when I turn up the wattage.

He didn't look up. "We talked about college before."

"You talked. I mostly listened."

"Take some college classes, Junior. You graduated high school in juvie. Took a couple college classes in jail. Why not give it a shot for real, now that you're out? You may qualify for a grant if you take something relevant to getting a job."

I finished studying a framed photo of a stream and trees and said, "How do I do that?"

"Let me worry about it. Go introduce yourself at the registrar's office, find out how to register, what you'll need. I'll help you with the process. You are twenty-two, the right age. You'll fit in. You've had it tough, and maybe you've quit trying. Now's your chance for a life. A real one. You like living jail to jail?"

"It's all I know." I rocked back on my chair. College? Seriously? "I wouldn't know where to begin."

"I told you. Get a schedule and come back. I'll help you navigate the process. Deal?"

"What the hell. Okay." I got up, shook his hand and couldn't believe I might go. No one in my family ever thought about going to college. Mom and Dad made a career out of beating us kids and getting high. We were always homeless. Never stayed in a place longer than months. Then they gave us to the preacher.

I left Mr. Millers office, walking, thinking. I flashed back to my tenth year, my sister's twelfth. My folks came under the spell of the preacher who convinced them we were too attractive to be out on the streets and needed to be taught the evil ways of the world. The godly people of Holy Oak took over our upbringing. They raped us over and over, raised torture to an art form while they "prepared" us for the world. Our parents played good little parishioners and turned blind and deaf to our programmed hell, showing up only when they needed money. They'd threaten to take us with them. The preacher would always pay.

I need to get home and get high. Take another taste of Miguel's shit. Who am I to think college is in my future? Screwing and getting high is all I've known. I'm pretty good at those things, praise God and the good people of Holy Oak traveling church.

***

My red-haired neighbor came down the apartment stairs as I headed up my walkway.

She stopped in front of me. "Getting pretty close to the first day," she said.

"I'm sorry?" I had no friggin' idea what the lady was talking about.

She tapped the catalog under my arm. "Midland Community College."

"Oh, that. I've sort of been thinking about going. I don't know. I'm not really college material."

"You should go." She put her hand on my arm. "It's a good school. I used to teach there, you know."

My inner asshole voice said, "How would I know that?" My outside voice asked, "What did you teach?"

"Botany, Plant Genetics and a little Yoga for fun. Right now I'm dabbling, working to create a new hybrid tomato in my apartment." She must have realized her hand still gripped my arm and jerked it away like my arm burned at a thousand degrees Fahrenheit.

"Long as it still fits on a hamburger," I said.

She smiled politely at my feeble attempt at humor. "What's your major?" she asked and immediately turned red. "My gosh, I haven't asked a young man that in dec—well, a very long time." She patted her hair self-consciously.

"Didn't know I needed one." I lifted the pile of papers and the catalog. "All this is new to me."

"I could help you. I know most of the teachers there. If you have time, I mean. If you're interested."

"How about now?" I said.

Her eyes widened.

"Or, we could do it another time."

"No, no," she said. "You are a very decisive young man. Let's do it."

I followed her down the stairs to her apartment. She fumbled nervously with the key and turned to say, "Please don't mind the mess. I was not expecting company today."

"No problem," I said. "I'll keep my eyes closed."

"Ah," she said. "I see. You are a kidder, aren't you?"

"Guilty as charged," I said.

She pushed open the door, and I followed her inside. She turned on a lamp, and I stopped dead at the threshold. Holy crap!

Everything was red. As in tomato. Bright red, huge, tiny and every size in between, tomatoes.

"I kind of have a thing for tomatoes," she said. "I know it's pretty silly. You could say tomatoes are my life."

No shit, Sherlock. She loved her tomatoes. Every surface, every square inch of wall space, every picture frame starred tomatoes. Hundreds of salt and pepper shaker tomatoes crowded onto a set of narrow shelves. Little boxes shaped like tomatoes clustered on a glass-topped table itself a giant tomato. A tiny gleaming gold crate held a pile of crystal tomatoes. There were little tomato twinkle lights strung and hung around the doorways. A large poster of Andy Warhol's Tomato Soup Can decorated the far wall.

A foam hat in the shape of a tomato draped over an arm of a chair; a shawl with a repeating tomato pattern hung on the other arm. Bowls in the shape of tomatoes clustered on an end table, and on the wall behind it, a framed chart that looked like an antique listed every conceivable type and color of tomato.

"I feel like we've met somewhere before, it'll come to me. Would you like something to drink?" she asked. "I have beer."

"That would be great, ma'am." I didn't know what to call her.

"Oh, please, call me Patricia."

"Everyone calls me Junior."

"Oh, what's your father's name?"

"Nothing good."

"Okay." She busied herself at the fridge. "Make yourself at home while I get us something."

I wandered around a bit, stunned by it all. On the wall beside the giant soup can, a framed stock certificate for one hundred shares of Campbell Soup company congratulated Ms. Patricia Keystone on her "joining the Campbell's family."

"Here we go." Patricia set two bottles of Heineken beer on the table. "I hope it's cold enough."

"I'm sure it will be fine," I said.

We clinked bottles, and an hour and a half and two beers later, we were laughing about teachers and classes and college in general.

I dug this lady. She sounded so nice. I hadn't been near nice in maybe, ever.

"Come on, Junior. What are you afraid of? You're a smart guy. I can tell."

"But Patricia, psychology? You think I could take psychology? I can't even spell it. Pottery would be more my speed." I frowned.

"Don't you dare sell yourself short, Junior. I won't have it. You can do this. You go every day, read the required textbooks, take tests, and be surprised you've passed another class."

"I don't know."

She put her hand on my arm. She did that a lot as we talked. After a while I realized that was just her way. How she related to people.

"What's the worst thing that can happen?" she said. "You learn something. Take the basics; English, math, history. You get your feet wet. Try psychology. Heck, give chemistry a shot. You might like it."

"What about weightlifting? For me it's a piece of cake."

She patted my arm and smiled. "Your muscles are big enough. Let's work on that brain of yours, shall we? Oh my god." Her hands flew to her mouth. "Piece of cake? I know where we met. The accident. You saved my life."

"Yeah, that was me." My face felt hot. Crap, I must be blushing. "I pulled you out of your car. Anyone would have done the same."

"You're my guardian angel, Junior." She stood and came over and hugged me. "How can I ever repay you?"

"Get me through that?" I pointed to the college catalog and my papers. "We'll be even."

"We'll start with that." She snapped her fingers. "Come on, bring them here. Let's get you enrolled."

With Patricia's help I decided on a list of classes. She helped me fill out the forms and I signed them.

I felt excited and hopeful, two emotions that were strangers to me. I made a vow to get to know them better as time went on.

I couldn't help thinking I'd made a friend in Patricia. Made me almost feel guilty about staring at her tits all those times and beating off.

Almost. Shit, I'm human, aren't I? Mostly?

WEST TEXAS DEAD

Chapter Twelve

Kailey and Shinto

The police department gym smelled of sweat, old leather and liniment. I felt stronger just being there.

"Shinto? Why do I love boxing so much?" Shinto pulled the laces tight on my second glove and I clapped them together.

"Because you get to hit shit," she said. "And it feels good."

"The first time I got hit didn't feel so good. I was fifteen and mouthed off to my boyfriend of the moment. He socked me in the jaw and pain went off in my head like a bomb. When I came to, he'd gone and my jaw hurt for a week. I've been picking losers like that ever since."

Shinto held the heavy bag steady for me and grinned around it. "Now's your chance, Tyson. Hit 'em back."

I slammed that thing with lefts, rights, combos, jabs. Over and over, dancing on my toes. I put my hips into it, swiveled, shifted weight. "I will never—" Bam. "Get caught like that—" Bam. "Again." Bam. Bam.

Shinto rocked back on her heels. "Not bad, killer. My first fist in the face? When I turned thirteen and told my dad that I'm gay. Pow." Shinto grimaced. "Asshole didn't quit until he got tired. One last kick to my stomach and he went out to the garage for another beer. I gathered my wits and what stuff I could cram into a duffle bag and split. Been on my own ever since." She smiled. "Off and on."

"Until we got our paws on you." Uppercut. Roundhouse. "Mom was so happy when we did. Made me kind of jealous."

"Your mom has a cloud waiting in heaven, Kailey. A big fat one."

"You had some older girlfriend back then, right? A redhead."

43

"Flame Gallagher. You think you made bad choices? That bitch was a piece of work. Haven't thought about her in forever."

I switched to southpaw. "Whatever happened to her?"

Shinto shook her head. "Don't know and don't care. Come on Kailey, hit the damn bag."

I stepped close and popped its middle with uppercuts until my arm ached.

"That's better. Dad's still alive, you know."

"What?" A good excuse to stop and catch my breath.

"Yep," Shinto said, "and it's all my fault."

"I don't understand. What's your fault?" I panted in through the nose, out through the mouth.

"Mom died when I was five. I got scared and prayed he would live forever. He's seventy-eight and still going strong. Bigger asshole than ever. Guess I have to be careful what I pray for."

"You goob," I laughed.

Right about then a vision in pink sweatpants, department issue tee and matching hairband bopped into the gym. "Ladies," it said.

Shinto turned and smiled. "Heather. What are you up to, girl?"

Heather barely cleared the minimum height requirements for the force at five-foot three, a life-sized doll with brown hair pulled into a French braid down her back. Her green eyes glittered as she shook out a jump rope. "Sweat is fat crying, people." Her wiry muscles flexed as the rope became a blur, crisscrossing in front of her and then behind, slapping the cement.

I sniffed. "My sweat's about all cried out. Let's get out of here Shinto, before I get too awesome. How about the Bar Steak House?" I grabbed a towel and mopped my face. "I've been craving a Goldbrick for a while and I can see it, vanilla ice cream in that tall glass with butterscotch hardened on top and nuts dripping down. Oh, god, and the whipped cream. YUM."

"Shut up. Christ!" Shinto said. "How do you do it, Kailey? You stay so thin and eat anything. If I ate like you I'd waddle like Barney the dinosaur."

I spread my arms. "I'm a metabolic marvel."

"Bitch." Shinto grunted.

Heather added, "Goldbrick on the lips, a lifetime on your hips."

We glanced at each other, turned to her, and said in unison, "Bitch."

Laughter followed us all the way to our lockers.

***

On friday night, the Bar Restaurant on Wall Street filled beyond capacity. People came for the steaks with chimichurri sauce, but I came for the dessert. I couldn't wait for my amazing Goldbrick ice cream sundae, but first I needed to fight my way to the counter. We worked our cop mojo on a couple of nerds and stared hard until they quit their stools. We high-fived each other and perched on our bar stools like victorious Vikings. I leaned back, taking it all in; the old silver tin ceiling reflecting back loud conversation, the odd shriek of laughter, and the whir of blenders.

I ordered for both of us, and when the kid at the counter slid my Goldbrick in front of me, I swear it gave me an out-of-body experience. I'd been away in Dallas for a long time and dreamed of this moment. I bragged on Goldbricks to Derek every late night we went out drinking. Enough to give him a contact sugar high. Which reminded me—

"I never told you about Derek," I said casually, as I slid a spoonful of caramel-laced vanilla into my mouth.

Shinto scowled at my dessert. "Derek who?" She looked up and seemed pleased with the distraction.

"Derek, who kept me sane in Dallas," I said.

"Finally, something interesting." Shinto propped her chin in her hand. "Spill. And don't leave out the juicy parts."

"You gotta remember, that FBI forensics school was pretty tough."

"Ah, poor baby."

"After classes me and some of the others would leave campus to unwind."

"Including Daryl."

"Derek. Yes. After a while it became just me and Derek."

"He on the job?"

"Police sergeant from Nacogdoches."

"Hot?"

"Like a scruffy Brad Pitt with edges. Let's say he gives a whole new meaning to classmate."

"I knew it," Shinto said. "You seemed way too happy."

"I'll show you happy." I pulled out my phone and thumbed through a few of the dozen selfies we took. I gave up and handed her the phone. "Slide to the right."

She busied herself with my Dallas love life and I got busy with my melting dessert. I slid one drippy spoonful of into my mouth and glanced up to see a busboy palm a customer a small glassine bag with one hand while he took money with the other.

Seriously?

"Shinto, I'm witnessing a drug buy." I mouthed the words around my ice cream.

"What?" She didn't look up from my phone.

"Shinto, gimme the phone. Concentrate. Drug buy, nine o'clock." I swallowed. "Latin kid. Busboy with the weird hair and Joe College in the Midland Tech sweatshirt."

Shinto followed my gaze. "Got them. Thing is do we care?"

"I do if you do," I said.

"I sure don't want to watch you suck down any more of that dessert. You ready?"

I stood and felt for my off-duty Sig Sauer. "If they split up, you take the short one. Oh, and Shinto—"

"What?" She was already up and moving.

"Try not to kill anybody."

The busboy a short Hispanic man, shouldered a tray of dishes and headed for the kitchen when I tapped his other shoulder and whispered in his ear. "Busted, asshole. I'm a police officer. I want you to walk quietly to the end of the bar and put down those dishes."

He did as he was told and turned to me all attitude. "Shit, chica. You ain't no cop. You're too fuckin' pretty to be a cop. You need little Pepe to make you feel better?" He cupped his crotch and licked his lips, enjoying himself. "We can go out back for a little piece of heaven."

I grabbed his shoulder and felt him tense. Awesome. He was going to bolt. Sure enough, he pulled the tray of dishes to the floor between us and ran. I slogged through the plates and caught up with him in the kitchen. He whirled and kicked me hard in the shins. Son of a bitch.

I hooked his arm and twisted it behind him. He yanked loose of my grasp and hauled ass toward the back door, yanking pots and pans off shelves to trip me up. Little sucker was quick but I gained at every step. He made the back door about the time I got close enough and I launched myself.

We stumbled through the door and out into the alley. Our momentum carried us into a row of dented metal trash cans. We knocked them over and fell wrestling into a slick mess of discarded food, papers, cans, and unidentified slime. He punched and kicked me. We rolled together, squishing in the goo. He clawed at my neck, and that did it. I spit out a piece of soggy carrot and slugged him hard in the eye. My fist slid off his cheek into a piece of liver.

He rolled over, scuttled to get away. I yanked him back by his pants, and they slid to his ankles. His hairy brown butt smacked me in the face as he pried frantically at my hold on his khakis.

I seized his balls hanging right in front of my nose and squeezed. Maybe I twisted harder then I needed to. Nah.

He howled and cupped his wounded nuts. I stood up to cheers from the wait staff, cuffed him, pulled up his pants, and marched him toward the street to search for Shinto.

"Police brutality, you fucking bitch. I'm going to report you, pig." He sneered.

"Are we through here?" I said.

He kicked at me and slipped on a piece of wet lettuce. I yanked him to his feet.

"Now Pepe, this has been a little bit of paradise."

Shinto rounded the corner. Her arrest had been uneventful and she practically glowed. Me on the other hand? Smelly slop dripped down the front of my shirt.

"Nice look." Shinto smirked.

"Thanks." I raked a clump of cold frijoles from my hair and heaved it at her.

Chapter Thirteen

Junior

Took me a while to find the Fine Arts building. I didn't mind. It felt unusually cool this morning, and I liked the walk. The grounds crew on mowers wheeled up and back on the thick green lawns. The smell of mown grass added the right spice to the air. A white sign with a black arrow pointed the way. I checked my schedule before heading up stairs. Elementary Drawing. On the second floor.

First door I came to, I peered through the frosted window and saw people sketching at easels. Bingo. I opened the door and a woefully overweight woman with neon pink hair flounced over to me.

"My god, you are beautiful," she said. "Turn around. Yes. You could pose for GQ. That jaw, your nose. Love the shoulder-length black hair. Where have you been all my life gorgeous?"

I pushed her hand away from my face. "Lady, I don't know who you are. I'm here for the elementary drawing class. Is this it?"

"No. Oh, I'm so sorry." Her hands flew to her mouth, and she giggled. "I thought you were the nude model I hired. I'm Mrs. Young." She wore some kind of multicolored tent-looking dress and large hoop earrings. Bright blue eye shadow caked on her eyelids. She extended her hand and smiled shyly.

"Junior Alvarez." I shook her damp hand. "I take it this isn't elementary drawing?"

"Sorry, sweetie. That's next door. By the way if you do ever want to model, nude or clothed? Let me know. It pays well." Her hand traced its way down my bicep before I could pull away.

"Pay?"

"Handsomely." A small grin played across her face.

"What do you have to do to model?"

"Sit on that podium over there, and let students draw you. You have to sit still for at least twenty minutes at a time though. Harder than it sounds. You get a ten-minute break, and that's about it."

"I could be interested. How much?" I stared deep into her eyes, dialing up the mojo.

She flicked her hair back and cooed, "Decent money."

"What's decent?" I jumped up on the podium and sat on the chair.

"One hundred dollars an hour." She stared at my crotch.

"You're joking." I switched positions, opened my legs, flexed.

"Remember you can't move." She licked her lips. "I could teach you some tricks to stay still."

"Teach away, teach, I'd do about anything for that kind of money." I winked.

Did she just moan?

"Come back later, after your classes are over, and I'll help you. I'll get a list of agents, if you like doing it. They can hook you up with more jobs."

"Thanks, Mrs. Young. I'll be back around three." I jumped down off the chair and slowly made my way out of the room whistling, watching her.

"See you then, Junior." She turned and gathered drawings up off her desk.

"One hundred dollars an hour to sit still. What the hell?" I laughed to myself. "Free money. I don't have to smash anyone's face in. I think I'm beginning to dig this school thing."

Three o'clock came around, and I swaggered into Mrs. Young's classroom. The male model finished wrapping a robe around his white, saggy body. No wonder she went wild when she saw me, if that's what she's used to. I might make some serious cash at this gig. Mrs. Young busied herself rubbing a finger and smudging black stuff on paper at an easel propped on a table. A lanky blue-eyed girl in jeans and a green-striped long-sleeved shirt, hair in a ponytail pulled high on her head, kept nodding with each stroke of the teacher's pudgy finger, as if Young were drawing a masterpiece.

Mrs. Young saw me, patted the girl on the back, and headed my way. "You came. I'm glad to see you." She smiled.

"Yes, ma'am. I thought I'd get a feel for what you want me to do from earlier."

"Craig, come here." She motioned to the model returned to the room now fully clothed.

"What's up?" He yawned.

"This is Junior, and he's interested in modeling. Could you tell him how you do it and what's involved while I finish up with Susie?"

"No problemo." He looked me up and down, his expression said he was convinced I'd suck at such a difficult task. "Come on over to the throne, and I'll show you some things."

I followed him to the raised platform in the center of the room. The "throne" was a straight-backed wooden chair, typical school issue. He sat down with his legs together, hands on his knees.

"There are standard poses they always want." He shifted through a few, arm on the chair back, legs crossed, Indian style. "Then there are poses that certain teachers want. They want to get creative. You have to know your own body limitations. Otherwise you'll get wicked cramps, appendages that fall asleep. If they twist you into a pretzel or something, you say no or demand more money. Sometimes that works. Hardest thing is remembering exactly, to the smallest detail, the pose you were in before you took your break. If you screw up, the students and teacher pitch a royal fit. Any questions?"

"Sounds easy." I threw him a bone. "But I know from experience whatever sounds easy is usually the hardest."

"You got that right. Dude, I gotta bounce."

"I appreciate your help."

Before he left he said, "There are books you can study for poses and shit. Ask Momma Young to hook you up."

"Thanks, man."

"If you decide to do this, we'll probably see each other again. These college artistes love gang posing. Like an orgy frozen in time. Twisted. Literally." He laughed and headed out. "Have fun," he called over his shoulder.

The old lady came up behind me. "Did Craig help?"

"He said you might have some books that explained posing."

"I do. Why don't you pose for Heather and me right here?"

"What do you want me to do?"

"Just take off your shirt and get comfortable on the chair."

Heather got a new piece of paper, and Mrs. Young sat at another easel as I perched on the chair and peeled off my T-shirt. I glanced down at the fine weave of raised scar tissue where each church member used various pieces of dirty glass and needles to carve crosses above my right pec. My *blessings* on display. On my back, a generous crisscross of raised belt and whip lashes.

"Oh my," the woman whispered.

"Awesome," said the young girl.

Chapter Fourteen

Kailey

"Momma, where's my phone?" I lifted the sweater off our old sable couch.

Momma laughed as she rolled her wheelchair toward me. It makes me happy to see her smile.

"When's your next doctor's appointment?" I fished my hand behind the cushion. "Here it is." I held it up like I'd won a prize. "I wish I would remember to put this thing away, not that anyone calls."

"You need to go out with someone besides Shinto, Kailey."

"I'm swearing off men, Momma, remember? No room in my life and no time."

"There are nice guys out there."

"Neither of us have had much luck in that department."

"Don't you say that—"

"Daddy drank, Momma. A lot." I turned to go back to my room.

"Don't speak about your father that way. Kailey Jo Carmichael, your father worked hard. He did the best he could. He loved us." She sniffled. "In his own way."

I knelt in front of her, gently took her gnarled hands in mine. "Momma, I'm sorry. I'm really thinking about me, all I've lost with Emma. I couldn't go through that again. Besides, I've got you, Shinto, my department. That's life enough for me at the moment."

"All I'm saying, sweetheart, is be open to love."

"Love is for little girls, Momma. I put away Barbie and Ken a long time ago." I grabbed the phone and escaped to the kitchen. How can she be such a hopeless romantic after all Daddy put her through?

My phone vibrated. *Message Waiting.* I thumbed it and read as I scanned the room for my purse.

"Momma, gotta go back to work. One of the guys called in, and they need me to cover. Will you be okay?"

"The visiting nurse will be here shortly. Everything is under control. Kailey?" She shifted in her wheelchair. "You just worked eight hours. Be careful. I love you. I know the sacrifices you're making for me. You're a blessing and an amazing daughter."

"Love you too. Gotta go." I kissed her, smelled her lavender perfume. "Be real with the nurse, you hear? Tell her what hurts."

Once in the car I sat still for a moment, baking. Dang air conditioner wouldn't kick in until I got moving. My mom, always thinking about others first. She saw the good in everyone, even Daddy. After all those years of her heartache and his drinking? After he put her in that damn chair?

I cranked the radio to drown the voices in my head. The first few notes of George Strait's "All My Exes Live in Texas" came on, and I stabbed a finger at the radio to turn it off. Not soon enough. Images of Emma bouncing in her car seat, chubby little arms and legs waving, flooded me. She loved that stupid song. Every time it came on she'd laugh and dance her silly sitting dance. I swiped at the tears streaming down my face and yanked the car into reverse.

I need to work. I need my days to drone on and on.

Thank goodness the police station was close. At least there I can put a world of hurt on someone, anyone. Best way to stop the pain is inflict it on someone else, any poor fool unlucky enough to get in my way.

I stood on the brakes and slid into a parking space. Took the stairs two at a time.

Chuck Dempsey, a big, well-built tall blond guy, leaned on a desk when I clocked in. "You taking Paul's shift?"

"Looks like it," I said as I rushed by him for the locker room.

Ten minutes later I rode shotgun with Chuck as we pulled away from the station. Paul was Chuck's partner.

"What's up with Paul?" I asked.

"His friggin' feet."

"What?"

"Doctor cut a bunion off his foot. You'd think he suffered an amputation the way he's carrying' on. Sorry to call you in. I know you just put in a full eight."

"No problem. I'd rather work than sit around at home."

"We may have some fun. It's a full moon tonight. Curtain call for the crazies."

***

Our radio squawked within minutes of leaving the station. "Gang fight on Garfield." I flipped on the lights and sirens, and we spun tires.

"Hope we get there before it's over," I said.

Chuck raised his eyebrows.

I cracked my knuckles. "I need the diversion."

He steered us through the next red light and yelled, "I'm betting we drive up, find a few banged up kids, everyone clams up, and we go about our business. Unless you feel like writing a report."

I laughed. "Not until they add writer's cramp to Worker's Comp."

"So tell me. How'd you like Dallas?" He took a hard right at the next corner.

"I liked it." I flashed mentally on my last night with Derek and felt heat rise past my collar. To cover, I rushed on. "Turns out I have a knack for forensics."

"No shit."

"I know, right? Something about piecing together a crime scene after the fact, the puzzle of it." I scratched my head. "I like using science to collar assholes who think they've gotten away with something."

We flew past cars and stop signs, the buildings a blur.

"Better you than me," he said. He slammed on the brakes.

I felt my seatbelt tighten.

"We're here. Lock and load."

We unsnapped, flung open the doors, and stepped out.

A crowd of six people turned and ran. Chuck laughed. "That'll save some paperwork."

The few that remained seemed determined to represent, whatever the shit it is that they represent. The gang leaned their backs against a brick storefront, arms crossed. In their early twenties, posing, acting all hard. They'd soften up soon enough with a baton cracked across their shins.

We posed, too. Put on stern cop faces and approached like we were tired of cleaning up crap. It's all crap, either way. I checked our perimeters as we walked. Chuck thumbed the radio on his shoulder and reported our location.

"Okay, everyone. Party's over. Let's move on." Chuck smiled.

"We ain't doing nothing. Why we gotta move?" A big kid with Fuck You tattooed across his forehead spit on the sidewalk.

I bet his mama's proud. "What's your name?" I pulled out my notepad and pretended to write.

"Don't have to give you my name," he said. "I know my rights."

"That so? Watch a lot of TV, do you?"

He scowled.

"See," I said, "Hollywood almost never gets it right. It's the darnedest thing. Besides, Mr. Fuck You, is it? Fuck You, this is Midland Texas." I turned to Chuck. "Officer? How far would you say we are from Hollywood?"

"Three thousand, four hundred and sixty-nine miles.," he said. "A long way."

"You're fucking with us," Fuck You said.

"You think? Now tell me your name, or we take you in and you'll wish you were in Hollywood."

"Fred," he said. He puffed out his chest.

"Fred?" my pen hovered.

"Medina." He spit again.

"Ah. Nice name. Freddie Medina. By the way, spit on the sidewalk one more time, and you'll lick it up or spend a week in jail. Seems there's a law against it, Mr. Medina."

Chuck took a turn. "Thank you, Fred. Soon's we get your buddies' names, you can move along. Oh." He slapped his forehead. "Almost forgot. We've had complaints. Loud music, fighting, folks hollering. Know anything about that?"

"Nope, officers." Freddie grinned at his merry band who all nodded in agreement.

"Quiet as a cemetery around here," said another vato in his baggy pants and wife-beater uniform.

"Ah," Chuck said, "you must be the poet of the group. What's your name?"

As he talked I noticed a young girl peeking around the corner of the building, a pre-teen. Thick mascara ran in black streaks from her eyes.

"You okay?" I walked over and crouched in front of her. "What's wrong, honey? Something I can help you with?"

Her eyes shifted to Fuck You Freddie like a frightened deer. "Nada, señora. Please go away."

She turned to go, and I noticed mud on the back of her blouse. "Stop. What happened to you?" I put a hand on her arm.

"I fell." She looked again at Freddie and shivered. Midland's hot, even in the evening.

"What's your name, and how old are you?"

"Please, ma'am, I'll go straight home." She eased away from me.

I looked over, tried to read Chuck's thoughts. He shook his head ever so slightly.

"You do that." I clapped my hands. "Run. NOW."

She whirled and scooted, her tennis shoes slapping pavement.

I rose and rounded on Freddie and his gang. "Looks like you cholos get a pass today. 'Cause it's too nice a day to ruin it dealing with you, frankly." I tucked my notebook back in my belt. "For your sakes, you should all know, cut-off age for statutory rape in Texas is sixteen."

"We never touched that girl." Freddie grinned at his boys. "Did we?"

The other two shook their heads, without Fuck You's bravado.

"Glad to hear it," I said. "Because the way it works is if one guy rapes her, you all get charged with raping her."

"Hey, that's bullshit, man." One of Freddie's boys kicked at the pavement.

"I know. So unfair. Now get out of here."

Freddie's two friends ran off. He followed at a slow walk. Saving face.

Back in the cruiser, Chuck said, "I forgot what a badass you are, Kailey."

"How could I not be? What sort of mental deficient idiot tattoos Fuck You on his forehead?"

"That mental deficient idiot, apparently." He cranked the ignition and pulled away from the curb.

About an hour later the car radio squawked to life and we got a domestic violence call.

"Here we go." he said and yanked us into a quick U-turn. We pulled up to a white two-story home with columns on either side of a red front door. The manicured green lawn and red roses in bloom were accented by subtle lighting pointed at the roses and trees. We heard chamber music as we approached. A man and woman in the house shouted in the background. Chuck knocked on the door and yelled, "Police."

He knocked again and yelled louder. "POLICE. Open the door or we break it down."

"Hold on; I'm coming," an angry male voice called out.

A guy in a suit opened the door a crack. "What seems to be the matter, officers?"

"You tell us," I said. "We're hearing complaints. Mind opening the door?"

He narrowed his eyes and widened the opening as far as his arm could reach. "There. Happy?"

"Happier," Chuck said. "Mind if we come in? We can all be happy together."

"Do you have a warrant?"

Chuck shook his head and said to me," Can you believe it? Second TV lawyer of the night."

"Here's how it works," I said. "Despite what you learned from the University of LA Law. For domestic complaints we are required to interview all parties, determine what happened, and make an arrest, if it's actionable."

"Technically, we're not searching for a thing," Chuck said. "No search warrant required. I suggest you do the smart thing and invite us in."

"Fine. Whatever," he opened the door all the way and stepped aside. "She's uh, she fell, and I was about to call the paramedics when you got here."

We pushed inside and saw a woman cradling a young child weeping in her arms. Chuck pushed the man to one side of the room while I ministered to the woman. She wore a set of green satin pajamas. The top button on her front dangled by a thread, her upper lip puffed out on one side and trickled blood. Her right eye would soon be completely swollen shut. I knelt in front of the two. "Hi, ma'am. I'm Officer Carmichael. What's your name?"

"Mrs. Quigley. Amanda Quigley. That's my husband, Ronald."

"Who is this little beauty?" I tugged on the little girl's sleeve. "Hm? What's your name, honey?" Three, maybe four years old. She turned toward me, and my heart clenched. Curly blond hair and blue eyes. Emma reincarnated.

"Lisa," she said, her voice muffled by her mother's shoulder.

I couldn't help myself and reached forward to stroke a curl on the delicate little head. "Well, Lisa. Everything's going to be okay. I'm going to talk with your mommy here. Would that be all right?"

She sniffed and nodded, wiping her nose on her mother's top while her mother continued rocking her.

"Ma'am, can you tell me what went on here?"

Amanda glanced over to her husband. "My husband's a lunatic." She shuddered. "And an ass. Lisa was up watching TV. He stormed in. I could tell he'd been drinking. He slapped her, grabbed her by the arm, and slammed her against the wall. He yelled at her to go to her room then kicked her for not moving fast enough. Lisa ran to me, and I comforted her. He came over, yelled something a child should never hear, and hit me too. He's a maniac." She glared at her husband. "YOU'RE A MANIAC! GET OUT OF MY HOUSE."

"You mean my house, bitch," he yelled from across the room.

"Settle down, Mr. Quigley," I heard Chuck say.

Amanda shrieked, "I want him out. I want a restraining order. I want him in jail."

Little Lisa sobbed in earnest. "Mommy, my arm hurts."

I heard the click of handcuffs and glanced over at Chuck.

"You don't have to do this. Why are you doing this? Amanda, tell them you're fine. AMANDA."

"I'm calling the wagon," I said. I keyed my mic and put in a call for dispatch to send paramedics. I turned back to Amanda. "Ma'am, please, calm down. It's not doing you or your daughter any good. I've called for medical. We'll get you squared away in no time."

"Is he going to jail?"

"That is our plan for the moment, yes."

"Lock him in with the biggest, angriest gay man you can find. Then lose the key."

I squelched a smile. "I'll see what I can do. If you ladies will excuse me?"

I stood and consciously kept my hands from balling into fists. When I got to Chuck, he steered a handcuffed and defiant man toward the door.

"May I?" I said to Chuck. "You'll want to check with Mrs. Quigley and Lisa for our report. I'd be more than happy to escort Mr. Quigley to the squad car and secure him safely in the backseat."

"Excellent idea, officer." Chuck grinned. "Be careful with him. Don't hurt him."

"Wouldn't dream of it," I said.

I grabbed the guy's arm and squeezed his bicep.

"OWW."

"You're with me, Mr. Quigley." I guided him toward the front door. "In case you're interested, we've called the paramedics for your wife and daughter."

I marched Mr. Quigley out the double oak front doors and down the brick staircase outside. We rounded a bunch of rose bushes and I stuck my boot out. Dear Mr. Quigley flew face first into the thorny patch.

"Get up." I stood over him as he lay bleating like a sheep.

"You did that on purpose," he sputtered. "Do you know who I am?"

I studied him while he struggled, his arms secured behind his back as his legs kept snagging on the bushes. I grabbed his shirt and pulled until he almost righted himself and then I let him drop back into the bushes.

"OW. YOUR CAREER IS OVER, OFFICER. I KNOW EVERY JUDGE IN THIS CITY."

"What a coincidence," I said. "Me too."

I grabbed his handcuffed hands and yanked him to his feet as the paramedics pulled up. The lead lieutenant came up to me. Thank god I knew him. "Battered mother and daughter inside that need attention."

"What about him?" the paramedic looked at me quizzically.

Quigley sobbed. "Help me. She hurt me. Police brutality."

I smiled my sweetest smile. "Poor guy tripped as he came off the steps and fell into the rose bushes. Nothing a little iodine and Band-Aids can't fix. Folks in the house are why I called you."

"I like your style, Kailey," the lieutenant said.

"Back at you, Cameron."

"Oh, for Christ's sake—" Quigley didn't get a chance to finish.

I pushed and pulled him to the squad car. I opened the door.

He turned and whispered, "You will pay for this." He leaned his head toward the house and sneered. "So will they."

Somehow, he cracked his head on the doorframe when I shoved him into the backseat. Then, I might have stomped on his ankle before he could pull it inside. I slammed the car door and propped my hands on the roof, seething.

Chuck walked up. "We all good here? Kailey?"

"Good to go, officer," I said. "Who we got in holding? Has Big Jamaal been pinched for drunk and disorderly yet? About time for it."

"We'll call in. Why?"

"Got a cellmate for him."

Hours later, at the end of our shift I made tracks for my car. The parking lot lit up like daylight. Typical police department policy.

Chuck's voice stopped me with my key in the lock. "Hey, Kailey, wait up."

I turned around to see Chuck walking toward me.

"Got a sec?"

"Two or three. What's up?"

"You know that domestic of ours?"

Where was he going with this? "Not that senile yet, Chuck."

"You seemed, I don't know, to take it kind of personal."

"Really?" I flashed back to that sweet little girl's face and saw Emma's right beside it. "Your mind's goofing on you."

"Uh huh. What about the husband?"

"The asshole? What about him?"

"You seemed to have it in for him."

"Maybe." I played at nonchalant. "A little. He deserved it."

"Ten-four. He certainly did." He hesitated. "Can I ask you something?"

"What?"

"This thing you've got against guys, is it going to keep getting in the way?"

"Whoa, hey. What?"

"Jesus, Kailey. I mean, it's no secret. Everybody in the department knows."

"Knows what?"

"Come on. You know." Chuck shuffled his feet. "Forget it." He turned to walk away.

"Hell, no. I'm not forgetting anything. What is it I'm supposed to know Chuck, that everybody knows?"

"You got a big chip on for guys, that's all. I mean, I get it. We all get it. You and Shinto are together, and—"

I started laughing then. I laughed so hard I think I scared him. "Chuck," I choked out between gasps, "Shinto and I are friends. Good friends. Very good." I wiped tears from my eyes. "But we're not, I mean I'm not, oh my god. I hate to wreck your lesbian fantasies, but—" I walked over and planted a kiss on Chuck's forehead. "You're a pretty good detective, Chuck. You are. When you don't jump to conclusions."

I got in my car, cranked the engine, and rolled down the window. "Have a good weekend. Say hello to the family."

I drove off, thinking about what Chuck said. That's what they all think? That Shinto and I are together? That I'm gay? Good. Let them think what they want. Next time I see Shinto at headquarters I'll walk right up, kiss her on the lips, and explain it to her later.

In the meantime, my love life is my business. Such as it is. Closest I got to love I left behind me in the parking decks of the Dallas airport on my last night. With Derek.

***

I heard footsteps behind me as I hefted my considerable suitcase collection into the back hatch of my Toyota. The flutter in my stomach jumped to my throat. I recognized the gait and the clomp of his Tony Lamas. I froze as the steps got closer and I felt his hands on my shoulders, pulling me up straight. His arms encircled me, and warm breath tickled the hairs on the back of my neck.

"Going somewhere, gorgeous?" he whispered in my ear.

His hands slid down and around me, cupping my breasts through my department-issue T-shirt.

"Have I told you how sexy you are in a gray T-shirt?"

I twisted around to face my sergeant lover from Nacogdoches. His laughing blue eyes, much bluer than mine. His soft lips with that quirky little smile that always seemed to be teasing me, when they weren't kissing me.

"Derek, we said good-bye last night. Don't make it any harder on us."

"Too late," he said as he grabbed my hand and pulled it to his crotch.

I felt the heat pressing hard through his Lee jeans, and my knees almost buckled then and there. "We can't," I said.

"We can," he said as he put his mouth on mine and pried with his tongue. We fumbled our way to the backseat door, and I reached behind me to yank it open. We tumbled inside, gripped by an insistent fever that even the cramped backseat of the Toyota couldn't cool.

Desperate hands pulled at buckles, snaps, buttons, and zippers as we squirmed for position. Him on the bottom. Me with my legs apart, trying to slide over.

"Climb on, woman," he said.

I felt his hands on my hips, pulling me down as he thrust up inside me.

Oh. My. God.

My orgasm filled every crevice inside me with sizzling bright light and kept it there for what seemed like an eternity. Even afterwards, collapsed on top of him in a sweaty heap, I didn't want it to end. Ever. Yet, it would. It had to. I was due back in Midland and Nacogdoches called to him.

Our wondrous, magical time together in Dallas, courtesy of our departments and the FBI, had to end.

Chapter Fifteen

Junior

I stopped outside Mr. Miller's office, shifted my textbooks and binders to my other hand, and knocked.

"Enter." The voice came so soft I barely heard it through the door. I stepped in and saw my parole officer bent over a pile of papers with a marker in his hand, muttering and circling things on the pages.

He looked up and pointed. "Have a seat, Junior. I'll be with you in a second." Finally he scooped stacks of paper into a ragged pile and plopped the mess into a box overloaded with a dozen similar stacks. He leaned back and grunted. "I am sure some idiot bureaucrat convinced his equally idiotic superintendent they needed all those forms filled out in triplicate or the world would crumble. Yet the only world crumbling is mine. Junior?" He leaned forward and clasped his hands in earnest entreaty. "Please tell me something, anything, to brighten my shitty day."

I couldn't believe I actually felt sorry for the guy.

"Don't know if this counts Mr. Miller. As of five days ago, I am officially a college student. Me. Who knew, right?"

He slapped his desk. "That's what I'm talking about. What are you taking? You like your classes?"

"I really do. With your help and a neighbor friend who used to teach at Midland, I think I made some good choices. The work's interesting. Homework's not too hard."

"You're on your way, Junior. I can feel it. Tell me something you learned you didn't know before."

"Uh . . . I don't know . . ." I turned over the top book in my stack. "I'm taking geology, and it's cool. Did you know there's this San Andres Formation goes right under Midland? Right under us? It's true." I tapped my foot on the brown linoleum tile. "Dig about five thousand feet down, you'll hit rocks over two hundred thirty million years old from the Permian Period. That's why Midland is called the Permian Basin and why there's a crap load of oil." I put the book back in my lap and felt myself grinning like an idiot. What the hell is happening to me?

He leaned forward and held his hand palm out. "Gimme five, man. Look at you. A budding geologist."

"It's one class."

"I'm proud of you, Junior, and I know it's one. That's how it starts. Take one class at a time. Show up. Do the work. You learn something."

"That's what she said."

"She?"

"That neighbor, old lady lives across the way from me. Turns out she was the one in the wreck. You know, on my first day?"

"Then we're both right. You're making an effort, son. You are. Thank you for making my day."

I handed him the paperwork my student aid advisor gave me for him to fill out, and while Mr. Miller flipped through and scribbled his signature, I felt good. In a weird way I never felt before. Mr. Miller gave me permission to feel proud of myself. For something I accomplished. The feeling didn't suck.

***

Back out on the sidewalk, I hauled my stack of books, homework, and myself toward my hovel. Dry heat in summer is brutal in this town. The air rippled, trying to fan itself. I rounded the corner of the apartment building and ran smack into my neighbor. The Tomato lover.

"Howdy, neighbor. Having a good day, Junior?" She looked at me like she really cared if my day was good or not.

"I am having a fan-fuck-I mean, a fantastic day. You?"

"I'm good . . . I've been fixing lunch, and . . ." She wrapped her arms around her body. It made her green blouse tight around her magnificent boobs. "Hey, are you hungry?"

The old me would have had a field day with that question. The new me simply nodded and said, "I'm always hungry."

"Then that settles it. I made a salad and tuna for sandwiches. That is, if you like tuna." "Just one thing," I said.

"What?"

"I hope your salad has plenty of tomatoes."

She hesitated for a second, and I thought I might have hurt her feelings. Then she let out a belly laugh that got us both going.

"As it happens, I did, Junior. Nice, firm, round tomatoes."

My old self about lost his shit, pushing to get a rise out of me. I ignored him. "Then lead on."

I followed her to her apartment, staring at her butt. I'm still human and she couldn't see me. I inhaled two sandwiches and half her salad and thought, I could get to like this normal life stuff. Who knew people could be so nice?

"Patricia, I'd love to sit and chat with you; that was the best lunch I have ever eaten, I swear, but I have two tests coming up."

"What am I thinking? You need to study. You can't sit jabbering with an old woman when you have work to do."

"Patricia." I grabbed her hands in mine. "Stop with that. You're not old. Frankly you're friggin' hot. If the time and place were different, who knows?" I let the words die an uncomfortable death.

She flushed and pulled her hands free. She stood all aflutter. "A man needs his strength, and you might get hungry later, so . . . I mean . . . I'll wrap this up, and you can take it home and eat it whenever you get hungry." She cleared the table and slammed through a couple cabinets, pulling out plastic containers. "Studying is hard work, Junior. I'm proud of you for pushing through."

Second person today who said they were proud of me. Definitely a record.

She finished snapping lids on plastic containers and filling baggies with sandwich squares. She handed me the food and patted my arm. "See you later, Junior." We walked to her door. I tried to thank her again. She silenced me with a finger on my lips. "You don't have to thank me. That's what neighbors are for. Besides, you remind me a lot of my son." Her eyes turned sad and I saw tears glisten for a second, before she hastily shut her door.

***

I sat at the kitchen table and studied as much as my eyes and spongey brain would let me. Started on geology, slipped into algebra, and cracked open the reading for English lit. Big mistake.

I awoke with drool all over my paperwork. My ass needed a break from sitting, and my brain can absorb only so much schoolwork. I remembered Miguel invited me, semi insisted, I come to his party. Said if I didn't show, questions would be asked and answers provided by a beat down. Party sounded better.

It was dark in the house when I walked up. The music loud. My eyes adjusted. I grabbed a long-necked cerveza from the refrigerator and wandered around. Best to get the lay of the place before I decided where to hang. A lot of the kids I didn't know. They looked young. Babies.

I spotted a bowl of X, popped a tab, and gulped it down with a swig of Corona. It'd take a while for the Ecstasy to hit. May as well get comfortable. I wandered into the living room and spotted Miguel. He grinned and motioned me over to his harem. He sat in the middle of a couch with chicas pressing in on both sides.

"Junior. Hey, man where you been hiding?" Miguel interrupted my fantasy, a smirk curled around his lips as smoke from a lit joint filtered through his moustache. He passed it to me. "Que pasa, hombre?"

"Boring shit," I said. "You?" I sucked in a quick toke. Passed it on to a girl with hot purple hair and a nose ring.

"Plans, man. Big plans. We're having a meet tomorrow night for a score next week. You'll fit right in. Fact, we could use you for it."

The joint came back around and I hit it again, inhaled deep, and squeaked out, "I could use some spending money. What time and where?" Exhale.

"Meet here around ten."

I passed him the joint.

He took a hit and waved me off. I was dismissed.

I ambled over to a black-painted wall and kicked back, leaning into the corner. Five feet to my right, a huge velvet neon painting of two reclining nude women added class to the place. I drained my beer and watched the party swirl around me.

About fifty teens and a few tweens spasmed in place to the music. Every one of them blasted, hammered, high, and otherwise ripped out of their minds. The thumping drumbeat pounded deep in my gut while the X warmed my body.

I pushed off the wall and headed for a dazed druggie nodding off all by herself. The X had me going, and I went with it. Maybe I'll hurt her a little, not enough to do too much damage. She opened bloodshot hazel eyes and smiled as I approached. She was about my age, maybe a little older. I got closer and saw crude teardrop tattoos. She'd been in jail a few times. She struggled to straighten up. I yanked her upright and leaned in close.

"Hey, baby," I said, "want to party?"

She grinned and pawed lazily for my arm.

I planted a hard kiss on her lips, made sure to bite down a little.

She flinched and slurred, "That hurt." Blood trickled down her chin. She grinned and attempted to punch me. I caught her slow-motion jab midair and twisted her arm behind her. I pulled her to me and grabbed her breast and squeezed hard. She winced. I turned her face to me and asked, "Want more?"

"Show me what you got, bad boy."

I smashed my mouth onto hers and bit her again as she rubbed my crotch. I picked her up and forced her to the wall. Pulled up her skirt. She didn't have panties on. Nice. She pushed me away far enough to unbutton my jeans.

"Now this is what I'm talking about." She pulled back to get a better view. "You're bigger than most; I like that."

I bitch-slapped her and shoved into her. She felt willing and wet. She moaned loud and I covered her mouth. She threw her head from side to side. I pulled out. She knelt in front of me to give me head. I yanked her up, turned her around, and mounted her from the back, slamming her head into the wall. I pinched her breasts and pulled on them.

She squealed, "Stop, stop. You're hurting me." She wiggled to get away.

I got her skinny neck into the crook of my arm, pulled her toward me and slammed my cock deep inside her. She groaned and I came hard.

Yesss.

I let her go, and she held out a hand. "How much you got big man?"

"Piss off, skank." I slapped her hand away and shoved my junk back into my pants, buttoned up, and headed for the door, followed by my demons.

"Asshole." She countered.

The old Junior laughed, content. The new one, not so much. I got home and kicked the door closed. What the hell? That sex back there ranked about as low as a toss-off in a jail cell. Who was I kidding? Am I really changing or making a big show of it for an audience? Maybe my parole officer? My school? My neighbor Patricia? Me?

Chapter Sixteen

Kailey and Shinto

"Captain." I stood at attention. No idea why he called Shinto and me into his office and asked us to close the door.

"Officers, our town has a problem, and I think you two can help solve it." He looked down at a file on his desk. I sneaked a peek at Shinto. She raised her eyebrows.

"It's delicate. Our complaining citizens are connected, and our mayor is on the warpath. No one is willing to testify, yet they want this *problem* to go away. Time to go undercover." He leaned back in his chair. Captain Samosa is a by-the-book bear of a man with receding gray fringe around a balding pate, a slipped halo around his dark Mexican head. I smiled.

"We have a situation at Magic Hands Massage. It seems the masseuses give great massages. I've been told after a wealthy woman customer comes back several times, there is one man and one woman that ask certain questions. About whether the woman is happy in her marriage or relationship. Innocuous questions, and they still give the woman a great normal massage. After a few more weeks of getting to know those clients, each time the massage gets a little more intimate. A slip of the sheet. Then if the woman doesn't react too much, they may massage the breast which leads to more intimate touching. Then they ask for money for these extra pleasures. If the woman is amenable they offer to go all the way for a sizable donation or tip."

"Gross." Shinto scowled. "I'd break a hand if anyone touched me without my invitation."

He ignored her. "We need to catch these scumbags in the act of offering their services. You can carry a small recorder in your purse and camera on your blouse that you can hang up in the room."

We both groaned.

I frowned. "How far do we let them go?"

"Far as you can."

I shifted on my feet. "I've never had a massage, Captain. What do you mean hang our blouse up?"

"To get a massage you have to disrobe."

"Take our clothes off?" I cocked my head. "Seriously? With cameras rolling?"

"It's for a good cause." He chuckled. "Only a couple of female officers will view the recordings. They will be discreet."

"I'll bet."

"Plus, the good citizens of Midland will pay for the massages. Come on, ladies. I wouldn't ask you to do this, but it has been an ongoing problem for a few months, and we have to catch them. The owners of Magic Hands Massage have appealed to us. They are trying to run a legitimate business. If nothing else you will get some great relaxation and work the kinks out."

Shinto looked at me with a do-you-kill-him-or-should-I face.

"When do we start, sir?" I asked brightly.

"Soon as you leave my office, call and make an appointment. Here are the names of the two suspects in question. Shinto, you take the woman, and Kailey, the guy."

"Yes, sir."

"I'm on it," Shinto said.

"May take a few weeks to get them comfortable with you. Play it up. Be two bored wealthy oil wives. We've arranged for Jo James on Wadley to do your makeup, hair, the whole shebang. Chico's will dress you, and Christiani Jewelers on Wall Street will supply your Rolexes and diamonds. Keep the clothes spotless and the jewelry safe. Return them the minute you leave Magic Hands, or it's your ass."

"Yes, sir." We said in unison and left his office.

Shinto grumbled under her breath as she closed the door. "I've never had or ever wanted a big-ass diamond or a fuckin' Rolex."

"And I've never had someone put makeup on me," I said.

***

We didn't enter Magic Hands at the same time. I parked behind the business, picked my way around to the front trying to look comfortable in a white filmy blouse, tight blue silk skirt, and spike heels. I wore a diamond tennis bracelet with diamonds big enough to choke a duck. I twirled a six-carat diamond ring around with my thumb that matched dangling diamond earrings. I didn't know how heavy a diamond-encrusted Rolex could be until I wrapped it around my left wrist. The .40 cal in my stylish little clutch felt somewhat reassuring. But I still would have preferred a police escort.

Shinto emerged from her car about the time I reached the front door. Holy crap. I took a step back and stared. Her four-inch heels pushed her well over six feet. Subtle makeup accented her cheekbones and dark skin tone, which in turn brought out her shocking light blue eyes. She shook out long black hair that cascaded down her back, I'd only ever seen it in a braid, and the effect stunned me. The hairdresser had given her bangs and pulled the rest off her face with a silver barrette that matched long, silver earrings. Shinto smoothed her short black sleeveless dress and her fingers sparkled with diamonds. Silver bracelets tinkled as she moved toward me. Christ. Her poor masseuse didn't stand a chance.

I must have looked like a drowned, diamond-encrusted puppy in comparison. Great for the ego. I threw my shoulders back and teetered forward on stilettos my dresser insisted I could wear. Silly ass.

I told the woman at the desk I wanted a deep tissue massage, like I had a clue, filled out a lot of paperwork, and found my way into a dark waiting room with music piped in. Lots of bird chirps and rushing water, less music.

Shinto followed behind me and barely glanced my way as she imperiously scanned the room filled with men and women of various ages and dress. One empty chair remained.

A blond young man with a too-perfect tan came around the corner and called my name. I rose, and he checked my name off on his clipboard. He flashed an overly white smile and whispered for me to follow him. We entered a room with low lights and a bed with a padded horseshoe pillow strapped onto one end. A poster hung on one wall displaying human muscles with callouts arrayed down the side. Three walls were painted gray and one dark blue. The same music played in the background. A metal chair sat pushed up against the wall, and behind the chair were hooks. On the opposite wall behind my guy a small cabinet, sink, and a towel-warming oven completed the ten-by-ten room.

My masseuse pointed to the chair for me to take a seat, introduced himself as Liam, and asked me a lot of personal questions. He marked my answers down on his clipboard. When we finished, he asked me to undress and lie face down on the message table. He would return when I was ready. He left and I stripped. I positioned the camera and shot birds at the voyeurs back at the station. Then jumped onto the table, covered my tush with the sheet, and plopped my face into the hole in the horseshoe pad. I gripped the table tightly and stared at the herringbone pattern in the blue and gray carpet.

Liam returned and asked, "Is this your first massage?" He pulled the sheet down to the crack in my clenched buttock. It tickled and I squirmed.

"Yes."

"Relax."

Easy for you to say. I stiffened when he touched me, then slowly loosened up. I wasn't prepared for it to feel so good. His hands, slick with some kind of oil, smelled vaguely of exotic spice and the seashore. He slid them over my shoulders and down my back and returned to my neck. He used his forearm and elbow to go deeper into my muscles. Ah, yes, there.

"Tell me if the pressure gets to be too much or if you would like it harder or softer." His voice soothed as well as his hands.

"I will." I squeezed my eyes shut tight. He picked up my arm, and I held it straight out.

He chuckled. "Relax. Please. Give your arm to me. I'll pick it up and put it back. I promise I'll be gentle."

After a few minutes my mind drifted to another universe. My whole back got massaged, then my arm. He worked his way down both legs, rubbed both feet, then moved back up the other side. When he came to my ass he delicately massaged each cheek through the sheet. After a while he pulled the sheet off one side and stood with his head turned, to offer me a semblance of privacy, I guess. He asked me to turn over. I complied. The sheet moved with me quite discreetly, and I stuck my tongue out at the hidden camera when Liam turned around.

He removed the donut thingy, sat on a stool, and massaged my head and neck. Ruining my new hairdo. Damn. The rest of the session felt amazing, but nothing X-rated. Maybe next time. Hopefully there will be many, many, next times before I have to bust him. I could get used to this duty.

***

I returned to the station feeling like a relaxed noodle.

Shinto, there already, leaned on my desk with a smirk the size of Texas. Her hair coiled back in the familiar braid, all vestiges of makeup scrubbed away. "Hey. How did you do?"

I shrugged. "So that's how the other half lives. It did not suck." I knew my hair still shined with oil and probably stuck out at weird angles. "He didn't say anything. Just worked my body into a state of contentment and bliss." I checked the mirror in my desk, and saw clumps of mascara under my eyes, not on my eyelashes. Damn. I rubbed my eyes and made it worse. "How about you?" I gave up on the mascara and rolled my head from side to side, it felt so good.

"We had quite the gabfest. My gal is a talker. She wanted to know all kinds of shit not listed on the intake sheet. I think I got a lock on this. She's going to come on to me next session. I'm sure of it. You don't have to get another massage."

"Whoa there, girl. I like these massages. My guy might be slow, but we still need time to bust him."

"Want to put your money where your mouth is?"

"You're on. How much?" By then everyone in the station gathered around and began taking sides. "Shinto, seriously, how are we going to bust both of them at the same time?"

"That's a tricky one. Guess if one of us is asked 'the question,' we should see if we can get them to turn on their friend."

"What did you do to get her so talkative?"

"I'm not shy about my body, and she was kind of cute. I undressed slowly and deliberately while she asked me about illnesses or broken bones. By the time she finished I stood bare-ass naked. I climbed on the bed and let her drape the sheet over me. I told her I didn't need the sheet. By then she got it. We connected. I told her normal massages bored me and could she recommend anything else special? Maybe with a guy and her. A ménage à trois?"

"And?"

"She said she would look into it and have an answer next time I came in." Shinto leaned over and tapped a drum roll on the desk with her fingernails. "That's how it's done, ladies and gentlemen."

Laughter erupted in the squad room.

"Bitch." I laughed too. I couldn't help myself.

Chapter Seventeen

Junior

The screen door slammed behind me, and four heads turned and glared my way.

"Hola. Let the good times roll, eses," I said to break the tension.

"Ese yourself, white boy," Fuck You muttered.

"You're late, Junior," Miguel said. "We set a time, we make the time."

"Didn't know I had to punch a time card, amigo."

Miguel scowled. "Listen, pendejo, you get your ass here when I say be here. Comprénde?"

I shrugged and sat on the arm of the couch.

He turned back to the group seated around him on chairs and sofa. "As I was saying," he glared at me, and I stared back expressionless, "this is a simple operation. In and out. I'll have a stopwatch. You get in and get out, no more than five minutes or I'll deduct from your share. Got it?" Everyone nodded. "I have golf bags for you and shirts with the country club's logo on them. Do you have pants that aren't baggy?"

"No," four of us said in unison.

"Naturally. Yolanda will measure your asses and get you golf pants. Then you'll fit right in."

"This is how it's going down. I'll drive the four of you to the golf course. You'll pull your bags, walk slow, and talk to each other. If other golfers see you they won't get suspicious. Stay on the outskirts of the course where the fancy houses are. When you see a house with sliding glass doors, two of you will act like you are looking for balls and scout it out. Watch for dogs and alarms.

They got an alarm sticker, a sign, sensors on their windows, move on. The cops roll faster for rich folks. When you give the go signal, the other two will go around and try the door. If it's open, great, go into the bedroom and grab as much jewelry, cash, and anything else of value that will fit in a golf bag. If the window isn't open, break it with this. It's a multi-purpose tool that can break glass to get you out of a car submerged in water. It's quiet and fast. We'll do as many houses as we can in two hours, and then we are out of there. Any questions?"

I shook my head.

The kid known as Dog, whose parents had to have been bloodhounds, boomed, "That's cool." He took the tool, turned it over, and used it to break his plastic cup. Not the smartest guy in town, but he was big and fast and knew how to throw a punch.

The kid called Chigger, about the size of a flea and who could not sit still, piped up. "When we doin' this, man?"

"Depends. Today I have to decide who's working together."

Nacho piped in. "I'll work with the new guy."

I'd heard of and seen Nacho at parties. We hadn't spoken before. It surprised me that he volunteered to partner up since he was a member of the inner circle. "We'll go in," Nacho said. "The other two can be lookouts."

"Done." Miguel slapped his hands together and stood. "I'll text everyone when Yolo has your pants and we're a go. Adios."

Chapter Eighteen

Kailey and Shinto

Time to get back into character and undercover work. I liked taking on another personality. The clothes, makeup, and diamonds changed the way I felt about myself. That's what I'd been missing all my life, a little class. I sashayed out of the station locker room, and when I hit the common area, I got catcalls and whistles. So I did a twirl and bowed, blew them a kiss, and headed out to the difficult job of getting another massage. Being a cop is simply every kind of hell.

I showed up about five minutes late, wobbling in another pair of very high heels. I felt foot cramps in my future.

I entered and heard a loud crash and shouts coming from the back. I hurried through the reception area toward the commotion. A crowd of semi-dressed and naked patrons peered out of their rooms as I dashed by.

A door opened and a pretty brunette with big boobs in a tight white cotton T-shirt and khaki pants struggled to exit the room but kept being yanked back by her arm.

She kicked and shrieked, "Help! Call the police! Leave me alone, you crazy bitch."

I heard Shinto calmly say, "I am the police. You are under arrest."

I got to the room in time to see the girl lunge at a totally naked Shinto and head-butt her. They both tumbled onto the table and tipped it over. Arms and legs entwined the women bellowed. Shinto's sounded like more of a growl.

My eyes adjusted slowly to the dim light. I found the dimmer, turned the lights up to full wattage, and laughed. The table sat to the side, upended, and *my* masseuse stood handcuffed against the far wall dodging the two women rolling on the floor. Shinto landed a fist to her masseuse's nose. Blood spurted.

The woman shrilled and kicked at Shinto. I pulled handcuffs out of my purse and attempted to grab one of her arms. She saw me coming and landed a right foot to my jaw when I reached for her. She kicked, and I toppled over. My skirt ripped when I landed with a thud.

The woman turned from me and snapped a kick into Shinto's stomach. Shinto clamped onto the yowling woman's foot and twisted. The woman fell. I crawled over to her and got a fist in the eye for my efforts. I grabbed her hand anyway and secured one arm while Shinto pinned the other. I whipped the struggling woman around and secured her hands with my cuffs.

Shinto picked up the overturned chair, righted it, and calmly sat. She reached overhead for her hot pink thong hanging on the hook behind her. "Nailed it."

My masseuse hung his head while Shinto's girl shrieked, "Police brutality. You saw what she did to me."

I read them both their Miranda rights while Shinto dressed and the woman cursed.

"I'll call it in, have a patrol car take these two so we can return all our baubles." Shinto stood and stepped into a leopard print dress that tied in the front. Her hot pink bra lace peeked out of a deep V-neck. Her black spiked heels completed her ensemble. "I can't wait to return this stuff. Too girly-girl. Now leather and whips, that's what I'm talking about." She licked her lips and winked.

"Shinto, you know you look good."

She chuckled. "I do, don't I?"

I scanned down my ripped and bloody outfit, and it occurred to me that I might be in a world of hurt. I'd seen the price tag on this stuff. It would take months to pay off the blouse. I should have followed Shinto's lead and fought naked.

"Damn it, Shinto, you couldn't wait? I told you I looked forward to a massage. Now all I'll have is a black eye and memories. Not real good ones either." I scowled at the female masseuse, panting and all hollered out.

"Kailey, stop whining. Dudes in the squad room may treat you with pussy gloves. I won't."

What could I do but laugh?

Chapter Nineteen

Junior

I'd never participated in a robbery, much less been in on the planning. My offenses were all based on impulse. If I see it, I take it. If a woman catches my eye and I'm in the mood, WHAM, she gets all of me. This was a whole different bag.

A big part of me worried about getting popped and disappointing my newfound friends, Patricia and Mr. Miller, particularly. The other part, the poor as a prison rat part, needed money. I wouldn't get paid from my modeling gig until the end of the month and I welcomed a new way to turn on the money tap.

The text came Tuesday at ten in the morning while I sat in class. Today is the day. We are on. Three p.m. sharp.

I got there at two thirty, found a shirt, cap, and pants all folded in a neat pile with my name on top. A chair in the middle of the room held a box of black garbage bags, a box of latex gloves, and a hairnet for each of us. Son of a bitch. These guys know what the hell they're doing, like they'd done it before. Cool. I get to learn from the best.

I dressed, found a spot at the kitchen table, and waited for the rest of the crew to arrive.

Yolanda rushed in. Her subtle perfume trailed behind as she snatched a beer from the refrigerator. She sat across from me and chugged half of it before swiping the back of her hand across her face. If she'd been a guy, I would have expected a huge belch.

She was bangin' in a librarian kind of way; dressed in a tight pink blouse and purpley skirt. Long black hair piled on top of her head said she was all business. She stared at me, silent. Man she cleaned up good.

"Thanks for the gear." I wiped sweat off my beer bottle with my thumb. The kitchen smelled of stale party.

She smiled. Multiple gold earrings climbed up her ears and a diamond in the side of her nose winked. The girl had definite flash. Cunning and intelligence camped behind her stare and I watched her size me up. Years in jail taught me who I could blow off and who I needed to watch. Yolanda I needed to watch closely.

"Looks like you either have a job or a doctor's appointment," I joked.

"Job."

"Where do you work?" I continued my interrogation.

"Claydesta Bank. I'm a teller."

"That's cool. How long have you lived in Midland?" My megawatt smile in place, I slouched in a casual, unassuming pose.

"All my life. You?"

"I'm new to the area. Are you with Miguel?"

"Since I was ten." The statement said volumes.

"Damn."

"Yeah." She laughed and sucked the rest of the beer down, slammed the bottle on the table, and said, "We run Midland." She stood when Miguel blew in.

"I see you made it on time today." He smiled and then kissed Yolanda. He looked over at me. "You ready for this gig?" He sported a bandana wrapped around his head, a ponytail, and a wife beater shirt. The tat of Jesus on his left bicep bulged as he grabbed Yolanda around the waist, claiming his property.

"Gotta tell you, Miguel," I said. "I've never done this kind of thing before."

"Not to worry. Today, we pop your cherry. Nacho will take the lead. Do what he says, and you'll be fine."

"When?"

"Now."

"Damn."

I heard a car with loud music squeal to a stop in the driveway. Nacho, Dog, and Chigger slammed into the house together, all talking at once. The party clicked into high gear and I got amped. This might be fun. Me with a posse. Backing me up. Hell yeah.

We dressed and looked almost presentable with hair tucked in our hairnets and ball caps. We piled into a black SUV and headed off to find booty at the country club.

***

Miguel's plan ticked by like a well-tuned Ferrari. Amazing.

We sauntered along like country club pricks. Picked our houses. Checked doors and windows for easy access. Most were unlocked. Basically kept on schedule, fleecing the rich folks. We were in and out of each house in less than five minutes, each of us buzzing on adrenaline. Miguel was a genius and we were thieving machines.

We returned to the house lugging golf bags with no room for clubs, carrying heavy trash bags full of jewelry, phones, purses, and lots of cash. Couple dudes slung TVs under their arms.

It blew me away to see how stupid people were. To have so much and leave it lying around for assholes like us.

A few of the guys howled, jumping for high fives and running their mouths.

"Man, what a trip! What all'd we get? Let's see." Dog stuck his nose in the nearest bag.

Nacho dragged over one of the trash bags and emptied it on the kitchen table.

Chigger cracked his knuckles. "Did you see the old guy drive up in his golf cart and ask how long we needed on the hole? Said his foursome wanted to play through."

"What did you say?"

"Told him we needed about ten minutes." Chigger snorted. "The old dude said 'Great he appreciated our kind gesture.'"

I heard the toilet flush.

"When was that?" Miguel slouched his way into the kitchen zipping his fly and frowning more than usual.

"At the last house," Chigger said as he dug through the loot.

Miguel stroked his chin. "He talk to you both?"

"Just me. Told him we were hunting for our balls, and he left." Chigger held up a woman's gold Rolex and slipped it on. It slid down, way too big for his skinny wrist.

Miguel grabbed his hand and wrenched the watch off. "Fucking pendejo."

"What did I do?" Chigger rubbed his arm.

"I told you not to talk to anyone. That guy is going to remember you when he hears about the robberies. You're out of here. Gone. Today. Disappear back to Mexico, Chigger. Before I forget how patient and reasonable I am."

"What was I supposed to do?" Chigger whined.

"What I told you to do. Get out of my sight. Now. Or you'll never make Mexico."

Chapter Twenty

Kailey and Shinto

Captain Samosa stood at the podium. "Now that our fine officers Kailey Carmichael and Shinto Elliot have busted the infamous massage duo, we can all be assured the good citizens of Midland Texas are free to have good, healthy, and sex-free massages."

I tried to look bummed about it. "Sorry, gentlemen, and I use the term loosely. Show's over."

Every male officer in the meeting groaned.

John Deltoro piped up, "Damn, why'd you do that, Shinto? Don't ya love us anymore? At least feel sorry for us poor sons of bitches that need a little relief, since you won't give it to us."

She punched him and laughed.

"We have another pressing problem that we haven't faced in our town before. Some of the houses adjacent to the Midland Country Club golf course have been robbed. Whoever did it came highly organized and slipped in and out before we got called to the first burglary. We haven't been successful in finding any fingerprints, hair, or descriptions. We'll alert the media and see if anyone on the golf course saw anything odd or out of place, someone that didn't look like a golfer. Keep your eyes open and be alert to any information from any of your informants."

"How much did they get away with?" one officer asked.

"Over two million dollars' worth of jewelry. Another million in coins and other valuables. We're still putting together descriptions of missing property." The Captain glanced down at some papers. "Next on the agenda, the county fair is coming to town. We will need volunteers to keep crowd control when the bands play on Friday and Saturday nights."

He sighed. "In the next few months our calendar will be full. The DAR is going to hold a Fourth of July parade, and we need volunteers. Lastly the Woman's Club is holding its annual fashion show at the Claydesta Atrium. They've asked for volunteers, two men and two women from the police force to be in the show. This year the show is dedicated to our fine men and women of the Midland Police Department. The sign-up sheets will be posted. Your work schedules are on the board and have been emailed to you. Any questions?"

"No, sir," we all said in unison and stood.

A short brunette, her uniform painted on, came in the squad room. The buttons were straining to contain her ample body. She wore a big smile and held her finger to her lips as she came up behind Shinto. She grabbed her in a bear hug and lifted the much taller Shinto off the floor.

Shinto grunted, frowned, and turned. Her face lit up, and she planted a big wet kiss on the woman's lips. "Terri, I'm so glad you're back. Are you okay?"

"Better than I deserve to be, baby."

Shinto turned to me. I must have looked stunned, because she chuckled, and so did Terri. "This is Kailey, Terri. I've known her since we could walk. Kailey, this is Terri Poindexter. She is a dear friend and works undercover most of the time. She has been deep undercover for about a year and just wrapped up a case, and I see is back in uniform." She slapped her on the back. "So to speak. How are the kids?"

"They ask about you."

"Sorry I couldn't get over more. How is Gary?"

"He's Gary. What can I say? He's the best."

"We all worried when we heard about his heart problems. I understand his valve replacement went well."

"Yep, he's better with that pig valve in him. He oinks when we make love but hey, who doesn't like a little piggly wiggle once in a while? Speaking of pig, let's all grab some barbeque for lunch. We can meet over at Big Bubba's on Wadley. I'd love to catch up. Kailey, please join us. Though, we might bore the pants off you. What the hell, if you are a friend of Shinto's, you're already bored. This woman doesn't have a life outside of this police force. We are lucky for it, but she needs to get laid. I've kind of made that my mission."

"Shut your damn mouth, bitch." Shinto actually blushed.

Who is this woman that can make Shinto blush? I need to know her. "Hell yes, I'll be there," I said. "Add me to your mission. I've shared my love life with her. Fair is fair."

***

"About Shinto's love life," I said.

"Come on, guys. Big Bubba's menu is a lot more interesting than my love life." Shinto flapped the menu and held it in front of her face.

"No, it's not." Terri and I chorused in unison.

I was getting to like this girl. As promised, we'd met after shift at Big Bubba's barbecue. Famous for brisket, ribs and Gut Buster fries only a masochist would order. Two beers down, we'd yet to order.

"Shinto helped me out of a jam a few months ago. Some loan shark was hassling my Gary and I couldn't break my cover to set him straight."

"Shinto to the rescue," I said.

"She broke the asshole's nose and one or two more bones. End of loan shark." Terri peeled the label from her Lone Star. "I like to think I returned the favor a few weeks later."

"Terri, that's old news. No use making it young again." Shinto slapped the menu on the table. "Let's order."

"I'm kind of a newshound myself," I said. "What did you do?"

"Terri…." Shinto said.

The two women exchanged looks and Shinto won out.

"I might have introduced her to someone who needed her um, in a different way than I did. One thing led to another," she glanced at Shinto, "…and that's all I'm going to say about that."

"Oh, hell no. You cannot leave me hanging like that."

"Oh, but she can," Shinto said. "I'm having the ribs. Who's with me?"

"I'll worm it out of you later my friend," I said.

"Worm away, Kailey." Shinto drained her beer and burped. "You have my permission. You know what happens to worms on fishing trips."

"That's not even remotely clever."

"I thought it was," Shinto said. "Terri?"

"Clever. Definitely clever."

"Terri did tell me one thing I didn't know for sure before tonight."

Shinto narrowed her eyes. "Enlighten me, oh wormy one."

"Now I know you at least have a love life." I drained my beer and let out a bigger belch than Shinto's. "I'll get the rest later. Worms are patient."

Chapter Twenty-One

Junior

"What are we going to do with all this?" I asked Miguel as I pawed through the loot. I could use a new flat screen TV. I dug out a honey with a remote. Nice. I put it back and picked up a brand new Playstation. Now we're talking. Toys. I've never had my own toys. About damn time.

"Why do you need to know?"

"Curious is all."

"We have contacts in Dallas. Don't want anything showing up here that could tie us to the robberies."

"Makes sense."

"Damn straight," he said as he typed on a spreadsheet on his computer. He held up a diamond ring and squinted at it through a jeweler's loupe squished in his right eye. Each piece we snatched he examined and cataloged. This was some serious shit, and Miguel didn't miss a trick.

"How does this work? When do we get our cut? Can we take some of it home?"

"You get it when I get this settled and I get paid," he snarled up at me. "Now get out of here so I can work."

I raised my hands in submission. "No problemo."

"Junior." Miguel hefted a gold chain in his hand as if weighing it. "I know you're kinda short. You did good today. Come back later tonight. We'll divvy up the cash and some of the stuff we want to keep."

Now we're talking. "I appreciate that. Serious. I'll be here, thanks."

Time to bolt. No A/C in this house and my pits dripped like faucets. My shitty little window unit back at my apartment called to me.

The prospect of a quick payday energized me. I said my good-byes and left, whistling some lame-ass tune heading for home.

Chapter Twenty-Two

Kailey

My partner, Mike, had the phone glued to his ear, so I ambled over to the bulletin board. An envelope pinned to it held a boatload of free tickets to the Midland RockHounds Minor League Baseball game. I hadn't been to a game since high school. I grabbed five and headed to the squad car. I slid into the passenger seat and waited.

The door flew open, and Mike leaned in and scowled at me. "You think I'm your lousy chauffeur?"

"I think you're an excellent chauffeur."

"You drive," he said.

Wahoo.

I hopped out and ran over to the driver's side, probably with a huge shit-eating grin on my face.

***

Just before end of shift, I pulled to a curb, and slipped the envelope of tickets from my uniform pocket. "Would you like to go to a baseball game with me?" A bus squealed to a stop behind us. The air brakes needed work. I heard the whoosh of the doors open and watched an army of people disembark.

Mike looked over at me and raised his eyebrows. "I think the Mrs. wouldn't be too happy about me dating another woman."

"No, no, I meant your whole family. I'm kind of alone these days, and my mom is always on my ass about getting out and doing things. When I was a kid my family loved the RockHounds. Saw these tickets stuck to the bulletin board. I checked and they're for tomorrow night when we're off."

"I think that would be nice, Kailey. Thank you for thinking of us. Are you ready for a wild couple of kids?" His smile looked surprised and grateful at the same time.

"I'd love that more than you know."

***

We juggled our hot dogs, peanuts, and beer as the color guard marched out to stand behind the pitcher's mound, and the whole stadium fell silent. A soldier limped out to the middle of the field and said, "Please join me in the Pledge of Allegiance and our favorite song."

We all stood, and every person, including the kids, placed their hands over their heart and said the Pledge of Allegiance, and then the kids kept their hands over their hearts and belted out as loud as they could the song "We're proud to be an American." They knew every word by heart and stomped on the metal bleachers in time with the song. It took my breath away.

Every adult and child in the stadium stood and sang in full voice and with total love of country. Gave me chills. Whoever said patriotism in America is dead has never been to a Midland, Texas, baseball game.

By the seventh inning stretch Midland had Frisco seven runs to zip.

I stood and asked, "Anyone need anything?" I needed a bathroom break.

Lexie, Mike's youngest daughter, a cute preteen, asked, "Can I go with you, Kailey?"

"Sure, honey. Anyone else?"

"I'll take another beer, if the line isn't too long." Mike held out a ten.

"You got it. We'll be right back."

Lexie and I stood in the beer line. A boy came up and said, "Lexie, um, hi."

"Hi, Oscar." Lexie blushed.

He cracked his knuckles and asked, "Are you going to be at the dance next Friday night?"

She squirmed. "Don't know. You?"

"Want to go together?"

"Me?" Lexie's blush got deeper.

"Sure. I'll text you, and I'll have my dad bring me by, and we can go on a date."

"Oh, okay. I'll have to ask my parents, but, yes, I'd like that."

I looked over at the hotdog queue and felt my heart pound and my mouth go dry. He stood with his back to me, adding mustard and relish to a fistful of dogs. No mistaking that tight ass and well-defined frame. He'd cut his hair since Dallas and might've lightened it a little. He turned around to hand his haul to a young boy of about twelve—and I saw it wasn't Derek.

What the hell, Kailey girl? You miss Derek so much you're seeing him everywhere?

I smiled to myself. He'd no doubt get a kick out of that. I might have to call that boy up soon and banish some demons.

In all that time our line never moved and I lost my appetite for ballpark fodder.

"Lexie, honey," I said, "I think we picked the wrong line. Let's head back to our seats before the game starts."

Lexie didn't seem to care one bit. She skipped ahead of me, no doubt to ask her parents about the dance.

We scored one more run and the game ended eight to zero.

Dry heat seared the starry night as the stadium crowd swelled around us, funneling toward the exits. I hugged Mike and his family in the parking lot and said good-bye. When I hugged Lexie I whispered in her ear, "Have fun at the dance."

She blushed and nodded.

Chapter Twenty-Three

Junior

"I'm here, Papi. You call, I come." I stomped on the lone ant crawling across the dirty white cracked tile in the entry. Miguel sat on the puke green couch years past its prime, eyes glued to the fifty-five-inch TV. He raised his hand. I shut up and glanced at it. The well-endowed blonde anchor's red dress hugged her every curve. Her stylish black-rimmed glasses didn't hide her smoking hot tamale brown eyes. I could use some of what she was selling. She frowned as if reading my thoughts and shuffled papers on her desk as a photograph of the golf course appeared behind her. I flopped down next to Miguel.

"Disturbing news to report this evening." The camera cut to a panorama of the golf course. Her voice hardened. "A series of brazen robberies has been reported. It all happened yesterday around three in the afternoon to houses facing the Midland Golf Course. What can you tell us, Ken?"

The face of an older gentleman with his pot belly barely contained in a tan suit stood in front of a luxurious Hudson River brick house. Sleepy pecan tree branches dipped low over a perfect green lawn. "Luckily no one got hurt, Karen." Several kids with skateboards shot past him on the sidewalk waving at the camera. "If anyone saw anything or anyone suspicious, please contact Midland Police Department at the number on your screen. The thieves got away with approximately four million dollars in property and cash. It's sad that our community can't feel safe anymore. Be sure to lock your doors and windows, folks."

The camera faded, and our buxom beauty returned. She smiled into the camera and cooed, "And after the break we will hear about the weather and sports from our two favorite guys."

"Four million? I wish." Miguel switched off the set, scratched his balls, and stood. "Junior? Man, I been meaning to talk to you. I thought you did good Tuesday. Nacho confirmed it. He's happy with you." He crooked a finger. "Follow me. I want to talk to you about something."

The house felt a lot bigger inside than it looked from the street, and it surprised me. All it did was give Miguel and his crew more space to junk up. Black trash bags filled to the brim were stacked by the sliding glass doors. A swag lamp hung lopsided from the ceiling, its light shining down on a nude statue in a cage as some sort of substance curled its way down the bars. Class all the way. Beer cans and cheap wine boxes competed for space with ashtrays spilling over with cigarettes, cigars, and God knows what else on every available surface.

I'm no Martha what's-her-name, but conditions in the house sucked even by my standards. Artificial flowers on the table behind the couch hung low with the weight of dust and neglect. Velvet paintings everywhere, with Jesus in one pose or another in most of them, the only exception being female nudes possessed of outrageous tits. Jesus opened his arms to embrace me from a large statue on a coffee table. Don't know how much he helped the troops here, but it wasn't from a lack of trying.

I followed Miguel down the hallway toward the back of the house to the master bedroom he'd converted into an office. Compared to the rest of the house, this room sparkled. Clean white walls, florescent lights, computers, printers, an array of phones, and spotless beige carpet. Miguel definitely had his shit together.

"Impressive," I said, looking around.

"Take a seat." Miguel pointed to a huge, curved cowhide sofa. "Tell me about this college shit you're into. Why college all of a sudden?"

I bounced on the sofa. I gotta get me one of these. "New beginnings," I said. I stretched my arms out and rubbed hide that used to be a cow. "Last round at Midland Correctional sorta flipped a switch in me. Like it's now or never. I either get my shit together, or—" I inhaled the leather aroma. "I might be fucked."

"You got ambition," Miguel said. "I hear you. The short time I've known you I've been impressed. We could use a smart guy like you in our organization. What classes are you taking?"

"Basics. art, English, and math. Took geology as a lark. Dug it, pun intended."

"See?" Miguel said. "That's what I'm talking about. Pendejos I'm working with wouldn't know a pun from a gun. Frankly they'd much prefer the latter."

"Why you so interested in my college?"

Ignoring the question, Miguel continued, "What are you taking next? This coming semester?"

"Don't know yet. Just got the class catalog."

"I'd suggest chemistry. Some of the shit we're into, it might come in handy. Also, criminal justice. That CSI criminal investigation shit is smoking, man. You pick up tips on crime scenes, collection of evidence, how the cops use forensics. Good shit to know in our line of work."

"I never thought of that." I truly hadn't.

"Why not, right? If we know what they are looking for, we can prepare better. Tip the odds in our favor a little."

"But chemistry? Seriously? I've heard that's no skate class."

"You got brains, and I got faith in you."

"Certainly worth thinking about," I said.

Miguel's fat mustache framed his generous lips. He leaned forward and steepled his fingers under his chin. "If I were you, I'd more than think about it. Comprende?"

I understood just fine. Chemistry and criminal law, here I come. "Sounds good," I said.

He nodded, as if my class schedule was one more detail solved. "Now go grab a beer or something. I got work to do."

He focused on the huge computer screen on the end of his desk. A stock ticker crawled across the bottom. He tapped a few buttons, called up charts and graphs. He frowned and muttered to himself. He'd dismissed me, and as far as he was concerned, I'd left minutes before. Miguel, gangbanger, caper planner, stock trader?

I walked out with new respect and a newer list of questions. Chief among them, what the hell had I gotten myself into?

Chapter Twenty-Four

Kailey

Hungry, I stopped at a Starbuck's for a muffin and a cup of Kenya Roast coffee. I snagged a banana from a basket on the counter and heard "Kailey, as I live and breathe, what are you doing here?"

I turned and saw mother's dear friend standing behind me. Damn. "Gail, how are you? I haven't seen you in forever."

Her white blouse fit snug over pancake boobs and large belly. The woman had gained fifty pounds since I'd seen her ten years ago, her hair had gone a dull dirty gray but the close piggy eyes still held the malice she chewed for breakfast, lunch and dinner. She loved to gossip. "Haven't seen you in a month of Sundays, Kailey. Your mother said you'd joined the police force. Keeping our city safe now are you?"

"Which reminds me." I glanced at my watch for emphasis and put the banana back in the basket. "I've gotta run. I'm late for work and I need to change. Good to see you Gail."

"I'm never late for work, Kailey, that doesn't show respect for your job. Goodbye now, dear." Her smile reminded me of a feral cat toying with a new mouse.

I waved and practically ran to my car. Now I gotta find another Starbuck's. As I approached my car I noticed an ominous tilt over my front left tire. Shit. I glanced back at the Starbuck's. A double espresso would sure come in handy about now.

I called my captain and explained why I'd be late. After a half an hour, sweaty and dirty, I rolled home on my spare smelling worse than a desert armadillo. A nice cool shower and a change of clothes and I'd be a whole new person.

I stomped up the walk and banged through the front door. "Momma, I'm home."

Momma rolled out of the kitchen wiping her hands on a dishtowel. "My lands. Aren't you a sight."

"Had a flat tire." Sweat stung my eyes. "Why isn't the air on?"

"I hadn't noticed, dear." Her speech came slow and deliberate. Maybe she needed a nap.

"I'm going to clean up and change."

Ten minutes later I finished drying off and had on most of my second uniform when I heard a loud thud and moan in the hallway.

"Momma? Are you all right?"

No response.

I cinched my pants and flew from my bedroom to see my mother on the floor, her wheelchair upended beside her. "Momma, what did you do? Why did you try to get out of your chair?"

"I'm cold baby and my head feels like it's going to explode." Her teeth chattered. "Could you give me a cover? I'll be fine."

"Don't you move a muscle. You hear me? I'll be right back." I ran for the linen closet and fished my cell out of my pocket at the same time. I plucked a blanket off the middle shelf and dialed 911.

Momma's eyes had closed by the time I returned with the blanket. I laid down beside her and held her until the paramedics came.

Chapter Twenty-Five

Junior

I sat in the computer lab at school brain-deep in my geology paper. Books scattered around me. Ideas flew out of my brain onto the blinking screen. My phone pinged with a text message. I glanced at it. Miguel. I turned the phone off and kept my analysis going, deep in the ground. Next up, write about the substance of the rocks and then the history of the earth's physical structure in its relationship as a planetary body in the galaxy. Crazy, mind-blowing information. I consumed every sentence and wanted more. Maybe one day I'll go on a dig and get my hands in the earth and know I touched more than dust and dirt. Know its proper name. Know its origins. Cool stuff.

After another hour the lab assistant announced, "Ten minutes to closing, people." Shit. I shut the books, hit Print on the computer, and stuffed everything into my backpack. I stood and stretched. Gotta pay for hard copies of my work so far. I couldn't wait to get home and finish my thoughts. I'd plunged so deep in the earth I could touch lava. Hell, I was the lava, smokin', on fire.

I rounded the corner to the complex dreaming up a title for my geology paper when I heard loud music and saw kids milling around on the stairs all the way up to my place. The door to my apartment stood open. I took the stairs two at a time. A party in full swing, and one woman squealing, not having fun at all. What the hell?

I pushed inside and elbowed my way into my bedroom in time to see Freddie Medina on my bed on top of Patricia. He slugged her in the face and clawed at her blouse. She slapped him, and he grabbed a fistful of bra and ripped it away, exposing her breasts. Several guys

102

leaned against the wall passing a joint and elbowing each other, laughing.

I dropped my papers on the dresser. "Get off my bed." My guts seethed, but my voice came out calm as death. I grabbed Freddie by the ponytail and yanked his head back, ripping him off my friend. "I said get OFF!" I glared at the rest of the group. "YOU, OUT!" They slunk out the door muttering and shoving each other in the back.

I still gripped a hunk of Freddie's hair. I stepped back and used it to fling him to the side. He thumped against the wall and rolled to his feet spitting mad.

The forehead vein running through Fuck You pulsed red. "I'll kill you for that, ese." He smiled and smoothed back his hair. "Maybe some other time." He straightened his clothes. "Miguel told us to collect you. You weren't here, so—" He shrugged. "We took our little amusements."

"In my house? With my neighbor?" I stepped forward and snapped a straight, hard right at the center of his smiling face. His head rolled with the punch. Apparently he'd practiced getting his ugly mug smashed in. I popped him with a tight left hook to the body, and he gasped and fell to a knee. "Amused yet?" I drew back a leg to plant my size eleven on his forehead, when Chigger and Dog rushed in the room and pulled me off.

I shook free and whirled on them. "You double pieces of shit. What the fuck do you think you're doing disrespecting me in my house?" I looked over at Patricia. She'd scooted under the covers and rolled into a fetal position, sobbing.

"Miguel ain't gonna like this," Chigger said.

Dog nodded in agreement but said nothing, clearly the wiser of the two.

"Miguel wants to talk to me, he knows where to find me. Now get this pile of shit out of my place." I snapped a kick into Freddie's mid-section. "Take the rest of your fan club with you."

Miguel's two soldados hoisted their comrade between them and shuffled out. Fuck You mumbled something about me being a dead man as they passed.

"You first," I said and slammed the door on their sweaty backs.

When I turned around, Patricia had gathered herself enough to lie still beneath the covers clasped tight to her chin, all wide eyes and disheveled hair. I walked to the bed carefully, like approaching a skittish deer. Her eyes followed me as I got close and I sat on the bed beside her. "I am so sorry, Patricia. I didn't know they were coming."

Her eyes shifted to mine, and after several seconds she appeared to make some kind of decision. She sat up, still with the covers high, and tried to speak. "I—I—" Words dissolved into tears.

I scooted over to put my arms around her. I felt like all clumsy edges and hard surfaces closing around something soft and fragile.

We stayed like that for a minute or an hour, I couldn't tell, until her shaking subsided and she pushed away from me. "I am so embarrassed, Junior, for you to see me like that and for me to be so stupid to let myself—"

I grabbed both her shoulders and squeezed lightly. "No, please Patricia. It's me who owes you an apology. Those assholes never should have come here. If I knew, I would have—"

"Are those, those people, your friends?"

"What? No. Not at all. I work with them. Sometimes. Not long."

"Could you?" She made a gesture with her hand. "Turn around please?"

"Oh, god, I'm sorry." I got up and turned my back and heard the bed springs creak.

"I'm okay now. Thank you."

I turned back around and watched her fumbling at the bottom her blouse. No buttons left.

"Oh, my," is all she said. She gathered the two blouse ends and tied them together. "There. That should do it." She straightened. "I should have known. They didn't look like people I thought you might associate with, and I guess I thought they might be robbers or something. Stupid, I know." She chuckled, small and quietly. "When I saw them go up to your apartment, I didn't know what to do, so I stepped out of my place and told the young man with the awful tattoo on his forehead that you weren't home. I hoped they'd leave but he said they knew you and would wait.

"Then later they were making so much noise I went up and told them I would call the police if they didn't stop." She hugged herself. "When he grabbed me I've never been so scared in my life." She shivered.

I went to her and held her a second time. I thought it might be the only time I held a woman for her comfort and not mine.

She pushed away and asked, "What should we do? Call the police? I know your apartment must be a shambles."

"Police would only make things worse with those people. Trust me. If you are okay with it, I'd like to handle this myself."

"Only if you promise they will never come back."

"You have my word."

She smiled a weak smile. "Bless you. That's good enough for me." She straightened her back and then peered at me with an embarrassed smile. "Would you mind walking me to my apartment? I'm still a little nervous, I think, or I don't know—"

"Are you sure you're up to it? You could stay here a bit longer if you like."

She shuddered and covered it with a little shake of her head. "No, I mean I'm okay, a tiny bit nervous, like I said."

"I'm your guy. For this and anything else you might need. After all you've done for me."

She glanced around at my mess. "Maybe when I get home you could check to see no one is hiding out in my place."

"Consider it done."

I walked her home. Escorted her inside and walked through every room, opening doors and checking under beds. After we made sure all her windows were locked, I returned to my place.

The pendejos destroyed my apartment. Not sure where to begin, I went for the smallest room first, my bathroom. Everything in my medicine cabinet filled my sink. The bedroom mirror hung at an angle, every drawer pulled open and empty, clothes wadded up and stuffed in creative places. My shorts swung from the overhead light along with one of my socks. I straightened things as best I could, mainly dumping clothes and towels in a big pile in the hallway. I shut the door and headed for my kitchen. Eggs broken in the sink. Glasses and plates shattered on the counters and the floor. All the food in the refrigerator either half eaten or missing entirely. I walked over to the open door leading out to my landing. My books and papers from my classes lay scattered about like trash left over from a street parade.

I dialed Miguel.

Chapter Twenty-Six

Kailey and Shinto

The ambulance screamed off for Midland Memorial Hospital. I followed, my mind a hopeless jumble of recriminations and prayers. How did I not see this coming? Please God spare my Momma. Take me, spare her. I sent a new prayer heavenward at every intersection.

I screeched to a halt in the emergency loading zone and rushed in to the receptionist.

An ancient couple beat me there by half a second.

The old gentleman asked, "Where is our grandson Thomas J? Thomas J. Humboldt?" He continued without giving the receptionist time to answer, "Tommy called and said he fell off his skateboard and thought his arm might be broken. Damn fool. What good is a skateboard anyway? Why are they building skate parks? Tell me that. Waste of the taxpayer's money if you ask me. Kids break their necks and we have to pay the bills. Stupid government. What the hell is this country coming to?"

I tapped my foot on the floor, ready to jump out of my skin. I peered around them.

The receptionist smiled up from her computer. "He's with the doctor. Please take a seat. When the doctor finishes examining him, a nurse will take you back to see him."

The old gentleman cupped his ear and looked around the room puzzled, then shouted, "What?"

The stoop-shouldered woman next to him wearing a clean polyester housedress with yellow flowers pulled the old man by the elbow, her fingers knobby with arthritis. She put her mouth to his ear and shouted, "She said we need to wait over here." She pointed to the blue sofa in the corner.

He stood rooted to the spot in front of the receptionist. "Well, why didn't she say that so I could hear her?"

"Delbert, if you'd put in your hearing aids, you would've heard her." She tugged his arm and pointed to the side of the room. "For that matter you shoulda put in your teeth."

"I can hear fine, she didn't enunciate. Damn, younguns these days." He shuffled into the waiting area.

The receptionist nodded at me. "May I help you?"

I tapped my badge. "I'm Officer Kailey Carmichael. Ambulance brought my mother here. Margaret Carmichael."

The receptionist's fingers danced across her keyboard. "Your mother is having an MRI at present and a stroke alert has been called." She handed me a clipboard. "Please fill out her paperwork."

After numerous pages of questions and a copy of my driver's license, the receptionist unclipped her I.D. badge and said, "Follow me."

She led me through several doors to the emergency room. The place hummed with activity. The layout reminded me of a wagon wheel. At the hub, a ring of desks sported several computer stations manned by doctors and nurses in earnest conversation. Rooms faced onto the hub, some open, some closed off by drawn curtains. Nurses threaded their way around the ER hub, ducking in and out of curtained-off rooms. My escort led me to one room and gently slid open the curtain. I thanked her and stepped inside. Momma lay unmoving, an oxygen cannula in her nose, EKG leads hooked to a monitor on a ring stand, an IV in her arm connected to a clear bag of fluid. She looked pale and small lying there. I stepped over to straighten her blankets when a young doctor pulled aside the curtain. "Are you Mrs. Carmichael's daughter?"

"Yes. I'm Kailey, Officer Kailey Carmichael with the Midland Police department." Unimpressed, the doctor stared into his electronic tablet. I judged him to be about twelve going on thirty. I cleared my throat. "I think I've seen you when I've brought a prisoner or two to the ER."

"Uh huh. Great." He scraped a finger up the screen, reading. When he apparently got to the page he wanted he stopped and narrowed his eyes. "I'm sorry, who are you again?"

I leaned close to read his name tag. "Officer Kailey Carmichael, Dr. Clark. Please tell me how my mother is doing. If you can spare the time."

He looked at me puzzled for a moment before launching into his spiel. "She's had an MRI and we confirmed a stroke. We've given her a strong anti-thrombolytic to help dissolve the clot in her brain. We'll monitor her and keep her comfortable and transfer her to critical care as soon as a bed is available."

"Prognosis?"

"Too early to say, ma'am. We are doing everything we can."

For some reason that ma'am really pissed me off. "Will she wake up? Is she impaired? Will she recover her brain function?" I ticked the questions off on my fingers.

He clasped the tablet to his chest like a protective shield. "That's a wait-and-see proposition, Ms.—?"

"Officer—no, hell, call me Kailey, please."

"I've seen patients with serious strokes make complete recoveries. She's responding to treatment . . . She is lucky you were there and got help so soon . . . Her prognosis is good . . . She needs to rest . . . There's nothing much you can do here . . . You're welcome to stay . . . Your mother's been medicated, and we'll keep her in ICU for a few days . . ."

His practiced litany of med-speak faded as I focused on the sounds around me, the quiet bleeps of my mother's heart monitor. The gentle whisper of her breathing. The squeak of rubber-soled shoes in the hallway behind me as nurses hurried back and forth. The sounds soothed me as I stepped forward to grasp her hand. It felt crepe dry and cool. "You will get through this, Momma. Don't you worry. I'm here now."

The noises in the hallway escalated, and I heard the thuds of running feet and shouts from the nurses. "Police officer down. Incoming. Get the crash cart!"

Peering out of the curtains I saw Shinto rush by, holding tight to a gurney, her face bleeding. What the hell?

"Shinto?" I dashed over to her and followed beside her. I heard the EMT tell the nurses, "Bullet severed his brachial artery, upper arm."

"Excuse us, officers." One of the nurses in the crowd stopped us as the gurney continued with its crowd of attendants. "This is as far as you go. We'll let you know your officer's status when we can."

Shinto and I stopped. Attendants wheeled the gurney down a hallway and disappeared through a double-wide, automatic door. She turned and grabbed my shoulder. "It's Allen. Stupid son of a bitch took a bullet meant for me." Her face turned ashen. "Damn it. Damn him!"

She did a doubletake when she registered where we were and that I stood beside her. "Kailey? How'd you get here so fast?"

"I've been here. Mom had a stroke."

"What? Oh, shit, Kailey. Is she—ow. Hey. Watch it." A beefy nurse with a scowl clamped a hand on Shinto's shoulder and pressed her down into a wheelchair. "Hey no, no. I'm good. No need to—"

"You're bleeding, officer, and we tend to frown on that around here. Now are you going to be difficult or smart?"

I put my hand on Shinto's forearm and felt it tense up. "She is going to be a model patient. The best. Right, Shinto?" I squeezed, hard. It got my friend's attention. "This lady has a job to do, same as us. Now let her do it and tell me what happened."

The nurse smiled at me gratefully and guided us into another ER cubicle. She bustled about, ministering to Shinto while I coaxed the story out of her.

Adrenaline loosened her lips and the words poured out of her. "We got a call about a homicide this morning. Saw this kid splayed out in the middle of West County Road one twenty-two, blood everywhere. Called it in. We secured the scene. Your Mike got there with the rest of the crime scene crew and we left. About a block away bullets shot through the front window of our squad car. Allen shoved me out of the way and got hit."

The nurse pointed to the exam table. Shinto eased onto it. "The shattered window cut me a bit." She touched her forehead gingerly and then winced when the nurse wiped it with gauze. "Those windows are supposed to be fucking shatterproof."

"Are you hurt anywhere else?" the nurse asked.

Shinto shook her head. "I don't know."

"I'll get the doctor." The nurse exited the cubicle with a flourish.

Dr. Clark stuck his head in before the curtains could close. "There you are. I've been looking for you." He came over to me. "Your mom's been moved to intensive care." Briefly distracted, he grabbed Shinto's chart. "Well, well. What do we have here?" He flipped a page and read for a moment. "What are you doing, Ms. Carmichael, trying to fill our emergency room singlehandedly?"

"Officer Carmichael," I said.

The nurse returned with a tray of various implements. I saw a hypodermic needle, a vial of clear liquid, gauze, tape, and an assortment of sewing needles.

"Excellent, nurse," Dr. Clark said. "Do we have a double-oh needle? Ah, I see we do. Perfect. Let's you and I get one of Midland's finest sewn up and back doing her job, shall we?"

Shinto stopped the doctor short before he could begin. "Doctor, how's my partner doing?"

"He's in surgery."

We heard a commotion. Captain Samosa stripped open the curtain. "How is she doing, doc?"

"She'll survive, and if I can convince her to stay still, without a scar." He shot some Novocain into Shinto's head and started stitching.

Captain Samosa motioned for me to follow him. "They tell me Allen's stable, Kailey. Tell me about your mom. What do we know?"

"She's in intensive care from a stroke. I don't know if she's going to . . . going to be . . . if she'll ever . . ."

He put his arm around me and hugged me. I felt ten years old again. I didn't care.

Chapter Twenty-Seven

Junior

"Miguel? What the hell? Your gang of stupid wrecked my place."

"You need to get over here. You didn't answer your phone, asshole."

"I was in class. It's called an education. I'm not one of your kids, and I'm not on call, got it? I'll work with you when I can. That's it. "

"Screw you. Put your phone on vibrate. Be available for me."

"What's so urgent?"

"The Snakes are on the move."

"The who?"

"The Snakes. New gang just cropped up. They're moving in on my turf. I need everyone. This is going to get ugly, man. I need your help, Junior."

"I'll help when I can. I'm my own man, not one of your damn lackeys."

"Understood. I'll pay for any damage as a peace offering. I'll speak to Freddie. Now get your ass over here. We got a situation."

"I've got a shitload of schoolwork and my place is in shambles. Classes begin at eight tomorrow morning. I'll be to your place around two tomorrow afternoon. That's the best I can do."

"Mother fu—" cut off as I ended the call.

Chapter Twenty-Eight

Kailey

I stayed with momma for a couple of hours. Before I left the hospital, I sneaked in to see Allen in recovery. "You look terrible." I smiled and sat next to the pole with bags of hanging medicines. A heart rate monitor beeped.

He opened his eyes. The top of the bed rose until he semi sat up. "Hey, Kailey," he croaked. "Thanks for coming,"

"I wanted to stop in before I leave. Momma's had a stroke, and we're down the hall."

"Jeez, I'm sorry, Kailey. I know you and your mom are close."

I forced an upbeat tone I didn't feel. "We'll be fine. Doctors are optimistic."

Allen closed his eyes as if gathering energy. "Did they find who shot me?"

"No, I'm sure everyone's busting their butt to find the bastards. I'll be out there, too, soon's I leave here."

He opened his eyes and fixed them on me. "Get them, Kailey, okay? You and Shinto. Make them pay for—"

Allen's wife and kids blew through the door to his room, "Daddy, Daddy." The kids ran up to his bed.

He looked at me with a dumb grin.

"I'll leave you to your fan club, Allen." I patted the covers on his bed. "We'll get the bast—I mean, suspects. Count on it."

Allen's wife slid past me to plant a kiss on her husband's lips. "Sweetheart."

I felt extraneous. "I gotta bounce, officer. You get better. We'll take care of the rest."

Allen's wife grabbed my arm before I could escape. "Please don't leave because we came. It's wonderful how everyone on the force has been kind to us." She smiled and said, "I'm sorry, I don't think we've been properly introduced. I'm Cindy, and these two hellions are Thomas and Noah. Boys say hi to . . .?"

"Kailey. Kailey Carmichael." I shook her hand. Her expensive perfume wafted toward me. Platinum hair pulled back, bangs cut across her forehead. The woman wore her tailored suit like a second skin.

The boys said, "Hi" without seeing me and scrambled onto Allen's bed. Thomas, the spitting image of his father, grabbed the TV remote and clicked through the channels. Allen winced as Noah, a cute redhead, nestled in his father's free arm.

"Noah," Cindy said, "be careful. Your father's got a bad booboo."

"I'm fine, Cindy. Don't be such worrier. He didn't know."

I took the opportunity to bail. "I've gotta go. Good to meet you, Cindy, Thomas, and Noah."

"Oh, don't run out on our account." Cindy didn't even look my way when she said it.

Allen spoke around her. "Thanks for stopping, Kailey. Prayers for your mom."

"Same for you. I'll keep you updated on our progress."

I ran out of the room and bumped smack into Captain Samosa.

Chapter Twenty-Nine

Junior

Rolling up to Miguel's I noticed a lot more guys milling around than usual. Some I'd never seen. I felt the excitement electrify the air. Crap. I didn't want to be part of a gang rumble. Skirting the mob, I rounded the back of his house.

Miguel sat on a plastic folding chair on the ten-by-ten slab of concrete that served as a patio. He nursed a cerveza, deep in conversation with Yolanda.

"Hola."

"Hola, gringo. You missed a great fight."

"Oh, yeah? When? We talked late last night."

Yolanda kissed Miguel and left. He smiled as he watched her ass and then turned to me. "We whipped 'em. Lost only one of ours. Mouse was a casualty for the greater good of Los Demonios. His death will be celebrated." He raised his bottle in salute.

"Mouse's dead? How did the little guy go?"

"Bastards shot him down like a dog. Shit, man, we agreed on a safe meet this morning around ten. Over by the tracks where it's all industrial. They shot him down in the middle of the street."

"Just like that?"

"Yep." Miguel laughed and took a sip. "'Course he strutted around, talking smack, being a genuine pain in the ass. If they hadn't shot him I might have. Dude was toasted, buzzin' on something." He motioned me toward a galvanized tub filled with beer and ice. "Then all hell broke loose. We heard sirens and booked feet out of there. Later on television I heard the Snakes shot a couple of cops."

"Stupid," I said. "You don't shoot cops. Folks in blue got long memories."

I stared at Miguel to see where he might land on the subject of gunning down police. He stared back at me with a little smile. Didn't take the bait.

"Listen, bro," he said instead. "Something else you should know. Freddie is pissed. I mean fuck-you pissed. Watch your back, vato. He's a slow burn and has a longer memory than cops. Be careful with that one."

"Tell him to bring it. I'll show him what real pissed feels like."

"All I'm saying, man, is he is one crafty dude. I've seen him play out some freaky shit on people he thinks have crossed him. I'll try to talk some sense into him. No guarantees. When you least expect it, he will live up to that stupid tattoo on his forehead. That thing's a warning, not a statement."

"Noted."

"Now, let's talk about how school crap is more important than when I want you here."

"Let's do it. You've got a shitload of people you can use. I'm no use to you as a soldier. I need to get an education. I've got a thirst."

"You are one messed up dude. I've never heard of anyone who wants to go to school. But hey," he spread his arms like a benevolent genie, "let's see how far you can go. I'm feeling generous. Just remember you owe me." Miguel held his longneck out, and we clinked bottles.

"I'll do what I can, man." We chugged beer. I took a deep breath and felt better than in a long time. In the middle of godforsaken Midland, Texas desert, and I'm working it. Hell yes.

Chapter Thirty

Kailey and Shinto

Captain Samosa grabbed my shoulders and stopped my momentum. His blue uniform stood out in the sea of green scrubs. "Where are you going in such a rush?"

"Crime scene, sir."

"Hold up a minute, Kailey. We need to talk. Let's grab a cup of coffee at the cafeteria."

"But sir—"

"Not a request, Kailey." He turned and headed down the hall to the cafeteria and I followed, hurrying to keep up with him.

Minutes later I perched on the edge of a plastic chair in the busy, noisy cafeteria, waiting. My knee bounced involuntarily. I tried forcing it to quit, but I'd get lost formulating my next words and forget. Then it would start up again.

"Kailey, I know your mother is in intensive care. This is a tough time for you to be out on the street."

I blew on my coffee, waiting, dreading what came next. Fluorescent lights blinked over the deli meat station. That's me, dead meat.

"Allen is going to be in the hospital and will need physical therapy for I don't know how long," the captain said. "Shinto is going to need a new partner. I was thinking of you."

"I didn't know his injuries were that bad, sir. Besides, I have a partner. Mike and I have been together ever since—"

Samosa grimaced. "It's only temporary, Kailey, for now. Until Allen is a hundred percent. Mike is an old dog who can handle himself. I'm worried Shinto may go a little ballistic over Allen getting hit. You're the only one I can count on who can control her."

"You want me to babysit Shinto Elliot."

"I want you to do your job, whatever that entails."

"Yessir."

"Good answer."

"We'll get the assholes that shot Allen, sir. You can count on it."

"I know you will. I need to count on you for something else while we're at it."

"Sir?"

"Did you know Allen signed up to teach a class at Midland College?"

"I—what? No, sir I didn't." More important, why would I care?

"Introduction to Police Procedure. It's more of a public service class, but in our current political climate a great foundation for public understanding and trust."

"Sounds great, sir. He'll be an inspiration to anyone taking the class."

"He's not going anywhere anytime soon and classes start in a week. I want you to take his place."

"I'm sorry, what?" My mind reeled. Me? Teach a class? "Are you friggin'—I mean, seriously sir? I'm no teacher."

Samosa narrowed his eyes. "With all you've got on your plate, and I'm talking about your mother specifically, I believe you'd be most effective doing this for the department. Shinto and the others will have this investigation wrapped up soon enough."

"Can I think about it?"

"Think all you want. It'll make you a better teacher. Thanks for being a team player. I'll have Allen give you his notes and fill you in on procedure at the school." He stood and stuck out his hand.

I rose and shook it. "Yes, sir. I'll be happy to. I appreciate the unique opportunity."

"Cut the crap, Kailey. I know it's not what you signed up for." He chuckled and angled for the door. "Oh." He turned back. "One more thing."

"Yes, sir?"

"Keep me up to date on your progress. Last thing I need is the dean of the university busting my chops for our less-than-enthusiastic involvement in its programs."

"No worries, Captain. I've got your back."

He smiled. "I know you do. It's another reason I'm giving this to you. Keep me up to date on your mother as well." He strode off and didn't look back.

I flopped down on the chair and put my head in my hands. A minute later I heard his footsteps returning. I groaned inwardly.

"Here's a thought," Samosa stuck his head in the door. "Since you're partners now. How about you ask Shinto to co-teach the class with you? I mean, if you feel it's too much for you to handle alone."

Shinto would be so pissed she might hate me forever. "Perfect, sir. That's a great idea. I'm sure she'd love to help."

Finally, a break. Teach a class, mold minds, be a role model, with my smiling, happy-go-lucky, best friend by my side. We might have fun, if she doesn't kill me first.

An hour later I lugged all the binders from Allen's college course to Momma's room at the hospital. Shinto was already there, sitting bedside.

"How's she doing?" I asked.

Shinto shrugged and didn't speak. The shine in her eyes told me why.

I dropped the load on the only other chair and approached momma's far side. She lay with her eyes closed. The shushing sound of her breathing apparatus and beep of the EKG reassured me she still lived.

"What's all that stuff?" Shinto said. "Forensics homework?"

"I wish. I'll tell you later."

So many machines. So many tubes. Sweet Jesus help her. I picked up momma's cool hand and stroked her palm. "We're here, Momma. Shinto and me." She looked small and peaceful. I touched her forehead and brushed a stray hair off her brow, the antiseptic smell overpowering. "Better ways to keep us off the streets, Momma."

I sat on the edge of the bed stroking her hand and stayed like that until Shinto rose.

"I'm going to check on Allen," she said, "then I'll get out, see if I can't get a line on the investigation into who shot him."

"Sounds like a plan."

"Text me if anything changes," Shinto said.

I nodded.

"We'll get through this," she said.

"I know we will. I'll find you later."

Shinto left and I settled in for a long vigil. "I'm going to teach a college course, Momma. Can you believe that? Kailey Carmichael, molder of young minds. I kind of like it. What do you think?"

I pulled the chair with all the binders close and angled momma's tray table around to use for a desk. I opened the first three-ringed binder and sorted through all the stray pages and thumb drives. Could the Dempsey's be any more organized? I noticed Cindy's law firm name emblazoned on each page. Must be nice to have secretaries at your beck and call.

"Pretty dreary outside, Momma. Hey, maybe it'll rain. Think that's too much to ask?" I scooted forward and realized the tray table needed lowering. "You know the RockHounds won again? We are on a streak. Go team." I tried adjusting it, pushing and yanking. Stupid thing. I had both hands on either side of it, leaning my full weight on it, willing the contraption to lower when a nurse popped in to hang another drip.

"Here. Let me," she said and saved a piece of hospital property from sailing through the window.

"How's my mom doing?" I asked.

"Doctor should be in soon. He'll be able to tell you how she's doing."

"Thanks."

I flipped open the binder and settled in to study while the nurse took vials of blood and made entries on momma's chart. After the nurse left and I finished several pages of dry reading, I said, "Hey, momma, did I tell you I ran into Gail the other day? She has gained a boatload of weight and looks like hell. I know, I shouldn't say things like that." I waited, watching my mom carefully. Not so long ago she'd be shaking her head and rolling her eyes at what a judgmental daughter she'd raised. Nothing. Beeps and wheezes. I reached for another binder. This one featured page after page of crime scene photos. Stuff the papers never saw. Fun.

Several hours and binders later, I stood and stretched. "I'm going to get some coffee, Momma. I'll be right back."

I took the stairs down to the first floor where I snagged coffee and a muffin wrapped in plastic wrap. I paid and hurried back to momma's room.

I stopped by the nurse's station on the way and asked the nurse behind the computer when my mother's doctor would be by.

"And your mother is?" The nurse waited, hands hovered over the keyboard.

"Oh, sorry. Mrs. Carmichael."

"You just missed him," she said. "He'll be back tomorrow. Get here early if you want to speak with him."

How long was I gone on my coffee run? Five minutes? "Great." My luck continues.

I churned through everything and finished my first look-see into the course outline before I checked my watch. Damn. Nine p.m. already? I stood. "Well, Momma. I've got to go. I'll be back tomorrow. You behave okay? Get better. I need you." I leaned over and kissed her. My butt hurt from all the hours I'd sat in the room. I took the elevator to the second floor and stopped in Allen's room to say goodbye. A football game on his TV squawked from the remote speaker when I peeked in. "Hi there. How are you doing?" I said.

"Better every day." Allen said. "How's your mother?"

"No change."

"Oh, I'm sorry."

"I wish I knew more. I didn't get to see her doctor today. I stepped out for a minute and he came and went."

Allen adjusted the head of his bed. "They're good at that."

"What's yours telling you?"

"Looks like I'll be released tomorrow."

"Allen, that's great. Then after that?"

"Physical therapy. I'll be better than new in no time. What the heck are you lugging there?"

"Don't you recognize it? It's the notes on—"

"My Midland Police Procedure class."

"Yeah. That." I scrunched my face. "Substance abuse, photos of dead bodies, firearms, domestic issues, the law, and rules of behavior. That's a lot to cover in a semester, Allen. You really think these kids are ready for how graphic you designed this program? Shouldn't we dumb it down a bit?"

Allen sniffed. "Truth is truth, Kailey. Powers that be asked me to design a course to give the kids a real taste for our job. Not my problem if they don't like the taste." He lowered the head of his bed. "But apparently, Captain put you in charge. Course is yours now. Do whatever you want with it."

"You don't have to get angry. I didn't ask for this assignment."

"I didn't ask for them to take it from me. Trade places." He frowned.

Silence.

"Captain asked if I'd like Shinto to co-lead with me," I said. Anything to break the silence.

"Shinto?" Allen snorted. "Bet she had a lot to say about it."

"I haven't exactly asked her yet. I sorta hoped Captain Samosa might do it for me."

"Not a chance. He's more afraid of Shinto than any of us."

"You may be right."

"Love to see it, though." He laughed bitterly. "Shinto will have the class drop and give her fifty for every wrong answer."

"I better get going." I lifted the books. "Homework."

"Have fun," he said.

"See ya."

Three hours later, Shinto answered on the fourth ring. "Who is this? It better be important to wake me up in the middle of the night." I heard her yawn.

"C'mon, Shinto. You told me you never sleep."

"Kailey? What's wrong? Is everything all right? How's Mom?"

"Sorry I woke you." No way I could tell her what I needed over the phone. "I need to see you, Shinto. When would be a good time?"

"I worked a double today. We are short-handed with you and Allen out."

"You know what? It can wait. Go back to sleep."

"Bullshit. You wouldn't have called me if it wasn't important. Get your ass over here with lots of hot black coffee and an assortment of doughnuts. I won't be able to go back to sleep anyway."

"You sure?"

"Sure as God makes lesbians."

"I'll be right there."

I arrived in twenty minutes.

She opened the door half-dressed, sleepy-eyed, and sipping tomato juice. At least that's what it looked like.

"I come bearing gifts," I said. "Don't shoot me." I walked in, handed her the coffee, and deposited the doughnuts on her kitchen dinette.

"The coffee smells yummy. What kind of doughnuts did you get?" Shinto pulled out a couple of small dishes from her cupboard, and I flipped open the box.

"Jelly, lemon-filled, cake, and glazed. Some with sprinkles."

"Come to mama," Shinto said as she piled her plate with a red, a yellow and a chocolate. She plopped down on a chair, took a huge bite, and said through the chewing, "Now quit stalling. How's mom and why would I shoot you?"

"Momma is fine, no change. I'm here because I need a favor."

"Of course you do." She picked up her second doughnut. "What is it? Spit it out."

"Has the captain talked to you about helping me take over Allen's course at Midland?"

"Not a word."

"Figures, the coward. He benched me, Shinto. Allen can't teach it. He's recovering. Captain got a brain fart and tapped me for the job. He thinks somehow, with my mom in a coma teaching will be easier on me than working the streets with you guys. Which is so much bullshit." I got up and paced. "Like I'm a teacher? I get nervous thinking about it."

"How hard could it be Kailey, you can do this with your eyes closed. Sounds like it might even be fun."

"I am so glad to hear you say that."

Ten minutes later, after Shinto stopped swearing at me and the "whole messed up goddamn world and the goddamn men who run it," I bit into a doughnut and lemon filling squirted out and fell all over my boob. "See, Shinto? This is my life. A big gooey mess."

Shinto started laughing.

I wiped goo from my blouse with my finger and stuck it in my mouth. "Can't waste good goo." I laughed, too, then. Rung out? Relieved? Who knew? I sat with my best friend in the entire world, who'd just said yes to sharing a crap job neither of us wanted any part of.

Maybe things weren't going totally to shit after all.

Chapter Thirty-One

Junior

I headed for the bookstore early. Patricia told me used books are the first to go, especially the cleaner, unmarked ones. The sign on the door said it opened at 9:00. I walked up at 8:30 and took my place behind a dozen kids who got here even earlier. No problem. I got to people watch, see more of what my fellow students were really like. Five years younger, on average, full of hopes and dreams, and not one prison tat among them.

Two girls in line behind me traded snarky comments and observations on college life. The debate centered on the sexual orientation of the professor in the drama department. I turned around and recognized them from one of my classes last semester.

"Hey," I said. Short and to the point. If not all that original.

"Hey yourself, big guy," the pretty Latina said. "Junior, right?"

"Yes. How did you—?"

"All the girls know your name, Junior." The blonde beside her giggled.

"Shut up, Brittany, you're embarrassing him."

"I think it's cute," Brittany said. "He's turning red."

"Now I know you guys are messing with me," I said.

"Maybe a little," the Latina said. "I'm Grace and the one beside me with the blond hair and blonde brain is Brittany."

"Pleased to meet you," I said. "Outside of class." I shook hands with each of them and felt like a total moron.

"What fun classes are you taking this year, Junior?" Brittany asked.

"Not drama; that's for sure." Grace laughed.

"Ah, I got a lot of catching up to do coverin' my basics. Don't know about any fun classes. One course I am looking forward to is police procedure."

"Yecch. I heard it's going to be taught by real police and they are going to show dead bodies and stuff." Brittany shivered.

Grace frowned. "No way, dude. I saw enough of that back home before Daddy brought us here."

"Where was that?" I said.

"Juarez. Cartel crap. No thank you very much." She scrunched up her face. "My daddy gets enough of that living here."

"Her dad's a lawyer," Brittany offered. "Big time. Like we're going to be. Sort of."

"How do you sort of be a lawyer?"

"Real estate law," both girls announced and then promptly laughed.

"Yeah. No guns," said Brittany.

"No dead bodies," said Grace.

"Yeah." I said. "I hear they drive down the cost of real estate."

Locks clicked in the front doors and the crowd surged forward, saving me from further inanities. A gray-haired woman with tight lips pulled the doors wide and got shoved into a stack of books by the crowd. I helped her to her feet on my way by but left her once she regained her balance.

The students and I flooded into the tiny bookstore wading through a sea of backpacks and Midland Community T-shirts. Like most other students, I pulled out my list and kept consulting it. In the end I located every book on my list except one. Introduction to Police Procedure would have to wait until another day.

I waited in a line of kids at the register. When I slapped my books on the counter to pay for them, I recognized the poor woman from the door crush.

"You doing all right?" I asked.

She patted her hair self-consciously. "Happens every semester," she said. "You'd think I would learn. Did you find everything you need?"

Not waiting for my answer, she took the top book off my stack and scanned it. She took the next one and scanned it as her glasses slid back down her rather large hooked nose.

"Introduction to Police Procedure," I said.

"Pardon?"

"Police Procedure? I didn't see a place for it on the shelves."

"That's because there isn't one. It's my understanding the professors hand out the materials they use in class."

"Ah, well, thanks, I guess."

She kept ringing up my books, and when she slid the last one onto her finished stack she said, "How will you be paying for these? Check, credit, or debit? Checks require two forms of ID."

I pulled my license and a copy of my parole assignment and laid them on the table.

She picked up the green piece of paper. "What's this? Oh. OH—"

"That's all I have."

"No, no. This will do fine. Just fine. Don't you worry." She ran my check, bagged my books, and ripped off a receipt in record time. "There you go, sir," she said. "Come back s—I mean, hope to see you, that is—"

I took my books and my receipt. I made sure to touch her fingers with mine to see her jump. "Thank you, ma'am. I'll be back to see you real soon."

Her eyes got big, and I blew her a kiss as I left.

I made my way to the police procedure class on Tuesday and took a seat in the middle of six rows of desk chairs. My knees bumped up against the desk part and I needed to stretch my legs to fit into the stupid thing. I pitied the poor kid who grabbed the seat behind me. He'd need to be a tall one to see over me. Not to worry. A huge blonde boy, had be an offensive lineman, swaggered up the aisle and tucked in behind me.

I recognized the medium-sized woman when she stepped up to the podium as one of the two cops who grilled me at my PO's office. "Good morning, ladies and gentlemen. You are in introduction to police procedure. When I call your name please raise your hand and speak up. We will make a seating chart next week. My name is Officer Kailey Carmichael, and this scary woman at my side," she nodded and grinned at a fierce-looking dyke in a chair behind her, "is Officer Shinto Elliot. We are with the Midland Police Department. The two of us will be sharing teaching duties. Shinto, would you like to say a few words?"

Shinto. That was it, the Indian-looking one.

She slapped Officer Carmichael on the back as she approached the front. "This class will be showing graphic photos of crime scenes and bodies. Later in the semester we will bring in blood and luminol. You need to feel and smell the blood to understand how we use microscopic evidence to catch people who choose to kill or ignore the law. We will examine bullet trajectories and see how to use lasers. If you believe you can't handle blood and seeing the horrible things people do to other people, then I suggest you leave and find another class."

Shinto smiled as several girls and my offensive lineman gathered their belongings and slouched out the back door.

Shinto took roll, and I raised my hand high like a good student. She took a moment to look me over before moving onto the next name on her list.

I felt her cop's eyes checking me out. What the hell was that all about?

I settled in for whatever the class and these two cops could teach me that I didn't already know.

Might not suck too bad. A couple of hot cops to keep my juices flowing? I might even learn something. I raised my hand. Time for some fun. "Will we be going to any crime scenes?" I heard groans and tittering in back of me.

Officer Carmichael spoke up. "No, Mr., um," she consulted her notes. "Alvarez. We will show slides, and for the final we will stage a crime scene and you will write a paper and solve the crime." She glanced at her partner, Shinto Elliot, and then went on. "One third of your grade will depend on how well you do. We will give you the tools you'll need and teach you how to use them. I suggest everyone take copious notes, and don't be afraid to ask questions."

I shot my hand up again. "Will this be based on an actual crime or one you two make up? Because we could use the Internet to solve one that's already been solved."

"Interesting point. We'll see," she sounded irritated. "Anyone else have any questions?"

I raised my hand again.

She rolled her eyes. "Yes, Mr. Alvarez?"

Good. She'd already learned my name. "What time does this class end?"

"They covered that when you enrolled, Mr. Alvarez. Now perhaps you will let some of the other students ask a question."

"Yes, ma'am." I smiled and she frowned. My work here is finished. I irritated the police without getting arrested. I win.

Chapter Thirty-Two

Kailey and Shinto

I gathered up my papers from the lectern as the students filed out to their next class.

Shinto came up and said, "That didn't go so bad hey teach? Grab some lunch at the cafeteria? I hear they have great catfish today."

"Where in the world would you hear that?"

"My auntie works there."

"You're on. I'm starving."

We found a table in the corner. I'd piled my tray with coleslaw, mashed potatoes, and steaming hot catfish, and my stomach growled like a begging dog. I squeezed lemon on the fish, grabbed my fork and speared my first bite when Junior Alvarez walked up. Un-frigging believable. First, he's mister Q and A and now he's interrupting my lunch. "Yes?"

"Catfish? Ooh, I don't know."

"Excuse me?"

"We're in Midland, Texas, professor. How could anything be fresh way out here?" Junior smirked.

Shinto growled as she slammed her tray onto the table. "Learn that in prison? We got lakes, genius. Oh, sorry." She grinned at me. "Too un-PC?"

He grinned back. "Go for it," he said.

Shinto did. "As I was saying, genius, my auntie works here. She told me this fish is fresh caught and delicious."

"What's she use for bait?" he said.

Shinto rose from her chair, and I put a hand on her arm.

"Pieces of students who ask too many questions," I said. "Cut us a break. And let us eat in peace. We'll see you Wednesday in class, yes?"

"Sorry to be a bother. Ladies I mean, officers." Junior touched a finger to his brow and shuffled off to grab a tray.

"Students these days." Shinto obliterated a piece of fish with several stabs of her fork.

"Oh, he's not so bad, Shinto. Lighten up. He's trying to be friendly."

"I don't like his demeanor or attitude. You know who he is, right? From the wreck? We interviewed him in his P.O.'s office? Why the hell would an ex-con take a police procedures class? I'd think he had enough of those to last a lifetime."

"Not going to worry about it. It's a free country, even for felons. Forget him. What do you think of our class? I think I'm loving this."

"You are delusional. I'm wondering why I'm even here."

"Captain's idea." I crunched into a bite of catfish. OMG. Heaven. "Go ask him."

"I saw you in there. You're a natural, girl." She snapped her fingers. "I know, why not teach it on your own? If you get into trouble I'll come by and save your ass. Like always. In the meantime, I need to get back to the streets. Still haven't collared Allen's shooter. A lot of bad shit going down besides that."

I spoke through a mouthful of mashed potatoes. "More than usual?"

"We're hearing about a new gang, the Snakes, slithering in to take over Los Demonios."

"Slithering in?"

"See what I did there?"

"Sounds ominous." I chomped on some tasty coleslaw. Really tasty. "Have you tried this coleslaw?"

"I'm trying to tell you. Miguel What's-His-Face is not a forgiving type. I don't give a shit about him or his Demonios butt-wads. It's the innocent bystanders that wind up dead in the crossfire." Shinto trailed her fork through her potatoes, not eating them.

"Take it up with the captain. I'm good with whatever you decide." I gulped some sweet tea and shivered.

"That good, huh?"

"This tea tastes like cat piss. I'll be right back." I took the tea to the cashier and said, "Tastes like something died in this."

"Wonder what it is this week?" She chuckled. Must be cafeteria humor. "Go get something else."

I grabbed a bottle of water from the cooler, always a safe choice, turned, and bumped smack into Junior Alvarez.

"Hey, professor." He grabbed my shoulders so I wouldn't fall. "We gotta stop meeting like this." He patted my shoulder and left me standing with my mouth open. I had no witty comeback. I'd think of the perfect one later. That guy is a piece of work. Better keep my eye on him.

I went back to the table and watched my co-teacher wipe her plate with a biscuit. "Shinto, if you don't need me, I think I'll go over and see how Momma's doing today."

"I'll be over later. In the meantime, I'll head to the station and tell the captain you love teaching so much you want to handle this gig by yourself."

"Thanks a lot," I said.

"Don't mention it."

"Fine. Tell him I got it covered. I'll sit with Momma while I plan my next class."

"You're the best," Shinto said. "After me."

"Don't you forget it."

She hurried off before I could change my mind. I bussed our trays and headed over to see Momma.

Twenty minutes later I waltzed into my mother's room. "Hi, Momma. I'm here. What have you been up to?" I scooted a chair up next to the bed. Silence with an occasional beep from her heart monitor was my answer. "When are you going to wake up?"

"Maybe I can answer that question for you Miss Carmichael?" A distinguished-looking doctor held a chart in one hand and held out the other for me to shake. "I'm your mother's doctor, Dr. Bisht." He said it with a charming lilt to his voice. Sounded like he came from India.

"Why is my mother still in a coma, doctor?"

"Because of us I'm afraid. We're keeping her in a medically induced coma until the swelling in her brain goes down. I know it feels slow, but she has improved. We're reducing her dosage, and we'll soon stop the drugs altogether to see how she does."

"That's wonderful."

"We are cautiously optimistic. You should know it will take a while to see what's involved and what's happened."

"Long as I get my mother back."

"Of course. If there are no other questions?" He waited in the doorway.

"I don't think so. Thank you, doctor."

After several hours and no change, mother slept on. Her color did look better, and she breathed without a tube down her throat. Thank God. I decided I needed some fresh air. "Momma, I'm going to run over to Shinto's house. Gotta work on some ideas for lesson plans. I'll be back soon. Don't do anything I wouldn't do." I bent down to kiss her as a nurse came in to give her a bath. Yep, time to go. No one needs to see their own mother naked.

Minutes later I pulled up to Shinto's house and noticed a car I didn't recognize in her driveway. Wonder if I should come back later. Nah, it'll take me a minute, and I'll have what I need for our next class.

Rather than burst in like usual, I rang the doorbell and waited. Rang it again and waited. I turned to go, when Shinto came to the door wrapped in a towel.

"Sorry. Did I get you out of the shower? I want to run some ideas by you for Friday's class. Funny, I just left momma at the hospital when they came in to give *her* a bath." I eyed Shinto's towel. "Must be the universal time for baths." I pushed around her and ran smack into Heather standing off to the side also wrapped in a towel. "Uh . . . oh . . . shit," I stuttered. "Jeez, I'm sorry. I am so interrupting something. Crap, this is awkward."

Shinto wrapped her arm around Heather. "Not in the least. You are the first to know."

Heather smiled.

"After Terri." Shinto hugged the petite woman.

"Your friend Terri. We ate at Big Bubba's."

Shinto nodded. "You can stop trying to worm stuff out of me. I would have told you then. I wanted to. But we're kind of paranoid about the department. If word ever got out—"

I held up a hand. "Say no more. I'm an idiot. And I am so damn happy for you. For you both."

"Thanks Kailey," Heather said. "Shinto tends to be a little paranoid."

"Shinto tends to be a lot of things. If she ever gets out of line, you call me."

"Oh, I think I can keep her in line."

They both blushed and I thought it might be the sweetest thing I'd ever seen.

"We've been together for a few months," Shinto said. "I'm trying to get her to see the logic of moving in and dumping her apartment. Grab a cup of coffee while we get dressed, and then we'll talk."

Heather returned before Shinto. "Shinto is changing her bandages, and I'm fixing breakfast."

I stood.

"No. Sit. I've got this. Shinto told me about your mom. I'm so sorry, Kailey."

"Thanks. Any progress on finding who shot Shinto and Allen?"

Heather got out eggs, green onions, chorizo, cheese, and potatoes. "We've got the bullets and the dead kid gangbanger. Lots of evidence to process. I've heard he's illegal. Shocker. We'll be tracking any relatives. You know how that goes. Is a communal omelet good for you?"

I couldn't sit still and jumped up to get the plates and silverware. "Perfect. It's for sure gang related?"

"Ninety-nine point-nine percent. Another shooting went down last night."

"I hadn't heard. Let's change the subject. I noticed a difference in Shinto lately. Her friend Terri mentioned it too. Now I see why."

"Thank you, Kailey. It's been amazing, but not without challenges. You know I was married."

I found the salt and pepper and put them on the table. "Yes, to Larry. Wasn't he a pilot?"

"Still is. We haven't been what you call close our whole marriage. Last June he asked me for a divorce. Come to find out, he got a woman he met in Dubai pregnant, and he is so happy. He's wanted a baby for a couple of years. I didn't. I've felt this distance and yearning for other women that I've suppressed all my life. When he asked me for a divorce I felt it was a sign." Heather plugged in the coffeepot.

"I can well imagine, if you weren't being your authentic self, as those pop shrinks would say."

"After my divorce I waited awhile and then asked Shinto to go to a movie. I was scared shitless."

"Me too." Shinto came into the room wearing a tank top and shorts. "Hell, I thought she wanted to go to a movie as friends. Not a date."

"Then I kissed her. In the movie. You should have seen her face, Kailey." Heather laughed and gazed at Shinto.

Shinto blushed. Second time inside fifteen minutes. "Oh, she surprised me, all right."

"I've known Shinto for so many years. You won't find a better person, Heather. Man or woman."

"Don't I know it."

Shinto piped up. "I am starved y'all. How about we eat before I die? We'll talk over your lessons for the little kiddies while we chew."

Chapter Thirty-Three

Junior

I munched on a piece of fish. Flaky, light, it actually did taste amazing, and watched my two teachers jaw back and forth. Who knew introduction to police procedure would be so interesting? That hot cop next to the ball buster didn't hurt. Yeah, interesting was definitely the word.

I finished lunch and headed home, walking with my armload of books. Me, Joe College. Who woulda thought it? I got to the corner and I kicked a rock, waiting for the light to change. This education thing might actually be my ticket.

Or, not.

The little green pedestrian light flickered on and I stepped off the curb. A car zoomed by, horn blaring. Missed me by inches. I didn't flinch, didn't curse his mother. What the hell? Jeez, I needed a beer, weed, something. Maybe a party? Hell, there's always a party at Miguel's place.

An hour later, four in the afternoon, and the party at Miguel's already raged. I recognized a few of the guys from college. I walked over to one. Blond kid dressed all imitation vato. Poor dude couldn't be more preppie.

"Hey, I'm Junior." I stuck out my hand.

He fist-bumped me like a real O.G. He must watch a lot of TV. "Hey, Junior. Levi. How's it hanging?"

"It's hanging."

He nodded. "I hear that. What classes you taking?"

"Got a late start on this college stuff. Still playin' catch up with the core classes. You?"

"Mom insists I take advanced calculus. I've been brushing up on my shit so I can get into SMU; her alma mater."

"SMU?"

"Southern Methodist, dude. My mom and dad got married in the friggin' chapel there. It's been their dream that I follow their footsteps."

"So you're engaged?"

"That's funny." Levi laughed and slapped his leg. "No, man, not that far gone. If I get in, you ought to come to Dallas. I'll show you around."

"Sounds like a plan," I said. "At the moment though I need a cerveza." We did the obligatory fist bump. I briefly hoped he'd get out of this party alive to get to SMU. Yeah, well. Not my problem.

I walked up the porch and into the house to grab a cerveza from the fridge. Yolo, Manuel's chick, stood talking with a dark-haired, dark-eyed young woman dressed in a pantsuit. As out of place as my fake vato outside.

"Junior," Yolo said, "this is Elizabeth. She works for me at the bank."

"Hey there, Elizabeth, good to meet you." We solemnly shook hands. "What do you do at the money store?"

She tugged on an earlobe. "I'm a teller, Junior." She blinked her long eyelashes several times. "What do you do?"

"Tryin' real hard to be a college student." I grinned, and she blushed. Yep, I thought, still got it.

Yolo wandered away and Elizabeth leaned on the kitchen counter, sipping her beer. "I'm starving," she said. "How about you?"

"I could eat. Probably nothing worth eating here. Not until they fire up the grills out back. We could hit up Taco Bell or walk down to Chili's, but I must confess I'm a starving student with no job and crappy prospects. If we go it'll have to be Dutch treat. I'm also cheap."

She giggled. "You're different Mr. Junior. I like that. How about I treat you? Since I have a job and you are starving."

"Oh, and I don't have a car either."

"My, my. You are a problem child. Guess we'll use mine."

She's sexy as hell, has money and a car. I'm in heaven. "Lead the way, chica. It's a date."

We finished our beers and headed out back to a red BMW convertible. "Sweet ride." I hopped into the passenger's side.

"My folks gave it to me for graduating college early. I love it." She squealed tires pulling away from the house. "What's your pleasure?"

"We are still talking about food, right?"

"Down, boy," she said, but her smile hinted at other possibilities. "Like cold pizza? I have half a pie from last night."

"My favorite."

She shifted into third and hit the accelerator.

I grabbed the handhold over the window as she slid into the next corner. She got the car straightened when—

BANG. BANG. BANG.

"Those are gunshots," I yelled. "Get the hell out of here."

She turned right, and we flew down Big Springs Street for about a quarter of a mile. Sirens wailed ahead of us, and she pulled to the curb. Two cop cars and a rescue wagon blasted by. She grabbed the rearview mirror and angled it to look around. "Wonder what the heck happened?"

"Sounded like guns popping off," I said. "Coming from the party. When we left I saw some gangbangers headed toward the house in a black lowrider. I thought they were part of the posse that hangs out there."

"I saw that car, too. It bounced like on springs. I thought that only happened in the movies. Want to go check it out?"

"How about that pizza? There's nothing we can do there. Be cops everywhere."

"I want to cruise by, see if everyone is okay."

"Go for it."

We drove by the house without saying a word. Police crawled all over the place.

"Oh, shit," I said.

"What?"

My imitation vato lay on the sidewalk where we'd stood talking a half an hour before. A bullet hole formed a tidy black dot in the middle of his forehead.

"I knew that kid," I said. "Levi. Had SMU on his mind. Now he doesn't."

"Junior." She put her hand over mine. "I'm so sorry."

"I didn't know him. I mean I met him earlier, but still—"

Jesus, what a waste. He'd seemed like a good kid. Several other kids were down on the ground. Some moving. Some not. I heard moans. Kids were having a party, for God's sake. I heard more wailing sirens. Another ambulance rounded the corner. I saw movement on the grass and spotted the ballbuster cop from my intro to police procedure class.

"Son of a bitch," I said.

"What?"

"That's my teacher. Dyke-looking one? Yep. That's her."

Just then Shinto, I think her name, glanced over and saw us.

"Tell you what. Let's leave before we get caught up in this shit."

"I hear you," Elizabeth said and pulled slowly from the curb as if afraid one of the cops might run over to write her a traffic ticket.

Out of the corner of my eye I saw my cop-teacher head our way and then stop as we pulled off.

We got to the end of the street and Elizabeth turned left and drove onto Loop 250. About three miles later she turned into a large housing complex. We passed large houses wound around a golf course to the condo side. She passed several buildings and headed to a covered parking structure without saying a word. After she parked and got out of the car, I followed her around a path to a condo on the end of a building. She let us in and collapsed on a light gray sofa. I flopped down next to her. I scooted over and took her in my arms and we sat like that for a long while, both of us numb. When it got dark she got up and motioned for me to follow her to the bedroom.

I followed, part of me amazed at what was happening, part of me not wanting to examine it too closely.

We undressed in the dark, quietly. Purposefully. We found one another under the sheets and the feeling of another human being, not as a quick lay or a bar pickup or a conquest, not even lust, really guided me. We moved gently. I felt her skin. I kissed her cheek and then her neck. I traced my finger down her belly as it rose to meet my touch. I followed my finger with my tongue. Her breasts stood erect when I kissed them. She moaned. I'd never listened to a woman before, focused on my own needs. The more I pleased her the more aroused I became.

She whispered, "Take me. Junior."

"Not yet." I played with kissing her pleasure. She pushed up. "Oh, God. Oh, yes, there. Don't stop. There, there, oh." She came. I pulled her up to sitting, and she was a rag doll in my hands. I laid her down on her stomach. God what an ass. I pulled her up and glided myself into her from behind. She moaned. "Oh, yes. There," she insisted. After a while I turned her back over and slid in as her body rose to meet me. She grabbed my neck and pulled me down to a deep kiss as we found our rhythm. I lost all thought and time.

"Baby, I can't last much longer."

"Now, now, NOW." It was all I heard her say, all I needed to hear before I exploded.

We lay together a long time alive and safe, connected in a way I'd never experienced.

Chapter Thirty-Four

Kailey

I smiled as I hopped into my car. Shinto and Heather. I would never have guessed. Naturally it made me think of my own prospects. Derek and Dallas were so far away. Looks like celibacy will be my lifestyle for a while. Kailey Carmichael, nun in training?

On the way home I couldn't help thinking X-rated thoughts about my Dallas lover. He made that forensics school a real pleasure in so many wonderful ways. A honking horn broke me from my erotic thoughts and I flashed the obligatory middle finger while I checked the time. Yep. Just enough to stop home, change, and sit with Momma for a few before I have to teach class.

I ran into the house, showered, and brushed my teeth. Tried to run a comb through my kinky blond hair and gave up. Frizz aplenty this morning. What the hell, I added gel, squished my hair, and blew it dry with the diffuser on my hair dryer. I ended up with ringlets, at best a blond mop. I hated ringlets as a kid. Now I've made peace with them. Momma loves them. To be super girly, I curled my eyelashes and brushed mascara on. Got mascara on my forehead and my cheek. "Crap." I tried to rub it off. One cheek shone bright pink and so did my forehead. Solution: apply makeup and blush. I pulled ringlets down on my forehead and stuck a couple of gold hoop earrings in my pierced ears and a diamond stud in my left ear above the hoop. I'd had it pierced when I found out I was pregnant with Emma; the diamond I chose for her. Then I threw on a pair of tight boyfriend jeans with ripped knees, a white T-shirt, and my favorite brown Roper boots.

I stuck my tongue out at the image in the mirror. Hell, I could almost pass for a college student, couldn't I?

I grabbed a banana on the way back out. Naturally I thought more about Derek. Bad girl, Kailey. You're going to see your Momma, for crissakes.

I rolled into the parking lot of Midland Memorial Hospital. When I got out, the dry Midland heat smacked me so hard it took my breath away. The hospital double doors sucked open, and I stopped a moment to absorb the cool rush of air conditioning. I used the stairs. Jogged six floors up to momma's room, my daily cardio.

Panting, I braced myself and scooted a chair up to her bed. When I took her hand it felt cool.

Then she opened her eyes!

"Oh, Momma. Momma, I'm here. Thank God."

She smiled weakly.

I jumped up and ran to the nurse's station. "My mother opened her eyes. She's awake. Get the doctor."

"Good news." The young nurse stopped typing on her computer and grinned. "Did she speak?"

"No. But she opened her eyes. Looked right at me. That's a good sign, right?"

"I'll page Mrs. Davis."

"Who?"

"Head nurse. I'm sure she will want to assess the situation. Dr. Bisht should be in this morning."

"Can't you tell him it's an emergency?"

She ignored me and paged the nurse.

Chapter Thirty-Five

Junior

Morning came, and I lay in bed not believing last night. I meet this amazing chick. We miss a drive-by shooting by seconds. She's upset. I'm right there, Mr. Comforter. I wondered what chance I might have at a rematch.

She laid with her back to me, hugging her side of the mattress. I scooted closer to test the waters, but when I put my hand on her back she shrank from my touch. Official forecast, chilly.

She sighed audibly. I knew I was probably supposed to say something. But what? No friggin' clue.

"Do you think she's okay?"

"Who?"

"Yolanda." She sat up in bed with the sheet to her throat. "Who else? Do you think she got shot?"

"I'm sure Yolo—Yolanda—is fine. First off, we didn't see her outside. Second, she has Miguel. He'd keep her safe."

"From a drive-by? Stupid asshole sticks a gun out of a car window and tries to hit as many people as possible."

"Exactly." I raised up on my elbow. "It's random. They're lucky if they hit anyone."

"We should go to the police," she said.

"What? Hey, whoa. Slow your roll."

She answered by jumping out of bed and looking for her underwear.

So much for our morning-after lovin' moment. I got up with her and threw on my clothes.

"We saw the car, Junior." She patted the bedclothes. Lifted pillows, searching for her bra.

I had fond memories of that bra. "Everyone there saw the car. Lots of people partying." I pulled on my shoes. Give it up, dude. Fun's over.

"Except they won't say anything. You know that. Everyone clams up." Spoken like a junior G-man.

I shifted gears. "But we weren't there when it happened. We go in claiming we saw something we didn't, they'll have our ass. And you have too nice an ass." Nothing. Not even a comment. I pressed on. "Police will look at us hard if we come forward. I don't know about you, but cops make me nervous. Plus, you have your job to think about."

"What about those poor kids that were shot?" Her clothes went on as quickly as mine. She just had more of them.

"Elizabeth." Oh my god, she would not let it go. "You saw the ambulance and the police. They showed up like that." I snapped my fingers. "Almost like they staked the place out. For all I know they did. Those who could be helped are at the hospital. The others are at the morgue."

"You don't have to be so unfeeling about it." She sat on the bed to put on her shoes.

"If I felt something for every vato who ate a bullet I'd be, I don't know what, gay."

She chuckled.

What? A ray of hope?

"I can vouch for the fact that you are not gay, Junior. Not after last night. But I need to get to work."

"I need to get to class. Drop me at my place?"

"If you can keep up." She winked and snagged her purse as she hurried for the door.

I beat her to the convertible by half a second.

We didn't talk all the way to my apartment. When she parked I leaned over. "Maybe my class in police procedure will have some

145

information about the shooting, Elizabeth. Give me your phone number, and we can hook up again soon."

"That would be nice." She dug in her purse and wrote something on a card and handed it to me. "My cell is on the back. My office number is on the front." I stepped out. She gave me a megawatt smile before she stomped on the gas. The car's momentum slammed my door shut for me.

Chapter Thirty-Six

Kailey and Shinto

"Momma, open your eyes again." I stroked her hand for a while.

Dr. Bisht hustled in. He checked her pulse and chart. "Good afternoon, Miss Carmichael."

Momma croaked, "Kailey?"

"I'm here." I smiled at her and then at Dr. Bisht.

He put the ends of his stethoscope in his ears and checked her vital signs. I stepped back and perched on the edge of the chair by the bed.

"How are you feeling, Mrs. Carmichael?" His voice sounded musical and soothing.

"Tired."

"You've been through quite a lot. Take it easy and rest. It's the best thing for you."

She took a deep breath.

He finished his exam and turned to me. "Progress." His cell buzzed. "The next few days she should be more alert. I'm pleased with her responses. Quite good, quite good indeed." He scrolled through a text on his phone.

"Is there anything I can do for her?"

"She has to do this on her own. It's helpful that you are here with her. I'll look in on her tomorrow."

"Thank you, doctor." I stood.

Dr. Bisht thrust his hands into the pockets of his lab coat. "The nurses have my contact information. They will call me anytime Officer Carmichael, if you have any concerns about your mother." His white coat flared as he left the room.

Mom didn't stir for the next full hour I sat with her.

I checked the time. Class kicks off in twenty minutes. I needed to get to Midland College.

I called Shinto on the way to tell her about momma.

"Christ on a Ritz," Shinto said. "Thank God. I'm heading there right now. Don't you worry. Teach that damn class. I'll talk to you after."

I reached the classroom with five minutes to spare and scratched my name and points I wanted to cover on the chalkboard. I sat at the desk shuffling through pages of Allen's presentation while the students filed in. I really needed to buckle down and sort through this crap. Maybe tonight.

I waited while the students took their seats. They seemed happy and streamed through to their desks, chatting and laughing. Made me wish for my days back in college.

Quite a mix of ages in this class. It might be interesting to ask what subjects they would like to learn. See what areas of police procedure interested them. Maybe a questionnaire would be in order. Not too shabby, Kailey. Thinking like a real teacher.

In the meantime, I stood and dove into Allen's first lecture. Fifteen minutes into the presentation the door eased open and Junior Alvarez slunk in. I stopped and waited for him to arrive at his assigned seat and said, "Glad you could join us, Mr. Alvarez."

He had the decency to look sheepish and pull out his books with no comment other than a subdued "Sorry."

At the end of the hour I erased the chalkboard, gathered my papers, and shoved them into my purse. It pays to have a large hobo handbag. A stab at my heart reminded me I used to carry all things Emma in it. Now I carried my gun, handcuffs, badge, and lipstick. I heard a noise and looked up to see Alvarez standing in front of my desk. "What can I do for you Mr. Alvarez?" I used my police voice.

"Please, call me Junior, Ms. Carmichael."

"Don't make a habit of being late, and I'll think about it."

"It's a deal." He smiled. "It won't happen again."

He didn't have a bad smile, frankly. Jesus, Kailey. Check yourself.

"Are there any handouts I missed?" Junior asked.

"No handouts. If you copied what I wrote on the chalkboard, then you have everything you need for today."

"Yes, ma'am." He stood rooted in place.

"Anything else, Junior?"

"Well," he looked at the floor. "I was wondering, will you be covering Midland current events in class?"

"Maybe. By next class I'll pass out a questionnaire to see what everyone might be interested in."

"Cool."

"Specifically what are your interests?" I shouldered my purse and headed toward the door. He hurried ahead to get the door. I squeezed by and noticed, even up this close, he wasn't bad on the eyes, but his rough swagger nailed him as a product of the system.

"Normal stuff," he said. "How police handle crime. From first call to locking up the bad guys." He shrugged.

"I appreciate your interest, Mr. Alvarez. Junior. I'll see what I can do."

"Thanks," he said. Nothing more. He turned and took the stairs two at a time, disappearing into a sea of students. Interesting guy. I watched the crowd swallow him up. My stomach grumbled and reminded me I'd been neglecting it.

First food. Then the hospital. Then homework.

***

Shinto rose when I blew into momma's room and we hugged. Both of us blubbering like fools.

"No change, honey," Shinto said. "She opened her eyes and smiled at me. Once. I about lost it. Nothing else to report since."

"I'm glad you were here."

"Where else would I be? I'm off. I think Heather might have made dinner."

"Go be with Heather. I have plenty of homework to occupy my brain. I'll call with any news."

"Any time, Kailey. You hear?"

I heard and I loved her for it. She left me with my teacher homework and I settled in where I could keep an eye on Momma and read without moving my head. I reviewed the last couple of lessons. Tried to find a thread to tie the upcoming classes together. I worked on my questionnaire. After a couple of hours, my eyes got bleary and my brain denied having anything to do with something so stupid as a questionnaire.

I sat thinking about strokes and watching Mom sleep.

My cell rang. "Kailey Carmichael," I answered.

"Officer Carmichael? This is Barbara Tonkin."

"Hi, Barbara, what can I do for you?" Barbara was Samosa's assistant. I leaned back in the recliner and closed my burning eyes.

"Captain Samosa asked me to call and find out how your mother's doing and if you might have any time to come in. We have officers out with the flu and are shorthanded. We could use your help."

"When do you need me?"

"ASAP."

"I'm at the hospital. My house is on the way. I'll stop and change into my uniform and be right there."

"Thank you, Officer Carmichael."

"Barbara, please call me Kailey."

"Thank you, Kailey. See you soon."

I got to the station and scooted around a flurry of activity. Larry grabbed me at the front desk. "Kailey, help me. I've got Mr. and Mrs. Williams over there." He pointed to a couple deep in conversation off to my left.

"Their son Levi stood outside some party and got shot and killed by a drive-by shooter. Could you please take them into an interview room? They don't know he's dead. We need to know what kind of kid he was."

"Any paperwork on the shooting?"

"Just a second." He hit Print on his computer and then slid the printouts into a manila folder.

I read the file on the fly and hurried over to the Williamses. He wore a dark blue suit with a green- and blue-striped tie. She dressed in a flowing caftan and high stilettos. Her perfume reminded me of a garden in the middle of a desert. Midland boasted more millionaires than anyplace else in America and this couple obviously belonged to the club. I ushered them into an interview room.

Mr. Williams furrowed his brow. "We are making a fuss by coming. It's probably nothing, but we need help. Our son, Levi, has disappeared. That's not like him. He's a great kid, and when he didn't come home last night I, well, his mother worried something might have happened."

Mrs. Williams placed her hand on her husband's arm. He shook it off. She frowned and looked down.

"Frankly," he said, "I think it's about time the boy got some cojones and stayed out all night. It's what boys are supposed to do."

I glanced quickly at the coroner's photo of the dead boy in my folder. "Do you have a current photo of your son?"

"I do." Mrs. Williams opened a small blue clutch and rifled through for the photograph. "He graduated from Midland College and is going to SMU in the fall. He's taking a couple of classes this summer for fun." She spoke rapid fire.

"For fun. Hell, it's so he won't have to work in the oil fields. Kids these days want it all." Mr. Williams huffed and raked thick hard fingers through jet-black hair. Worry etched craters in his sunburned face.

"Tell me about your son."

Mrs. Williams grunted and pulled a photo from her purse, a proud smile on her lips. "He is perfect. Always a good boy."

"What did he wear yesterday?"

"A white T-shirt and jeans, I think, or did he wear khaki shorts?" A quizzical expression flitted across her face. "He had on jeans, definitely." She nodded in agreement with herself.

The father cleared his throat. Puddles filled his bottom eyelids. It softened the tough-guy image like throwing a switch.

I took the photo from her shaking hand. "Thank you. I'll make a copy and return it." I opened the folder and double checked. No doubts. My eyes flicked up.

Mr. Williams stared into my soul, his voice ragged. "He's gone isn't he? How did it happen?"

Chapter Thirty-Seven

Junior

I wandered over to the school bookstore with my first modeling paycheck sitting fat in my new bank account. I cracked my back and twisted my shoulders. Who knew modeling could be such hard work? I've never itched or felt body aches as much as when I'm sitting still, posing. I'm sick of using the computer lab to do homework. The bookstore offered deep discounts to students.

I must have been standing for too long. Coke-bottle-glasses cashier materialized next to me. "May I help you?"

After hearing a long explanation of each computer, tablet, and PC, as well as megahertz, memory, and ram, half of which I didn't understand, I walked out with a thirteen-inch MacBook computer, paper, printer, and more questions than answers.

Think I'd better sign up for computer science next semester.

I crossed the street to my apartment. This is what it feels like to be an adult? Wish my parents had tried it. Screw them. I'll do it for all of us. I added a little more giddy-up to my step and scaled the stairs to my apartment.

Several hours later I got the computer connected to the printer and printed out a page of gibberish to make sure the thing worked. I called the local cable company, gave them my Student ID number and they did the rest. I followed their directions for how to get online and *Click. Bam.* I'm a certified nerd. No more getting kicked out of Computer Lab right when my ideas are popping. I can work from home or anywhere I want.

I thought about going to Miguel's, but it was probably still hot with cops. I don't need to be associated with what went down there and get my probation revoked. Miguel and company can get along without me for a while.

Maybe Elizabeth? Nope, that chick is obsessed with the murder. She's also good friends with Yolanda. Hell, that left only one thing, sleep. I stripped and slid under the sheets at ten and zonked out instantly.

I woke sober, wired. I showered and threw on my clothes, grabbed my backpack, and slid my sleek new computer into the compartment. Halfway out the door, I froze. There sat my brand new printer, and I remembered how easy the gang could get in. Might as well tape a Steal Me sign to it. I dropped my backpack on a chair, strode to my kitchen and opened my oven. The assholes would never think to look there, and neither would I. Damn thing smelled of burnt cheese. Caked-on gook blackened every surface. Perfect.

* * *

"Mr. Alvarez could you stay after class? I'd like a word."

"Yes sir, Dr. Walker." Startled, I gathered my work and awesome new computer and waited for the rest of the class to file out. I stood in front of the guy who lived and breathed dirt and igneous clay.

"Mr. Alvarez, you have a unique and fascinating way of studying geology. I'm impressed, sir, and I'm not easily impressed. You have potential. I wanted to speak with you about focusing on geology as a career path."

I left his office taking the stairs three at a time.

I have potential? Me? Junior Alvarez, professional skater on the fringes, keeping it real and not real successfully, has potential? That was a new one. Scum of the earth? Yes. Worthless? Always. Dear old dad delighted in telling me how sorry he felt for screwing my mother in the back of his pickup and getting me as his punishment. Well, kiss my ass, Dad. I got potential, and by god a career with a future staring me in my ugly puss. Hah. I drew stares from my peers as I leapt up the stairs to class. Oh, hell yes, my peers. I could get used to A's. Last semester I got on the dean's list. Who knew there was a dean's list? There are no boundaries for this vato. A future? I felt buzzed, electric, hopeful. I almost quieted that little voice inside that wondered how long it all would last.

Chapter Thirty-Eight

Kailey

"Mr. and Mrs. Williams, I am so sorry to say that your son, Levi, was a victim of a drive-by shooting last night."

Mr. Williams slumped in his chair. His wife wailed a shrill "Oh, nooooo" and covered her face with her hands. The sound must have roused him, because he leaned over and wrapped his arms around her. They stayed like that for a long minute, not saying anything, swaying slightly in their grief.

I felt their pain acutely, filtered through the tragedy of my own loss. They wept for all the promise and love lost to that random, brutal act of senseless violence.

Mr. Williams looked up; his gaze bore into me. "How? Where? Why?" he croaked. They were all the words his vocal chords could manage.

"No, no, no," Mrs. Williams murmured to herself, her eyes closed. "No, no, no." Her whole body trembled with the pain behind each word.

I cleared my throat. "I'm sorry to have to do this," I said.

Their heads snapped up.

"If we are to catch the animals who did this to your son, I need to start with his friends. Can you tell me who they might be?"

"Roberta?" Mr. Williams queried.

"Yes, forgive me." Mrs. Williams opened her eyes, and I watched an amazing transformation as the quivering, blubbering woman changed into one with steely resolve and clear eyes. She cleared her throat and brushed hair back from her face. I saw a glimpse of a formidable woman used to getting her way and navigating the treacherous waters of Midland's moneyed class. "I have their names, addresses, phone numbers, and their parents' names in my phone." She thrust her diamond encrusted cell at me. "I have them grouped. Check under Levi. If any one of the names on this list gives you any trouble, call me." She cleared her throat. "I will straighten them out."

I grabbed the phone. She held onto it for a second, mascara streaming down her pampered, translucent skin. "Promise me," she said. "When you do your job, which I fully expect that you will, and you find who did this, tell me." One last tug before she let go. "Promise you'll tell me who killed my precious boy. Will you do that for me, officer?"

"Yes, ma'am," I said.

"Do you swear it? From one mother to another?"

"How did you know I was—?"

"Oh, my dear, please. Do you swear?"

"You have my word."

"That's all I need." She stood. "Come, Curt. We are through here." She held her hand out and pulled her husband to his feet as if he were a big, lumbering child. "Keep the phone as long as you need. I'll get another."

I watched them leave and marveled at how deceptive first impressions can be.

Chapter Thirty-Nine

Junior

"Hey, Junior, how ya doin?" Brittney hooked her arm in mine. She flicked her hair back with a toss of her head and marched in step with me.

"Brittney, hey, girl. How ya doing yourself?""

"Since you asked." She stopped and counted on her fingers. "I got up late. I couldn't find a parking spot. Spilled latte on my best jeans. Plus I need to sweet-talk my calc professor into an A or my dad will kill me."

I copped a serious attitude. "Sounds like you're doing great."

I smiled and she laughed.

"Can't complain. Much." She slapped me on the shoulder. "Dude, why aren't you at any of the parties around here?"

"Didn't know about them, babe."

A screech behind us startled me, and we turned in time to catch Grace as she flew into us. "Guys, guys. Did you get your papers done?" She panted.

I peered at my watch. Business Law 101 clear across campus began in two minutes.

"Of course." Brittany dismissed her question.

"Did you, Junior?"

"Not until about two this morning. Don't know if I'm cut out for business law. I won't let it beat my butt. I'll pass it if it kills me."

Grace confessed, "I barely got it done. If Dad didn't help me I wouldn't have finished. I got hung up on torts and bailments. He had to explain the whole concept over and over. Old Mrs. Kingston drones on, so I can hardly keep my eyes open, and I love law. I can't wait to get into real live criminal and civil cases. Trusts, property, bailments, torts, and consumer protection are all so boring." She rolled her eyes. "I come from a long line of distinguished lawyers, and I'll be damned if Kingston will ruin it for me."

Brittney commented, "Maybe if you didn't spend so much time with Ken you might be able to do your paper, girl."

"Ah, Brittney, jealous of my bubba-licious?"

I opened the door to the classroom with thirty seconds to spare, and Brittney whispered on her way by me, "Give me a break. Bubba-licious my ass."

I asked Grace as she passed, "Wait a minute, is your dad 'The Carlos Sanchez' of the Sanchez, Sanchez, and Sanchez Law firm? The criminal lawyer on TV who gets everyone he represents off?"

"Yep," she whispered. "In five years I'll be the next Sanchez on that door." She stood tall and scooted passed me to take her seat in the desk next to mine.

I leaned over after I sat. "I thought you two were only interested in drama, Grace."

"It's perfect practice for presenting to juries. I'm learning how to nuance my performances to suit my audience. My dad told me to take the class. I'm learning how to lift an eyebrow and how to modulate my voice for effect." She demonstrated, and it was a sight to behold.

These girls are funny, smart and sweet. Weird, the females I knew before Midland were only out for number one or drugs. Evolution. Who knew it would happen to me in the middle of Nowhere, Texas? It stopped for the dinosaurs during the Paleozoic Era and picked back up for Junior Alvarez in the Vato Era.

After class Grace and Brittney fell in step with me. "Comin' to the party tonight, Junior?"

I countered with "We have a lot of law homework, and the quiz tomorrow."

"Let's go to the library and do an intensive study group of three," Brittney said. "We'll shoot questions at each other until we know tort law inside out. Then we divide up the chapters on real estate law and share answers. Any of them that don't make sense we hash out until they do. If two heads are better than one, three heads ought to kill it."

I'd never been in a study group. Sounded like it might be a trip. "Let's do it. I don't have another class until four."

The girls and I headed for the library.

Two hours later I understood a lot more about real estate law and torts than I ever would have studying on my own. Those two ladies were smart, and I thought I did pretty well myself. Each of us brought something to the discussion.

"I think we nailed it." Grace slammed her book shut. "All that's left is for you to pinky swear you'll come to the party with us."

"Sorry. I do a pinky swear and I lose my Man Card. What kind of party is it?"

They both chattered at once.

"Hold it! Chill. One at a time, guys."

They stared at one another, and Grace pointed at Brittney. "You go."

"Okay," Brittney said. "Our sorority has been invited to a campus fraternity party. We can bring a plus one, and since Grace is all tied up with Ken, I thought you could be my plus one. It's not a date, Junior. Don't give me that funny look."

I had zero idea what funny look she might be referring to.

"It's a plus one not a date. You don't want me to be that lonely girl in the corner, do you?"

"Somehow, Brittney, I don't see you as that lonely girl at all."

She laughed.

"Then it's settled. You'll come? Please?" Grace pleaded.

"Girls, I don't have anything in common with your friends. Or sororities and fraternities for that matter. I'd stick out like a sore thumb."

"We like how you stick out." That comment got both of them giggling. "We want you there. We need you there."

"Pretty please?" They begged in unison, one on either side of me, clinging to an arm.

"It's a Nuts and Bolts party," Grace said. "You'll meet bunches of people from this school that are a lot of fun and really nice."

"What's a Nuts and Bolts party?"

"Seriously? You don't know Nuts and Bolts?" Brittany said.

I tried hard to appear interested. "Nope. Never heard of it. In all my party experience, that is a new one."

Grace answered. "You pay your five dollars at the door. If you're a girl, they hand you a nut. If you're a guy, a bolt. Nuts and bolts."

"I get that part," I said.

"Then you have to find the nut that threads onto your bolt. When you do, you take it to the bartender for a special drink. Same old stuff: Skippy, kegs, Jungle Juice."

"Skippy and Jungle Juice?"

"Skippy is cheap vodka, beer, and frozen pink lemonade concentrate mixed all up. Jungle Juice is usually purple . . ." Brittney scrunched her forehead.

Grace saved her. "Jungle Juice is Kool-Aid and grain alcohol. Now you will come, right?"

"The nuts and bolts are for drinks?" I asked.

"Junior, you dirty boy," Grace said, all wide-eyed and innocent. "What did you think?"

"Never mind."

They started up again. "Pleassse?"

Grace batted her eyelashes and tugged on my arm. "Our sorority sisters will be so jealous. They all think you are hot."

"They don't even know who I am."

"Junior," Brittney said, "you are new at school. You make all the other guys look like such boys. You are modeling for art classes. I mean, duh."

"Duh, yourself. Fine. I'll see you tonight unless there are more rules I don't know about."

"That's all; promise. Meet us at my house," Grace said. "At eleven-thirty, and don't be late. We'll all go in together."

"Don't have a car, babe."

"Where do you live?"

"Across from the college at the Chaparral Apartments. I could meet you on the corner of Garfield and Siesta Lane."

"Date."

The two girls each reached up and kissed my cheek and ran off clapping their hands and giggling.

***

Speakers thumped in the windows of a two-story brick house. Large blue Greek symbols and a banner over the front door announced NUTS AND BOLTS to everyone walking by. Who has to have a title for a party? Weird shit. Decorative white-gone-yellow shutters hung lopsided from every window. An assortment of trash littered the front lawn. This should be interesting. Never been to a bash like this, and I'm friggin' sober.

We paid five dollars at the door. The girls were given a nut, and I got my bolt. The girls immediately tried to screw their nuts onto my bolt, giggling the whole time. Neither matched, thank the god of stupid party tricks.

We ambled into the crowded first floor. A frat smog of sweat, beer, marijuana, and cheap aftershave closed in behind us. We each grabbed a red plastic cup and handed it to a blond frat boy standing by a keg. Just looking at him I wanted to punch him in his entitled pretty-boy face. Lucky for him I resisted the urge. He pulled the tap on the keg of warm beer, flipped his long hair back, and said, "Hey, man, find your screw mate, and you get to go up to the second floor for a cold one." Cute.

Brittney glued herself to my side.

A chubby angel-faced baby who couldn't be old enough to be at this poor excuse of a party came up to us. "May I try?" she held up her screw, and her face turned the brightest red I'd ever seen on a person.

"Sure. What's your name?" I held my bolt at her boob level, secure between my thumb and first finger.

"Calista. We're in the same English class."

I'd never seen her before. "Yeah, right," I said. "Good to see you again."

Her nut, way too small for my bolt, didn't come close, though she tried it three times.

"Ah. Sorry we don't fit, Calista. Maybe at our next party." My finger rubbed her palm. I smiled and moved a little closer.

She took a swig of beer, swallowed wrong and coughed, gasping for breath. I patted her on the back, which seemed to make her cough more. Brittney took over and led the poor girl away. Ah, I still got it. Women swooning at my feet.

The music changed, and Ken and Grace moved to the middle of the room to dance.

After my second lukewarm beer and more women trying to nut my bolt, I'd OD'ed on over-privileged brats flashing hand signs and hitching up pants, posing, talking trash. I decided to explore. My shadow, Brittney, disappeared into a flurry of giggling sorority girls. I stepped around amorous couples draped on the staircase. At the top, a guy dry humped a girl against a wall. Classy.

The second floor sported a pool table. A few guys slipped money on the rails and waited for their turn at a game. I grabbed a cup of jungle juice, tasty, stood and watched for a while. I got bored and wandered, checking out the place. Several dark bedrooms held couples in varying stages of undress. I watched for a while, felt vaguely like a perv, and moved on. I checked out a bathroom that held a crying girl, barfing. She looked up and shrieked, "Shut the door, asshole!" before she resumed hugging the throne.

I slipped down the staircase and followed it to the basement. Hello, a large sign announced, *Drink a Skippy at Your Own Risk!* A large bucket with pinkish liquid and a ladle sat next to a large plastic pot of ice. I grabbed a cup and sipped my first Skippy. I turned and watched a very drunk football player push another larger and hammered football player against a wall as they slow punched each other.

I'd had enough fun for the night and climbed the staircase searching for Brittney and Grace to say good-bye. This party sucked, and an early test awaited me tomorrow.

I hunted for them in the kitchen, front porch, and the dining room. I said screw it and headed out. I stepped out the kitchen door to the backyard and saw a circle of banger dude wannabes. They'd trapped Brittney and Ken in their midst and were shoving them from one part of the circle to the other. They hit Ken harder and harder with each guy he stumbled against.

Grace ran out of the house howling. "Stop it, assholes."

The dudes in droopy drawers laughed and punched him harder.

Brittney stepped between Ken and the next bully up. "Stop this nonsense. Do you hear me?" She looked tough with her hands on her hips.

A big pimple-faced dude flashed a gangsta sign at his buddies and swung a roundhouse at her head. He clipped her on the chin, and she went down.

"Ah, shit." Thick with rage, I jumped into the sweaty circle of tough guys. I kicked the first guy I came to in the ass, grabbed a fist full of his wife-beater shirt, and swung him around. His arms pawed at me, and I punched him in hard in the gut. He went down. I turned a half circle and grazed the Brittany-clocking jerk on his jaw. He slugged me on my bicep. I swiveled my side to him, hands up, open and ready. He took the opportunity to bull rush me low. The kid had some moves, I'll give him that. The other dudes jumped in for a gang punch-fest and left me no choice. I went full-on jail on their asses. Rushing Bull got the toe of my boot in his nuts and he went down, puking in the grass. I head butted the next guy and dislocated his jaw with my fist. I blew out another one's knee, and he screamed and fell to the ground clutching his wounded leg. Whiney bunch of pussies.

Grace rushed over to Ken and took a boxing stance, bobbed and weaved through a couple of drunk punches thrown by the skinny beaner about to hit Ken after I took care of his buddy. She connected with a respectable one-two punch. He went down with a whoosh.

I picked Brittney up in a fireman's carry and took Ken by the arm. Grace held onto his other side for support, and we staggered off from the party.

We were about a block away when Brittney began coughing. We stopped, and I let her slide until her feet touched ground. She stood on her own, a little wobbly, but she got better every second.

Ken shook so hard he bent over and put his head between his legs.

"What the hell?" I said. "I leave you guys for a nanosecond . . . "

"Thank you, Junior and Grace. I owe you both." Ken gasped between heaves.

"I didn't do much; Junior is our hero," Grace said, holding tight to her skinny bespectacled Romeo.

"Don't forget Brittney. What in the world made you step between a fist and a hard place?" I couldn't help myself and snorted.

She socked my arm. "I can take care of myself."

"Ow. I think I got stung by a mosquito."

She teared up. "Very funny and thank you from the bottom of my heart."

I wrapped my arms around her. "Why did that happen anyway?"

Ken straightened up. "Those guys crashed the party. I told them to leave when they started to harass Brittney."

"You did the right thing, Ken. Just need to learn a few moves. Maybe a few dozen."

He shook his head. "No fistfights in the corporate world. I'll fight with my mind."

"Even so." I nodded to Grace. "I suggest, my brother, that you keep that woman close by your side. Now you two need to get home, and girl, you ice that jaw and stomach, or you will get the third degree from your parents. Please don't tell them I had anything to do with this."

The three of them laughed. Brittney said, "How'd you like your first frat party, Junior?"

"What's not to like? Though I do plan to avoid any parties you three are going to from now on. Either that or Grace and I need to be there to chaperone. Where did you learn those moves, Grace?"

"Mom and Dad made me take every type of martial arts and boxing since I could walk. They said I needed to know how to take care of myself and not depend on anyone else. What about you, Junior? Where'd you learn to fight?"

"You don't want to know, honey. My family's a lot different from yours."

Ken piped up. "Least we can do is drop you at your apartment."

"Damn straight." I climbed into the backseat, glad to be distracted from the questions.

When we got near my place the street up ahead flashed bright with red and blue strobes. More police cars than I knew existed in Midland, Texas, crowded the curbs and front lawns. Crime scene tape drooped around the entrance to my building in ominous fluorescent yellow and black. Sleepy neighbors wrapped in robes formed a subdued audience three and four bodies deep. An officer corralled them with little effort.

"Great. Now I won't get any sleep. Wonder what happened?"

"Junior, why don't you come over and stay at my place? We have a guesthouse that's empty. My folks always insist friends can stay there," Grace said. "Go back to your apartment in the morning when all this blows over. Probably a domestic. Some couple got drunk and got in a fight. Dad's always telling me about those kinds of disputes." She turned around in the front seat constrained by her seatbelt and patted my knee.

Brittney said. "You saved us. It's the least we can do. Have a decent night's sleep and ace the test in the morning."

"How can I turn down a sweet offer from two hot young girls?"

Ken piped in and stepped on the gas. "Hey, buddy, one of those hot young girls is my girl."

After a while we turned onto a quiet tree-lined avenue. About halfway down the street on the right Ken pulled into the driveway of a large yellow brick home. Brittney and I got out of the back seat and headed down the driveway while Ken and Grace goodnight-groped each other.

Brittney seemed to know where we were headed, so I followed. High hedges lined one side of the driveway with the darkened house on the other. The generous driveway led past a home big enough to have a guesthouse behind it. We rounded a hedge, and I noticed a black-bottomed pool lit by soft lights pointing at huge trees. The pool sported a steep, curvy slide. A large, roofed patio had a fire pit and fans twisting slowly overhead. A massive built-in barbecue with a sink and a refrigerator in one corner and a large flat screen TV in another were situated behind a bar area. The bamboo furniture looked expensive. I'd never seen anything like it. I stopped in my tracks and stared.

Brittney tugged my arm, and we continued. We rounded the corner to come upon a small, English-type cottage straight ahead nestled between two big old pecan trees. Like on a postcard. Brittney found a key in a flowerpot full of yellow flowers and then she led us inside. Just as she turned on the light, Grace skipped up to us.

"Do you need anything else, Junior?" Brittney asked. "In the bathroom are razors, toothbrushes, and toothpaste. Soap is in the shower. The refrigerator is stocked with water and some food. The cupboards have some canned goods and breakfast bars. Help yourself. Want me to call you on the land phone for a wake-up call?"

"That would be great." I looked around. Nice. "You sure this is all right?"

"Don't be silly." Grace said." Cable TV's in the bedroom if you want to watch a movie or whatever. Brittney is staying the night with me, so we will see you in the morning. We'll all carpool to school. Won't that be fun?"

"Thanks for this, guys."

They both reached up and kissed my cheek and left me to my guest palace.

At six a.m. the strange phone sounded like a fire engine on full alert. I groaned and rolled over. "What?" I growled into it.

A too-chipper voice said, "Wake up, sleepy head. Time for school. We'll be over in an hour."

Showered, shaved, and in the process of brushing my teeth, I heard a knock on the door. "It's unlocked, come in." I spat, rinsed. "Thank you again, Grace."

I rounded the corner to the living room and practically ran into a man I'd seen photos of on bus benches and billboards all over town. He stood tall and ramrod straight in a starched white long-sleeved shirt. Gold flashed on the cuffs, and a green tie added the right touch of flair. His salt-and-pepper hair could have starred on any poster in a hair salon.

"I thought I should see who Grace brought home with her last night. I am her father."

His black eyes bore into me, unblinking.

I turned on the smile. "I'm Junior Alvarez." I stuck out my hand.

He whipped his hand up to my shoulder. I winced and stepped back and saw a large scorpion wriggling in his fist. He calmly walked to the kitchen. I heard the crunch and crackle of the scorpion body. He deposited the lifeless creature in the trash and then rinsed his hands. He turned. "Carlos Sanchez. What brings you to our home, Mr. Alvarez?" His penetrating gaze never wavered.

"The police cordoned off my apartment building for some reason last night and Grace offered. I'm sure I can get in today."

"Where exactly do you live?"

"Chaparral."

"Public housing," Sanchez stated. He turned and walked out of the guesthouse.

168

Chapter Forty

Kailey and Shinto

After the Williamses left the station, I felt drained. Maybe coffee would help. I wandered over to the pot.

Captain Samosa approached. "Carmichael."

"Captain?"

"Get yourself over to the Chaparral Apartments. There's been a murder. Time to use those new forensic skills of yours."

"Yes sir." Gulping the remains of my newly poured coffee I rushed to pick up my gear and exchange my uniform for crime scene coveralls.

The crime scene was across from Midland College. I grabbed my phone and cancelled my class for today, ducked under the crime scene tape and met Mike. "Hey, partner. What have we got so far?"

"Shinto and Allen are inside. They can give you more information. It's pretty bad Kailey. Poor woman didn't have a chance in hell."

"Allen is here?"

"Moving a little slow," Mike said. "But this one is all hands on deck."

"Who is it? Do we know?"

"Lived in that apartment with the front door open."

I pulled on latex gloves, a hairnet and bent over to put on my booties. I noticed a newly planted row of small oleander plants with a few white flowers. One bush listed to the side. Behind it, a squashed tomato looked definitely out of place. My eyes drew a line from it, up the outside wall, to the kitchen window. I knelt and saw the imprint of a shoe or boot in the smashed tomato pulp. I photographed it in situ and staked it with evidence flags.

After that I proceeded into a small, immaculate apartment decorated to the hilt in tomatoes. Tomatoes everywhere; framed in pictures, patterned in the furniture, Warhol's soup can art hung on the wall. This woman lived for her tomatoes. I wonder if she died for them?

To my left, a sunny kitchen. I opened the refrigerator, more out of habit than any forensic insight. I wanted to get to know this woman. Damn. I immediately wished my refrigerator were as clean and stocked with fresh veggies and things good for you as this one. She kept eggs in a clear bowl, not in the carton, nonfat plain yogurt and a perfect heirloom purple tomato as well as an eggplant, a head of red leaf lettuce and nonfat milk. Not a candy bar to be found. I snapped a photo of the contents. I opened the freezer hoping to find some chocolate ice cream. Nothing but ice cubes, a small zip-lock bag labeled stew meat, and single serving of frozen edamame. Who eats edamame in Midland, Texas? I snapped another photo.

I turned and noticed the window open over the counter and a broken drinking glass in the sink. Clearly, the perp's way in. I took a photo and hustled from the kitchen to look for Allen and Shinto. I heard them somewhere on the other side of the living room, probably the bedroom.

I stepped to the side of the logical footpath. Didn't want to contaminate any evidence Luminol might reveal. I hefted my equipment bag higher on my shoulder and remembered my instructor's admonishments: the role of a Crime Scene Investigator is to identify, document, collect and preserve evidence for presentation in court. Take a lesson from the botched case in California. Nicole Simpson and Ron Goldman changed forensics forever. Thanks to them, we know everything is important. If you don't believe it, there are guidelines and rules to prove it to you.

I rounded the corner to the bedroom and saw Shinto squatting next to the body of a nude and bloody woman. Allen faced the closet, talking on his cellphone.

"Look who's back on the job." Shinto rose and came over to me.

"Mom?"

"Hanging in there. Tell me everything," I said.

Allen clicked off his phone. "We got the call around one a.m. Found her like this; beaten, probably raped." He consulted a notepad. "Name's Patricia Keystone, fifty-five-year-old female."

"What's been done so far?" I noticed blood spatter on every wall in the bedroom.

Shinto leaned over the body. "I'm gonna get the asshole that did this."

"We're gonna get the asshole." Allen said. "She called nine-one-one," Allen continued. "Said she'd been raped and assaulted. The operator told her help was on the way and asked if she knew her assailant. She said yes but didn't identify him. The last words the operator heard her say were thank-you. Then nothing. Believe that? She must have died thinking someone was coming to save her."

I hope so, I thought. I hope this poor woman found some solace in a little bit of hope at the end.

I opened my magic bag of forensic tools and went to work.

Chapter Forty-One

Junior

I patted Grace on the back as the door to the classroom closed behind us. We were first out. The rest of the students remained inside, buried in their tests for the remaining minutes.

"The study group worked great. Pretty sure I aced that test. I'm telling you, we ought to schedule a study group every week if we can. Thanks again for letting me crash in your guest house."

"Listen, buster, it's the least I could do after what you did for us," she said.

"Catch any grief from your father?"

"Why should I?"

"No reason."

Grace grunted and said, "You really are a dork, aren't you?"

"I've never in my life been called a dork," I said. "That's a new one." The bell rang, and we were suddenly in the middle of a crowd. "Do you have another class this hour?"

"No, you?" Grace said.

"Nope. I am hungry."

Grace hooked her arm in mine and pulled me toward the cafeteria.

I grabbed a table and watched Grace as she waited for her order. She gestured and laughed with the hairnet woman behind the counter. I wondered what it might be like to be a normal person with a Disney family and a safe upbringing. Memories of sucking dick for grocery money and getting beat-downs so severe I pissed blood for weeks faded as I watched Grace giggle over something Hairnet said.

Maybe this is my time for normal stuff. Why not? Today will be my new birthday. No more dark shit. From now on it's college, new friends, women as actual people. I'll live straight. Improve. Make a future. Look out, world. Today a new Junior is born.

Chapter Forty-Two

Kailey and Shinto

I cleared a small part of the crime scene after six hours. Bagged, tagged, and photographed, the body lay waiting for removal to the morgue. I stood and arched my aching back. "I need some air."

Allen piped in. "Think I'll poke around the complex, come back and finish later."

I turned to my friend. "Join me for a cup, Shinto? Allen can guard the premises."

"I'll guard your premises anytime, baby." Allen Groucho-Marxed his eyebrows.

I didn't respond and Shinto chuckled under her breath.

"What do you say, Shin?" I said. "Is there a latte macchiato in your future?"

Allen banged the mirrored closet doors open. "Let's see. Oooh. Red in every color."

"Nice, Allen." Shinto sensed my irritation. To me she said, "Latte sounds perfect."

"Don't mind me," Allen grumbled. "I'll guard while you're gone." He flicked his high-powered flashlight over the racks of clothes. I stepped closer to the closet and peered in. The clothes were indeed all shades of red, dark purple at one end and light pink at the other. Coordinating shoes tucked neatly in their respective boxes with photos of the contents taped on the outside and spaced evenly apart. I didn't see one thing out of order or too close together.

Shinto snorted. "Don't mind him, Kailey. He's in full-on PMS, Poor Me Syndrome."

I turned and we left the apartment. "Wish I was tidy."

"Look what it got her."

We arrived at my car and shed our plastic garments. Threw the whole mess, hairnets and booties, in a trash bag in my trunk, tagged, and sealed it.

Thirty minutes later we returned, Starbucks in hand, in time to see Allen jump into one of the Dumpsters behind the apartments. "We got your coffee." Shinto raised a cup.

"Keep it warm for me. A tenant came by and said they saw a guy throw a knife in here. I've found lots of other shit; empty beer bottles, cat food cans, broken dishes, cigar butts, hypodermic needles, tons of shitty diapers, a broken-up gun, and one dead cat. I'm ready for a couple of showers."

"You rock. I'll leave your coffee on your cruiser." Shinto leaned over and put it on the hood.

"We'll handle the rest of the apartment. Thanks, Allen," I said.

He nodded and continued his Dumpster diving.

Shinto nodded her head in the direction of a guy who turned the corner with a backpack. "Who's that?"

The guy stopped and stared at the police tape. He looked familiar.

"Junior? Shit that's Junior Alvarez. One of our students," I said.

He walked up and slid his backpack to the ground. "Hey, my two favorite professors. What happened here?" He nodded at the apartment we were working.

"You know the woman who lives there?" Shinto asked.

"Yes, ma'am." His voice sobered. His eyes darted from Shinto to me and then the crime scene tape. "Is Patricia all right?"

Shinto advanced on him. "Did you give a report to the officers last night?"

"Wasn't here last night." He kept his voice light, his gaze unwavering. He didn't elaborate.

I said. "Did you do your homework for class, Junior?"

"Yes, ma'am, but class got canceled." He rested one black Doc Martin on the bottom stair step. "Is Patricia okay?"

Shinto narrowed the space between them. "No, she's not. Again, where were you last night? Know anyone might want to hurt her?"

"At a friend's house. Guest house, actually and no, I don't know anyone who'd want to hurt Patricia."

"Who's this friend, and where was this guest house?" Shinto asked.

"A schoolmate. A mile or so from here. In a nice part of town. Though come to think of it, yesterday I did hear Patricia screaming."

Shinto looked at me.

"You heard her scream?"

"I did." He nodded. "I knocked and asked if she was okay. She flew out of the door and slammed into me, begged me to kill it, kill it." He jerked a thumb at the apartment. "She found a tarantula in her bedroom, and it terrified her. She kept babbling something about always being afraid of spiders. She wouldn't let go of my arm. I talked her down enough to let me go in and kill the sucker, a big hairy one. I used one of my books and smashed the guts out of it on her wall." He scraped his shoe on the stair. "When I came out of her bedroom she sat in the hall still shaking. I thought she might pass out." He pulled on his backpack. "I sat her in her living room while I wiped spider blood off my book in the kitchen with a paper towel. She gave me an apple and a nutrition bar when I left. For my heroism, she said. She always did stuff like that. Nice lady."

"Are you messing with us, Mr. Alvarez?" Shinto said. "Because I would not recommend that at this juncture."

"Wouldn't dream of it. I know how you folks work. I'll know even more after this semester, right, professor?"

Shinto stepped forward, and I stopped her with a hand on her arm. "I am not a professor, Junior, as you well know."

"Are you going to tell me what happened to my neighbor, or do I need to read it in the Midland Star News?"

"Your neighbor, a one Patricia Keystone, was murdered sometime yesterday evening. You may have been the last person to see her alive."

Shinto crossed her arms over her chest. "What time did you go into her apartment, Junior?"

"Thank you for that, Officer Carmichael. Let's see." He looked up at the sky. "Seven. I got up late and had to book it to geology before the bell. Old Mr. Walker's a stickler for being on time. Five tardies in a semester and the old fucker drops you a grade."

I get a kick out of this wiseass guy, I thought; something about him. "We need a formal statement from you."

"I don't know anything. I saw her for only a few minutes."

"We need your formal statement," Shinto repeated. "Tomorrow morning at the station. If we can impose on you."

He shrugged. "Sure." His posture and face turned from carefree to jailhouse blank. "I'll see you guys later. Too bad. Patricia's good people," he murmured.

I watched him march up the stairs with exaggerated nonchalance, unlock, and enter a second-story apartment. Junior's apartment faced the dead woman's. Interesting.

"Obviously the squad didn't get everyone's statement. They missed him."

"He wasn't here," I said. "Supposedly."

"Did you see his face?" Shinto asked.

"Long scratch on his left cheek?"

"Blood on his shirt?" Shinto pulled on the glove and snapped the wrist of her left hand. "We need to get that guy into the station."

"I hate to think he did this. He seems so eager to learn in class, asks smart questions. We'll see." I handed her the coffee and bent to pull new booties on.

"They had a drive-by not too far from here," Shinto said. "Some college kid got killed."

"I know. I broke the news to his parents."

"Now this? And guess who lives within walking distance of both crimes?"

"That's not fair, Shinto."

"Your star pupil, Mr. Junior Alvarez."

"Come on."

"Told you I had a vibe about him."

Chapter Forty-Three

Junior

My backpack got heavier with each step. I acted all cool and casual but my heart slammed from one side of my ribs to the other. I flopped down on the couch, grabbed a fistful of hair, and yanked, hard. "Shit, shit, shit." I sat holding my head until my cell phone rang. "Yes?" I barked.

"Um, Junior?"

"That's my name. Who is this?"

"Elizabeth Parks."

I waited a beat. "Elizabeth?"

"Yes, Junior. I should think you'd remember."

I imagined I could see her blush through the phone. "Elizabeth I'm messin' with you."

She rushed on. "Yolanda gave me your phone number."

"I figured."

"It's been a weird couple days, huh? I thought I'd see how you're doing."

"I'll let you know in a few more," I said.

"I need to ask a favor."

"Name it." *What the heck could that woman need from me?* "What's up?"

She stuttered, "Yolanda and Miguel are having a party and invited me. I haven't been to one of their parties. I've only been to their house for lunch. I know it's short notice, since the party is tonight, but I thought if you wouldn't mind, you might be my date." She stopped, and I heard her take a breath. "I could pick you up."

Inwardly I groaned. Talk about bad timing. Too much homework
. . .Patricia dead in the apartment across the way . . . my fingerprints
and DNA probably all over her place. Proximity and my record are
going to wet the pants of the two policewomen downstairs. Her
timing couldn't be shittier if I lived in an outhouse. "Sure, what
time?"

Chapter Forty-Four

Kailey and Shinto

The poor woman's apartment combined every possible shade of red to overwhelming effect. Much of it because this lady had a strange fascination for everything tomato. Pictures, paintings, plates, pillows, knickknacks crowded onto every available square inch of display space, all in praise of the humble fruit. Add a brutal, sadistic murder frenzy by a psychopath armed with a knife, and blood spatter flung a full 360 degrees in multiple locations and red rapidly became my least favorite color.

Finding blood streaks and droplets took on a whole new level of difficulty. Red drops on red paintings, red porcelain figurines, a red wall in the bedroom and red rugs and tapestries throughout took exponentially longer than normal to locate. We took our time because it was necessary, and because this was my first dive into my new forensics niche. I wanted to get this right.

The techs and I dusted every inch of Patricia Keystone's apartment. We checked the backsides of cabinet pulls, faucet levers, the inside faces of cabinet doors, the entire contents of the fridge and the silverware drawer. Excessive? I don't know, maybe. But a monster had been at work here and I wanted him bad.

Next challenge was identifying areas of initial confrontation, spots where intense struggle took place, and the final killing zone. It helped us map the progress of the attack through the apartment to its final conclusion in the bloody bedroom.

We worked in silence for the most part. Subdued by the ferocity and humbled; we were witnesses of a sort to an innocent woman's last desperate minutes on earth. At times I had to take a break and go outside to get a grip.

It took us the better part of a day to gain a toehold in that place. By evening, we'd set up our laser and string to diagram the attack and begin puzzling out the movements of both players in the deadly struggle.

By late evening we were all dragging and needed a break. As the lead forensics person on the scene, I knew I'd be put through a bloody marathon on the stand. I couldn't afford mistakes because I'd been too tired to do my job. I needed to be extra careful to catalog and photograph everything two and three times over before I could hope to enlist Heather's help back in her lab.

I sent all the techs home for the night while Shinto and I stayed behind to finish a couple things. I wanted to ease the load on us for tomorrow and so I'd saved the ceiling blood spatter for last. Every ceiling. In every room.

"Shinto, you're taller. Want to help me with the spatter on the ceiling? I'll buy you dinner, after. You name the place."

I expected a little bit of pushback. At least one snarky comment, maybe two. Both of us were zombies by this time. Plus, Shinto had no filter on that sharp tongue of hers she could wield like a weapon.

"You got it, boss," was all she said.

Chapter Forty-Five

Junior

If I stay cooped up in here much longer I'm gonna punch holes in the walls and a handy-dandy repairman I am not. What the hell is taking Elizabeth so long? Screw it. I'm outa here. She can meet me on the street, up at the corner, whatever.

I clomped down the stairs two at a time, trying not to look at Patricia's apartment. Hard not to notice the bright lights leaking out of the covered windows. The police were still in there. Perfect. I made it to the corner as my date came sliding up in her slick red Beemer.

"Just in time." I hopped in the passenger's seat, leaned over, and planted a wet one on her hot pink lips. All of a sudden, the night looked a lot better.

More people than I'd ever seen at Miguel's swarmed the place, forced us to park a half a block away. Elizabeth unfolded from her car and fluffed her hair, smokin' hot in tight black pants, high heels, and a see-through black blouse with a pink bra. Big gold hoops dangled from her ears. She smelled great too.

I took her in my arms and nuzzled her neck, breathing her in. She shivered and in a husky whisper said, "Keep this up, Junior, and we may not make it to the party."

"All right by me. You look so good I could rip those clothes right off you."

"Easy, big guy. Let's at least pay our respects to Miguel and Yolanda."

Pay our respects? Who am I with, a debutant? I draped my arm around her shoulders as we weaved our way through the crowded front yard and into the house. Jane's Addiction thumped from speakers loud enough to make talk impossible. I pointed to the kitchen, and Elizabeth nodded.

We pushed through the crowd and plucked a couple of cervezas from the refrigerator. I popped the tops and handed her one. Waves of kids filed through the tiny kitchen. Soon we were backed into a dark corner. I bent my head and shouted into her ear, "Let's find Yolanda and then split."

She nodded.

Dog stood in the hallway with a very young chica. "Hola, vato, where you been, man? Haven't seen you around."

"Here and there." I turned to Elizabeth and winked. "I been busy."

He nodded approval.

She grabbed my hand and led me forward. I spotted Eduardo and Freddie on the couch fondling a couple of teens years from getting their driver's licenses. A fog of pot smoke hung over the room. Multicolored pills spilled across the coffee table, enough to dose the entire parole board for a week. I need to get the hell out of here. I spotted Nacho standing next to the sliding glass doors talking to Miguel and Yolanda. I tugged on Elizabeth's hand and raised my chin toward them.

Elizabeth waved to Yolanda as we made our way over to the power couple. The two women hugged. "Glad you could make it Elizabeth, and look who you drug along. If it isn't the infamous Junior Alvarez." She planted a kiss on my cheek.

Miguel fist-bumped me. "Hola, ese. Where you been, man?"

"Doing my thing, school and shit."

"Boring, huh?"

Freddie Fuck You Medina slouched up to us, his subtle-as-a-train-wreck tat half-hidden under a red bandana. "It's good to see you, Miguel." He looked bad. Scratches crisscrossed his face and arms. A bloody bandage wrapped clumsily around his hand.

"What happened to you?" I said. "Mama kick you to the curb?"

"Laugh your ass off, motherfucker. The joke's on you."

"Whatever, asshole. Ready to book it, Elizabeth?"

Elizabeth said, "See you at work, Yolanda. Thank you for the invitation." She hugged Miguel and Yolanda and we headed out.

***

Elizabeth linked her arm through mine after we got out of her car, and she snuggled close. Not what I'm used to. We wound around trees and a swimming pool as we followed the path to her condo. Last time there I didn't notice the vibe of this place. The whole complex trumpeted money, from the slow-opening wrought-iron gates to the golf course threading through the community. Wonder if it's the same golf-course houses the gang robbed a few months ago? Could be. All golf courses look the same to me. I chuckled.

"What's funny?" Elizabeth squeezed my arm before letting go to fish her key from her purse. The lock clicked, and she opened her front door.

"Happy to be with you is all." I grabbed her and pulled her into a rough kiss.

"What's the rush?" She pushed away and plopped her purse and keys in a large blue bowl on a table by the front door. She took my hand and led me into the living room.

I remembered comforting her after the drive-by shooting. I eased down on the couch and patted the cushion for her to join me.

She shook her head. "I have something I want you to try. You sit." She disappeared into the kitchen and left me sitting there. Too wired to sit, I stood and wandered around. The ceiling soared at least two stories. Light filtered in from windows high up. The walls were painted a light tan. A large painting on the wall featured a freaky owl with four arms. Each arm ended with a bird head. Crazy shit. A coffee table of carved dark wood looked picture-perfect with girl-type magazines at one end and a funky flowerpot on the other. Thing seemed friggin' old.

"Like my vase?" Elizabeth waltzed in carrying a plate full of cupcakes. "Antique store in Dallas said it came from an archaeological dig in China."

"Oh, yeah?" Digs tweaked my interest from geology class. "What's with him?" I pointed at the freaked-out owl.

"That's called *Guardian Owl* by Kenojuak, an Inuit artist."

"Cool." I never heard of Inuits and didn't want an art lesson right then. My interests ran to the more basic. Like how to get Elizabeth out of her clothes.

"I made these and wondered if you wouldn't mind tasting them. I've been experimenting."

"They look almost as good as you do." I reached for her.
She sidestepped my arm and set the cupcakes on the coffee table.

"I'd like to get to know you, first. You were so kind to me the last time we were together."

"I'm boring. I'd rather get to know your body again." I reached to catch her.

She stepped back and said, "Which do you prefer with your cupcakes, coffee, tea or milk?"

"Milk." *Wouldn't take her long to pour a glass of milk. Then we can get to the good stuff.* "Definitely. I'm a milk guy."

The cupcakes did look great, piled high with frosting. "Can't remember the last time I've eaten a cupcake. Seems like a lot of trouble to make a little round cake."

She returned with two glasses of milk and two small plates. "These are salted caramel." She pointed to the cupcake piled with light-brown frosting. "Chocolate cake with a whipped cream icing and coffee beans and that one has a salted caramel in the middle with a little candy topping for crunch."

"Really?" They didn't seem big enough to have anything in the middle. "I'm impressed."

She studied me and continued. "Those," she pointed to the two white ones in the middle, "are key lime with vanilla frosting. The last ones are the red velvet with cream cheese frosting." She waited with upraised eyebrows.

"I'll take one of each."

Her face lit up and she handed me a small plate with four cupcakes, a cloth napkin, and a tiny fork. What was I supposed to do with a fork?

I sat on the couch and watched her smooth her napkin on her lap, take the baby fork, and slice into a cupcake. She slipped the morsel into her mouth. Kind of sexy. My turn. I followed her lead, even used the baby fork, and I think I might have groaned with pleasure when the first taste of caramel hit my mouth. Holy shit! These are the sex my taste buds didn't know they wanted. I'd never tasted anything like them. I wanted to lick the crumbs off the plate but figured that might be bad form. "Oh, my god, Elizabeth, those were friggin' great."

"Really? You like them? I've been fiddling with my recipes for ages, and I think I'm pretty happy with these four flavors." She placed her plate of partially eaten cupcakes on the table and leaned forward. "Tell me about you. What do you do for fun?"

"What's to tell? I'm a guy going to college. For fun, how about I frost you?" I stood and held out my hand.

She didn't move.

Okay, fine. I sat back down.

She leaned forward on her elbows. "How long have you known Miguel and Yolanda?"

"A few months. They were the first people I met when I came to Midland."

"They seem cool. I can tell they like you. Yolanda said Miguel has plans for you."

I rubbed my face. "I have plans for me. Whatever their plans are I'm not sure I want to know. I've got school. I'm trying to get my shit together."

"They are involved in so many things."

What the hell is with all the Yolanda crap?

"Yolanda said she might throw some work my way, and I could make a lot of money."

Ah, so that's it.

"But I had to be careful and not report anything I made to the government."

"She must trust you, sweet cheeks." I scooted closer to her chair.

"Not sure that's something to get all happy about."

"Would you put in a good word for me? It might not look like it, but I could use the money. I'm kind of behind on my credit cards and rent."

"I don't know, gorgeous. I got people watching me, parole board and such. I need to keep on the straight and narrow and out of trouble."

"Please, Junior?" She leaned closer.

"Listen, I come from their world. I know it from outside the bars and in."

She pouted.

Damn, she was cute. I tried again. "What they do is illegal. Get it? Once you enter that world it changes you. Makes it hard to get out. Sometimes you don't." I grabbed her hands and held them. "You seem like a nice person, Elizabeth. I like you. A lot. Those are some really bad people you're flirting around with. If you mess up or don't follow their rules." I dragged a finger across my throat. No response. Like talking to a wall. "I'm trying to help you here."

"Then talk to Yolanda. I can handle myself. I'm stronger than you think, and I could use the money."

"Fine." What can I say? I'm weak. "Remember I warned you."

She nodded solemnly. "You did, but I'm a grown woman, and I make my own decisions. I appreciate your warning, and I won't forget it."

Hell, it's her life. I pulled out my phone. "I'll text Miguel."

He replied immediately: *Done. Bring her over tomorrow. Yolanda will set her up.*

I showed her his answer.

"Thank you, thank you." She clapped like a schoolgirl, which made me feel even shittier. "You don't know what this means to me. I hope someday I can return the favor."

"How about right now?" I stood and reached down to her.

She lowered her lashes and rose. I pulled her to me. She put her hand on my chest and held me at arm's length. Damn. She's strong for such a little woman. Little except for those tits.

"Let's enjoy the moments as they come," she said and moved closer. She kissed my forehead, my eyes, my cheeks, and then slowly came around to my lips. She teased with a light brush of her lips, and I shivered down to my toes. What the heck was that? She took my hand and I followed her to her bedroom like a puppy on a leash.

The room stayed dark until she clicked on a small lamp on her nightstand. Its stained-glass shade threw color splotches on the ceiling and walls.

She turned to me and stepped in close. I felt her breasts push lightly against my chest. She kissed me with lots of tongue. Now that's what I'm talking about. I sucked her tongue hard, and she pulled away again. Jeez what now?

"Easy, Junior. How about a long foreplay?"

"A what?"

"Trust me, you'll like it."

I remained still. "Tell me what you want, and I'll do it."

"Oh, such a brave man. Let me have my fun then." She took my shirt off and kissed my chest. First my neck then slowly down to my nipples, she ran her tongue around them. She moved onto my welts and scars. Kissed each with reverence. When she got to my Levis she unbuttoned every button with slow, deliberate fingers. Every time she brushed up against my dick it jumped. I closed my eyes. It felt friggin' great. She let my pants fall and giggled when she pushed me onto her bed.

"Watch me," she said. I did. I sat on the edge and watched her slink out of her blouse. Her black stilettos followed. She struggled a bit with those tight pants. Finally she stood in semi-darkness, a vision in hot pink bra and panties. Her gold hoop earrings glittered in the dim light. She stretched and then knelt in front of me. Took me in her delicate hot pink-tipped fingers and stroked me gently. I didn't think I could get any harder, but I did. She looked up and smiled and then bowed her head to take the tip of me into her mouth.

Shit. I held her head and pushed.

She raised her head. "Huh-uh. What's your hurry? Enjoy, baby."

When I thought I would explode, she stopped. No!

She chuckled low in her throat and stood. "Like what you see?"

I took one of her breasts in my hand and cupped it. I kissed and licked the outside of the lace bra. Had to stop myself from chewing through the damn thing. I reached around her back and undid the hooks. The bra fell to the floor. She stepped out of her panties, and I rubbed my hands all over her body.

She pushed my hands aside and sat on the bed next to me. When I didn't move, she laid down and spread her legs. I moved to hop on her, when she stopped me again. "No. My turn." She pointed to where she wanted my mouth.

An eternity later, after Elizabeth dropped me off, I crashed on my couch, images of her and me and the best sex ever flashed through my brain. I flipped on TV for diversion, something to bring me back to earth, and channel surfed until I found local news. The reporter rolled video of the previous night at the Chaparral Apartments. My building lit in flashing red and blue lights took up the whole screen. Yellow crime tape stretched across the front. Neighbors I didn't know stood around craning their necks at the TV cameras. The reporter at the scene talked to an old man with all of four teeth in his mouth. "Sir, what happened here?"

"Lady in apartment one twenty got stabbed to death." He scratched his head and leered at the camera.

"Do you know the lady's name?"

"She seemed real nice. Always friendly to everyone. Only talked to her once in the parking lot. Next to the trash bin. I had garbage to dump. They take the trash on Wednesday, so we gotta get our stuff in there before that. Sometimes they come real early, so you need to be ready." The old guy squinted at the camera.

The smiling reporter gritted his teeth and asked again, "Do you know her name?"

He rubbed his bare chest. "Let's see, Gina? No. Patty or Pat? Somethin' like that."

The reporter on scene narrowed his eyes and stared into the camera with manufactured concern. "Still a lot of confusion out here at Chaparral Apartments. Back to you, Brett."

The newsroom hack held up a finger and listened to his earpiece.

"We've confirmed the name of the murdered woman as Patricia Keystone, fifty-five years old. She is survived by her son, Henry." The blond-haired, blue-eyed man in a charcoal suit turned to his right.

The camera shifted to a buxom Mexican beauty whose smile would melt a polar ice cap. "I can't imagine the pain he must be in." She pursed her lips at the camera. "To know his mother was stabbed to death." She shivered. "Hope the police catch the person who did it, and soon."

The blond dude looked soulfully into the camera. "Indeed, Maria. If anyone has any information concerning this heinous murder in our city, please call the Midland Police Department. If you wish to remain anonymous call the number at the bottom of this screen. Now for Tom, our certified meteorologist, with the latest on our heat wave."

I clicked off the TV and sat numb for a moment. Stabbed to death? Something tickled at the back of my mind and made me get up and head for the kitchen. I opened the drawer where I kept my knife. Shit. No knife. I dug around and checked every drawer in the kitchen. The son of a bitch had vanished.

Chapter Forty-Six

Kailey and Shinto

"Done. I'm good. We've cleared this scene. Now let's see if Heather can find us a killer."

"The sooner I get out of this apartment from hell . . ." Shinto packed up. "This is the worst crime scene I've worked."

"The killer knew the victim," I said. "I'm ninety-nine percent certain. This was a vicious attack. We need to sift through her life and find someone who hated her enough to spend the time it took to torture and defile this poor woman. No one should have to endure the savagery she did." I looked around the bedroom one last time before I turned off the lights. "Management's going to have a devil of a time renting this out."

"It's public housing, girl. People are lined up waiting for an apartment. A little thing like murder only adds spice to it. The city will get a cleanup crew in, and it will be good to rent within hours after we release it."

"You're probably right." I said. "Do you mind taking the evidence to Heather? I need to check on Momma. She's going to be released today or tomorrow. I've got a lot of cleaning to do at the house. She will have a cow if she comes home to dishes in the sink and clothes on the couch."

"Say hi for me."

"Of course."

We hefted several loads of evidence bags into Shinto's SUV. I returned to the apartment and retrieved the lasers and spindles of colored thread and the lights. Last, we picked up the tarps we spread out after we secured the scene. We locked the doors and blocked them with crime scene tape. I'd be back the next day. I wanted to make sure I didn't miss anything.

Later on, back at momma's house, I cleaned for hours and collapsed on her couch. Dishwasher slushed along, washing machine gurgled. Not a speck of dust anywhere. I'd changed sheets from both beds and vacuumed the whole house. Momma will like that. I jumped in the car, exhausted. Checked myself in the rearview. Oh, yeah. A hag in the making. I turned up the radio. At least momma is improving. I'll take that trade any day.

I turned into the hospital parking lot and hurried to the elevator. Momma's floor was already selected so I hummed along with the elevator music as I waited to arrive at her floor. The doors opened to a crowd of people running, rubber-soled shoes squeaking on the tile floor, sirens whooping.

All the activity pointed to my mother's room. Nurses rushed past and I chased them, stomach clenching and white noise filling my head. I squeezed through a crowd of scrubs and white coats. One nurse sat astride my mother doing chest compressions. Another checked her vital signs, while a third shouted into a phone. A doctor pushed past me and told me to wait at the nurse's station.

I saw Dr. Bisht get off the elevator and hurry toward me. Someone turned off the bells, and I breathed a sigh of relief.

"Kailey," he said. "Wait out here. Let them do their jobs. I will come back and fill you in when I can."

I waited. What choice did I have? After what seemed like forever, Dr. Bisht came out and walked over. He had that look as he put his hand on my shoulder. I knew, but it wouldn't be true until he said the words.

"I'm sorry, Kailey," he said. "She had a massive heart attack, and we couldn't save her."

"She was doing better. You said so yourself. You said she might be coming home."

"This sometimes happens after a stroke. The trauma proved too much, and her body gave up."

"She wouldn't do that."

"She didn't have a choice, honey. I'm so sorry."

"I want to see her."

"Of course."

I approached her room like it might bite. Several nurses came out, somber and subdued. A couple looked disheveled, like they'd run a marathon. I waited, my hand on the door, staving off reality for a few seconds more. Then I steeled myself and stepped in. I saw her shrunken body, and sobs welled up from deep inside. I couldn't stop them. She was so small and fought through the pain of losing my father, losing the use of her legs, losing her granddaughter. I love her so much. She's my rock. My hero. I leaned down and kissed her cheek, brushed her hair back. *What will I do without you, lady?* I sat on the bed and sobbed while my world tilted, again.

Chapter Forty-Seven

Junior

Plan? I should have a plan, right? Pack up and run? Tough it out? Maybe the police will find evidence to clear me. Sure. When have I ever gotten a break? To hell with it. I'm innocent. I need to act like it. Go to class and do my homework, period, said the dead man on his walk to the gas chamber. Come on, universe. A murder? I've done a lot of shit, never murder. Police will see my rap sheet contains only petty stuff, won't they? A couple complaints from women. Crap. They'll peg me as an escalator, and if they don't find a suspect, good old Junior will fit the profile.

I trudged to my law class and sat next to Grace.

She leaned over. "Hi, buddy."

"Hey, babe."

"What's going on? You look like hell."

"Thanks." I ran both hands through my hair.

"Spill."

"My neighbor got murdered, and I think the police might like me for it."

"Holy crap, Junior, seriously?"

"Unfortunately. I have a rap sheet, Grace."

"You've been in jail?"

"Yep."

"Golly."

"I'd say that about sums it up."

"When did this happen?"

"Night of the frat party."

"You were with us."

"Not the whole time. Remember? It was a big party."

"Yes, but you saved us. I'm going to call my dad. He'll know what to do."

"Don't do that, Grace. That's sweet but unnecessary at this point. They want me to come in and give a statement, that's all. Could be I'm being paranoid."

"Could be you're being an idiot. I'm calling my dad, Junior. He says everyone needs representation, especially when you go in to give a statement."

"That's great, but I don't have any money to pay him. I probably couldn't even afford you." I pulled out my computer. "Case closed."

"I didn't think you were that stupid, Junior." She put her hand on my laptop. "Everyone needs help now and then. That's what friends do for friends. You helped us."

"Did you do your math homework for this afternoon? Can you say boring? What is the circumference of an acre? Four thousand forty-seven square meters. Aced it. Think that'll be on the test?"

"Junior, be serious."

"Class is starting."

"I'm not dropping it, Junior."

"No worries, Grace. Relax. I got this."

Chapter Forty-Eight

Kailey

I managed to get home through my fog of tears and collapsed on my bed. A million thoughts spun in my head. Funeral arrangements. Work. Calling family. Calling friends. I couldn't do that tonight. Tomorrow will be soon enough. I closed my eyes and fell into a fitful sleep. Dreams summoned my dead family to lie beside me. My baby came with them. I was in hell in my dreams. I was in hell when I awoke the next morning. My body ached, and my heart hurt worse. The weight of my anguish squeezed me until I thought my lungs might not be able to fight it.

I don't know how, but a couple hours later I stood outside Captain Samosa's door. I knocked softly.

"Enter," boomed the baritone on the other side.

I scooted in, stood ramrod straight, and tripped over my words. "Captain Samosa, sir, my mother died last night, and I might need a day or two to take care of the arrangements."

"Sit."

"Yes, sir." The chair screeched when I pulled it closer to his desk. "I'm on the Patricia Keystone case and I need to take care of things so I can get right back here to finish it."

He sat back in his chair. "Jesus, Kailey. I am so sorry to hear about your mother. I thought she was coming home yesterday. What happened?"

"When I got to the hospital they were working on her. They couldn't save her." My voice came from deep underwater. A flood threatened to gush from my eyes. "Heart attack, sir."

"I see." He sat forward, hands under his chin, tapping his chin with one finger. He sat in that pose for an eternity.

My steely resolve and professional demeanor had a time limit, and I needed to get out before I crumpled into a soggy mess. I cleared my throat as I rose from the chair. "I'll tell Allen and Shinto and check in with Heather before I head out."

"Sit down. You will do no such thing." His voice softened, and I knew I would lose my composure any second. "Go take care of your mother Kailey, and yourself. You have a lot to deal with. I know, I've been through this too many times." He cleared his throat. "I'm granting you one month's leave, effective immediately. We'll extend it to six weeks if you need the time. I will have our therapist get in touch with you. And you will talk with her."

He smiled sadly. "Kailey, I said you will take four weeks bereavement leave, and you will take every day of those four weeks. Do you understand? Also, I know you won't like this, you will have to be cleared for duty by Dr. Whittingham before you return to the field.

"But—"

"No buts. Those are your orders, officer." His phone rang, and he waved me out of his office. He rose and plucked his hat and coat off a coat rack in the corner. "Sorry to rush out. I have an audience with our mayor. We'll continue this later if you like."

I nodded and left. I didn't trust my voice to any more conversation.

Chapter Forty-Nine

Junior

"What in the holy bloody hell?"

"What's wrong, Junior?" Brittney said. Both girls grabbed their graded test papers and headed out of class.

I followed, reading mine. "I got a C plus."

"We studied our brains out," Brittney said. "I'm afraid to see mine."

"I got a B minus." Grace frowned. "What the hell?"

Brittany said, "I got a C. We need to figure out where we went wrong. Or, how to snag some extra credit. I'll check it out." She marched back toward the classroom.

"You do that, Brit. I need to get something to eat. I'm famished." Grace rubbed her belly."

"Me too." My stomach growled loud.

"I'll meet you both in the cafeteria. Save me a seat," Brittney yelled to us as she disappeared.

"You got it." I said to the heavy slam of the door.

***

My tray groaned under a mini buffet of food. Grace's too. We crammed as much as we could into our mouths before Brittney made her appearance. Too little time between classes, not enough for talking and eating.

I looked up when Brittany cleared her throat. "Jeez, you guys are disgusting," she said.

Meat hung from Grace's mouth. "Who me?" she said, spitting food as she talked.

My cheeks bulged with a mouth full of french fries and almost lost it as we all cracked up.

When we recovered enough to talk, Brit sat and said, "I've got the extra credit information. Maybe we could meet at your house tonight, Grace, and discuss it. It's formidable."

"Sure. What about eight at the guest house?"

"I'm in," I said as the bell rang. "I need to get to my next class, see you tonight."

I made it to the police procedure class in plenty of time. Got out my computer and booted it up. Everyone sat and fiddled or talked, waiting for Ms. Carmichael or Ms. Elliot. Ten minutes later I started packing up when Ms. Carmichael burst into class, her hair a mess and her eyes rimmed in mascara. She looked half drunk, like she'd partied all night. Maybe this will be an entertaining couple of hours after all.

Then, she went full-on business bitch and gave us the test from hell. After class I waited 'til the rest of the students left, packed my backpack, and approached her. I cleared my throat.

She stopped grading one of the tests she'd handed out earlier.

"Yes, Mr. Alvarez?"

I stammered, "Junior, please. I'd like to speak to you about something personal, if I could, student to professor."

She leaned back in her chair, rubbed her red-rimmed eyes, and said. "I have office hours for that. I believe the hours are posted online."

"Yes, and they start in five minutes."

She glanced up at the clock. "So they do. Sorry, I've got a lot on my mind. Give me a couple minutes, and we'll head there."

I followed her down the hall and around a corner to a small room that looked like every interrogation room I've ever been in. Déjà vu. No windows except a small one in the door. Dingy off-white walls hadn't been painted in a long time. No pictures on the walls. A functional gray metal desk with an industrial-issue black phone. Cozy.

"You okay, Miss Carmichael?"

"My mom passed away last night and I'm still dealing with it, making arrangements, all that."

"Jeez, that's tough. I'm sorry."

"Yeah. It's been a crappy couple of days." She stared off into the distance, sadness smoothing lines in her face. She seemed more like a regular person than a cop.

"I have no idea if my mom is dead or alive," I said. "She left me at eight years old with a group of very bad people. I haven't seen her or my father since." Shit, where did that come from?

Her eyes were swimming.

Wonder how long before the dam breaks?

"Seems like you are doing okay now." She cleared her throat.

"It took me a long time to get here. Longer than most. I'm a slow learner." This is getting way too deep into my shit. On to today's problem. "I wanted to ask you about blood splatter."

"Blood spatter, Mr. Alvarez." She corrected me. Irritation crept into her voice. "I put that on the test. Half the class missed it. There is a big difference between splatter, like dropping a carton of milk on the floor, and spatter, where we can analyze and catalog individual drops of blood. It's an important concept in police procedure."

"Spatter, then. Can you tell the difference between spider blood and people blood?"

"Oh, okay, I see where we are going. This isn't about the class, is it? You shouldn't be talking to me about this. Have you given your statement?" She sat up straight, and her eyes bore into me.

Man, this is one tough chica. "I've been busy with school and homework. I figure you guys can solve the case fine without me. Besides, I don't know nothin'."

"Come on, Mr. Alvarez, you're in college now. Lose the street talk and the attitude. If the police say we want you to come in, you need to get your ass into the station and give a simple statement. Unless you have something to hide."

"I have a record, and um, police stations give me the willies." I went for a little humor.

"I'll give you some advice then, sir. Get yourself a lawyer, go in, give your statement, and be done with it. Waiting will only make you look guilty. I shouldn't even be talking to you about this. We are through here. I suggest you leave my office and go give your statement." She stood. "Good luck."

"Thanks." For nothing.

Chapter Fifty

Kailey

I slammed and locked the door to the conference room after Junior Alvarez left. I always thought I had great instincts for sussing out suspects. This guy doesn't seem like the type to commit a murder so close to his home. That would be stupid, and he's certainly not stupid. I have too much to do to worry about it. For once I'll let the team of Shinto and Allen handle it. Mom's funeral needs my full attention.

Resthaven Cemetery on the outskirts of town had mature oak trees and lush grass amid the desert sand. I wanted to pick the perfect gravesite.

First, I needed to fill out a lot of paperwork and then follow a young woman named Terry Jobe to the first selection. I stood frowning at the grass and plaques next to what seemed like too small a space to rest in for eternity and felt my leg sting. "What the f—?" I looked down and saw my feet covered in fire ants. Dammit! I kicked and hopped from foot to foot.

Terry said, "Oops, sorry. I should have warned you. We keep spraying, so far the fire ants are winning."

"You could have told me." I stomped as many of the little suckers as I could.

"Really, I do apologize. Rarely does anyone come here in open-toed sandals."

"I'll go and get my boots and bug spray before I come back this evening when it's a little cooler. Have the grounds men spray before you show me any more sites."

"I will. What time will be good for you?"

"I'll be here at six."

"Again, I'm sorry for your loss, and for the fire ants."

I rushed for my car and home for relief. Fire ant bites are a long-term pain in the—wherever they bite you. The bites last at least a week to ten days, hurt like a bitch, and then itch worse. This is the only cemetery in Midland, and Mom always wanted to be buried here, so I'll suck it up, fire ants and the lovely Terry be damned.

Chapter Fifty-One

Junior

I got off the bus and hoofed it the rest of the way to Grace's house. A slight breeze made the walk tolerable even carrying a backpack in this desert heat at dusk. I heard the girls talking and laughing as I approached the door to the guesthouse. Sweet.

We worked on extra credit deep into the evening.

After we finished, Brittney drained her bottle of Heineken and said, "Let's play poker for pennies."

"I'm in," crowed Grace.

They both stared at me. "I gotta warn you, I'm really good," I said.

Grace winked at Brittney and got cards and a huge jar of pennies. I pulled out five bucks and plunked it down for my penny stash.

An hour and five Diet Cokes later, I said, "Who's cheating? No one is this good. One of you is cheating."

Grace smiled. "We've been playing poker with my dad since we were five, and he taught us to look for tells from other players. You raise your eyebrows when you have a good hand and you put your tongue over your front teeth when you have a bad one."

"I'm impressed. How much did I lose?"

"Your shirt, buster, all five smackeroos."

"I'd like a rematch, but I better get going, or I'll miss the last bus."

"Stay here tonight."

"I've done that once. I need to get back to my apartment. After I help you clean up."

"Besides," Grace said, "I think you missed the last bus."

I checked the clock on the wall. Shit, she was right. "I can't make this a habit, girls. Your dad and boyfriends won't appreciate me hanging out with you. I guarantee it."

"Please, Junior?" Grace batted her eyelashes. "You are not a threat. We love you. You saved our lives, and you are an all-around great guy." Grace slapped my fiver on the kitchen table. "You were too easy. Study up; we'll play again."

They both hugged me and ran out giggling before I could give it back.

After a wizz, I returned to the living room. Grace's father stood frowning, hands on his hips.

"Sir, hi. No worries. I'm outa here." I grabbed for my stuff.

"Sit, Mr. Alvarez." He pointed to the kitchen table.

"Yes, sir." We both sat facing each other, his black suit and blue tie still crisp at this hour, me in a raggedy-ass shirt and Levis.

He picked up the five from the table. "I'll take this as a deposit," he said, "for representing you." He slipped it into his pocket. "Don't worry about the cost. We'll figure all that out later."

"Excuse me?"

"Junior, my daughter told me everything. How you saved them at the frat party. How you've been working on your degree, and how honest you've been with my daughter and her friends. Even told them you had a record."

"They're nice kids."

"I'm glad you understand that. I intend for them to stay as innocent as possible for as long as possible."

"I would never do anything to hurt Brittney or Grace."

"Good to know. Grace told me what happened at your apartment and that the police want to question you. I took the liberty of checking the crime in question and your record in particular."

I groaned.

"Sir, I apologize. I asked Grace not to bother you. I didn't kill my neighbor. I liked her. She seemed like a nice lady. I got a chance for a new start here and I'm busting my ass. I don't do stupid shit anymore."

"The police don't care that you've changed, Junior. They simply want to solve the crime. Tell me everything, and I mean everything, that's happened to you since you've come to Midland, Texas. Tell me all about your contact with Patricia Keystone. Don't leave anything out. Do you understand? The most insignificant detail is important." He took his coat off, loosened his tie, and pulled out a tiny reorder.

"I've got all night."

"But sir, I don't have the money to pay your fee."

"How does five dollars sound Mr. Alvarez?"

I must have looked puzzled, because he added. "I'm sure you can pay me in some other way and in time. Remember, we both have my daughter to deal with. I'd rather answer to a judge than her."

"Sir, I . . ."

He waved my objection off. "I've got a feeling you are in a world of hurt, Junior, and it's only going to get worse, a lot worse. Let me—let us— help you." He steely gaze bore into me. "You in?" His finger poised over the recorder.

Chapter Fifty-Two

Kailey and Shinto

First United Methodist Church on Main Street has been our church for as long as I can remember.

Friends and family from all over Midland and Odessa poured into the pews to pay their respects. I sat quietly hidden behind a curtain and watched them file in and sit. My mother's casket overflowed with flowers. Arrangements cascaded around and down the pulpit.

Mia Emery, mother's friend and head organist played Mom's favorite hymn, "A Closer Walk with Thee." Oh, how Mother wanted to walk again.

Midland Police Department lined the church, all in uniform. I saw them through a blur of strangled tears. Sheer willpower held back the waterworks.

A dear family friend Christopher Spanks wore a full kilt and played bagpipes as we left for the cemetery. He'll play at the gravesite too. Wonderful man.

Mother gave me strength and hope for the future. She gave me the will to live after I lost Emma. She would not tolerate maudlin outbursts or anger. She would simply say, "I'm so sorry, sweetheart. God's will is sometimes hard to understand. We must persevere, and He will show us his path. Trust the Lord."

My heart ached for her and Emma. I felt an arm encircle me from behind. I stood, and Shinto held me close. My resolve burst. I convulsed with sobs. She held me for a few minutes and then pulled away and said, "Get it together, officer." She handed me a handkerchief. I handed her the box of tissues some guy from the funeral home gave me. We both sobbed and blew our noses. We got through Momma's funeral and even the graveside burial without another outburst. She would have been proud.

Chapter Fifty-Three

Junior

I've never gone to a police station willingly. My usual M.O. was to come grudgingly by way of handcuffs in the back of a police cruiser.

At precisely nine a.m. I arrived at Mr. Sanchez's law offices. His personal assistant called earlier and told me to arrive at his office dressed for court. I came dressed in my best clean white shirt, Levis, tennis shoes, and white socks. The sour-faced woman who led me into his huge office frowned when she saw me.

Mr. Sanchez looked up from his computer screen and said, "No, that will not do. Sharon, please bring us a white long-sleeved shirt, some khakis and loafers for Mr. Alvarez."

"Yes, sir." She left the office.

"Sorry, this is my only white shirt, sir." I smoothed my best go-to-court short-sleeved white shirt that I got in a thrift store. I'd even washed the sucker.

His secretary returned an hour later with a big bag from American Eagle Outfitters. "I guessed at the sizes," she said. She directed me to the men's room, and I quickly changed into the finest clothes I'd ever worn.

Thirty minutes later and two steps from the doors of the Midland police station, Mr. Sanchez quietly said, "Answer only the questions you are asked. Volunteer nothing."

I nodded.

"They have some statements from you already."

"What?"

"From the day you found out Mrs. Keystone was deceased. The policewomen you spoke to at your apartment complex made notes of what you said. Stick with that script. Any deviation from what you recall or told me is not acceptable. Agreed?"

"I understand."

We were immediately shown to a small beige room without windows. In one corner, a metal ball with blinking red light hung from the ceiling. The camera and microphone.

"Good morning, gentlemen. I'm Officer Allen Dempsey. Good to see you, Mr. Sanchez." He nodded and then squinted his eyes at me and said, "Junior Alvarez, I understand you are here to give your statement."

I nodded.

"You'll have to speak your answers, Mr. Alvarez. For the record."

"YES." I said.

Mr. Sanchez coughed.

I realized I must have spoken a bit too loud. "I mean, yes. That's why I'm here."

Officer Dempsey opened a folder. "How long have you known the deceased?"

"I met her when I moved in. She showed me the laundry room." I made eye contact, going for neutral and helpful.

"When's the last time you saw her?"

"I told Officer Carmichael and Officer Elliot, I helped her get rid of a spider in her apartment at seven that evening."

"Where did you go after you left the deceased?"

"She wasn't deceased when I left her and like I said before, I had a class in geology at Midland College."

Mr. Sanchez schooled me pretty good. I took my time, looked over at him for clues, and kept my answers short. The whole process took half an hour from the time we entered the station until we walked out.

Afterward, when he dropped me off at my apartment, I got out of his car and he rolled down the passenger window. "You did well today Junior. They learned nothing more than they already knew."

"Thank you."

"Do not thank me yet. All we did is frustrate them. They are not finished with you, son." He put the car in gear. "Call me if they attempt to follow up without me present." He raised the window and pulled into traffic before I could answer.

I slogged up the stairs to my apartment and knew in my gut he was right. Typical. Just when things go good for me, I trip and fall face first in dog shit.

Chapter Fifty-Four

Kailey and Shinto

I paced. Two weeks and the house has me in its grip. I can't bear to move or change a thing. Momma's reading glasses sit beside her chair where she last placed them. Once an hour I think I hear her wheelchair roll down the hall. It's worse at night. The smell of all the flowers in the house is nauseating, but I can't throw them out while they are still beautiful. It's been only a week, and I'm going stark raving batshit.

Why can't I continue my rotation on the force? Bust some sleazeballs. Knock some heads. Preserve and protect, right? More important, work the Patricia Keystone case. It'd keep me sane, but not according to Captain Samosa. Thank god for my teaching gig at the college. Those poor students are going to get my undivided attention whether they want it or not. I stepped over to my desk and stared at the briefcase full of their latest test papers. May as well go over them again. Give me something to do.

I wandered to the kitchen, grabbed the pitcher of lemonade from the refrigerator, and poured myself a glass. The doorbell rang, and I almost dropped it. I spilled half of it on the counter.

I swear, if it's another flower arrangement, I'll throw it at the deliveryman. If it's one of Momma's friends dropping off a casserole, I'll barf. There are only so many tuna casserole surprises one person can eat in a lifetime, and I've far exceeded my limit. If I never see another casserole, I'll be a happy woman.

I flung the door open, and Shinto and Heather stood there empty handed. Thank god.

Shinto sniffed as she strode into the living room. "We came to see how you are doing. Good thing apparently. You look awful. When's the last time you took a shower?"

"What do I need to shower for, if all I'm going to do is sit home and eat? Are you two hungry? I've got casseroles coming out the wazoo. I think I've gained twenty pounds." I grabbed my T-shirt, pinched my protruding stomach, and flung myself down on the couch.

"Oh, are we having a pity party?" Heather said and sat on the couch next to me. "I love pity parties. I'm a great crier."

"What if I am?" I sniffed. "What am I going to do without Momma?" Just the mention of her set me off on a crying jag.

"Oh, brother." Shinto said. "Listen, bitch, stop this and get your ass to the court-appointed therapy sessions."

I stared at her. "Momma's gone, Shinto."

"Don't start that shit. I know you're not going to therapy because the Captain told me. The sooner you go the sooner life goes back to normal. I don't do the poor-me shit. We didn't come over to hear you whine."

"Shinto," Heather cautioned.

"She knows I don't do the crying thing," Shinto shot back. She stood in front of me with her hands on her hips. "Get your ass to therapy."

"What am I going to say? I lost my mom and I'm sad?"

"I don't care what you say." Shinto huffed. "Say anything. Tell the therapist you loved your mother and kick dogs. Whatever. Go see the stupid shrink. Play the game. You're smart enough to do that aren't you? Then come back to work. That is what you need."

"I told the captain the same thing at the beginning. He told me I had to stay out a month. I'll croak if I have to sit here and stare at the walls that long."

"Go to the shrink. I'm sure you'll be back before the end of a month." Heather patted my back.

WEST TEXAS DEAD

Chapter Fifty-Five

Junior

I felt jittery and anxious after giving my statement to that prick of a cop. I jumped at every beep of a horn or class bell for days. I went to class every day expecting to be arrested. I sat home watching TV with an ear cocked for footsteps on the stairs. I did nothing but school, parole officer, and home. I didn't return Elizabeth's calls. I didn't want to put her in an awkward position if the cops were watching me. I didn't see Miguel or the gang, I kept my head down and worked my assignments. No arrest, nothing new.

I relaxed into my new role. Old Mrs. Young, the head of the art department, gave me twelve modeling gigs this week. All I have to do is pose with my shirt off. The students really dig drawing my tats, burns, and scars. This is the last session, and I've made a cool twelve hundred dollars sitting on my ass. Only problem is she pays me with checks. If I keep this up I won't be able to stay on welfare. I've got to figure this out. I don't make enough to pay for my apartment, food, and school. I hate to turn down the work, but unless they can pay me under the table, I'm going to have to quit. I'll talk to Young after this pose. I should call Elizabeth tonight and get out of this funk.

I stayed still, held my pose, wishing I knew about that meditation crap. Make this shit fly by.

The door to the classroom crashed open. Two cops entered and scanned the students before they zeroed in on me, a posing Adonis. *Posing asshole's more like it.*

Mrs. Young tottered over to them while the whole class stopped drawing me and gawked. She said, "May I help you, officers?"

The prick that questioned me at the station marched up to me without acknowledging her and said, "Mr. Alvarez, you are under arrest for the murder of Patricia Keystone." He said it loud so the kids in the back row could hear and jingled his handcuffs in front of my face. The whole class gasped. He smirked. I picked up my shirt, shrugged it on, and clasped my hands behind my back. Seems I've been doing that my whole life. Except this time I was innocent.

Chapter Fifty-Six

Kailey

I closed the door to the therapist's office, my release in hand. I felt like I thought cons must feel sprung from jail. I'm free! Free to get back to work full time and get back on the case. Finally. God. I felt better than I had in weeks as I strolled over to the elevator. Dr. Whittingham said all the right things, so kind and compassionate. She listened and gave me ways to handle my grief without making me feel like a whining little girl. For more than a month I'd felt frozen, paralyzed, waiting for something to happen that never did. Hell, if there'd been an incident where someone needed a police officer they would have been SOL with me.

The elevator doors whooshed open and there stood Jacob Kade, high school jock gone fat and doughy. He nodded to me. He had no idea who shared the car with him, which was fine by me. How does a fit, handsome teenager turn into a balding, fat lump in ten years? I felt like asking him what happened, but he buried his face in a newspaper as we flew down to the first floor. I glanced at the headlines on the front page; they were hard to miss: Police Arrest Neighbor for Murder of Midland Woman.

What?

How did I not know about this?

"Hey, Jacob, remember me?" I said.

The jock-gone-to-seed jumped and looked at me closely.

"Oh, hey. Carley, right?"

"Officer Kailey. I'm going to need your newspaper."

"What?"

The elevator doors opened to the sound of falling water from the indoor waterfall. I snatched his newspaper and walked out of the elevator car.

"But, you can't do that."

"Actually, Jacob, I can." I flashed my badge and watched his white doughy face go doughier. "Official police business."

I felt great doing it. Probably shouldn't have. Over a stupid newspaper. But man I felt good. Better than I had in a long time.

First stop, Samosa's office to drop off my clearance papers.

Then find Shinto and Allen. I had an idea who they arrested. More importantly, I wanted to know why.

Officer Kailey Carmichael, forensic specialist and righter of wrongs, on the job.

Chapter Fifty-Seven

Junior

I sat quietly on my ride to the police station. Kept my Doc Martins planted on the floorboards and stared in the rearview at the ass-wipe driving the car. This wasn't my first rodeo. The handle-less doors and the cratered seat felt almost like home. The signature police cruiser smell of vomit and cigarettes took me back to other rides at other times. The steel mesh cage between the front seat and me tempted me, begged me to hook my fingers in it and rage. For what?

Soon they'd have me back in the only life I'd ever known. Outside had me going for a while. Gotta admit it. I came so close, made friends, growing a new me. Almost got me believing I could survive as a productive citizen. Should have known it wouldn't last. Jail doesn't let go that easy. It doesn't like defectors. When you've been in the system as long as I have, it brands you with a hopeless reek to keep reminding you of that.

I sat back in the seat, handcuffs biting into my wrists. Officer Dempsey had squeezed them extra tight, enjoyed the theatrics of roughing me up in art class. The big man in front of all the students. Must have given him a chubby pushing a handcuffed sucker around. A sucker too smart to strike back.

Officer Asshole pulled me out of the cruiser and shoved me toward the building's double doors.

He led me to the same interrogation room from several weeks ago. I sat alone for an hour and a half before Officers Dempsey and Shinto Elliot showed up. Dempsey sat across from me and belched.

Officer Elliot stood against the door and frowned. At the belch or me I couldn't tell.

Officer Elliot pinned me with her gaze. "Hello, Junior."

"Officer Elliot," I countered.

"Still doing your exemplary work in police procedure class?"

"Yes, ma'am. The other day I aced a test. Only one in the class to earn an A."

Officer Dempsey sneered. "You've had enough practice with the system." He glanced over at Officer Elliot. "You allow parolees to take your class?"

"I made the dean's honor roll last semester." I leaned back on two legs of the metal chair and balanced against the wall.

"Model citizen," Officer Dempsey quipped. "Get it? We arrested you modeling." His guffaw died when he realized no one else laughed.

I glanced over at Officer Elliot. She frowned, definitely at the asshole, and said, "Mr. Alvarez, you have the right to an attorney. Anything you say can be held against you in a court of law. Do you understand your rights?"

"Yes, ma'am."

"You are charged with the murder of Patricia Keystone," Officer Dempsey stated. He leafed through a manila folder. "Do you have anything to say for yourself?" He looked up.

"I didn't kill Patricia." I so wanted to say and do more. Rip his face off, for one thing. The old me liked that idea very much. The new me had other ideas. Ask for Mr. Sanchez. Don't be stupid. This is serious shit. The new me won.

Officer Dempsey said, "Uh-huh. Well, let's talk about that, shall we?"

"I've been advised by my attorney, Mr. Sanchez of Sanchez and Sanchez and—"

"We know him," said Shinto.

"He told me not to talk to you, and I'm requesting he be called or I be allowed to call him before I answer any questions." The smart, new Junior thumbed his nose at them. No way I'm going down for a murder I didn't commit. I'm going to fight for me and fight smart this time. Which meant I needed someone even smarter in my corner.

"If that's what you want, I'll contact him." Officer Elliot left the interrogation room.

Shit Face stayed. "Why not admit you did it, Junior? Save us all some time. We have your fingerprints all over the murder weapon."

Outside I gave him stone. Inside I'd already smashed his face to pink goo.

"Don't be a wiseass, Junior. Clear up this mess and I'll get you a deal. Put a good word in, tell the judge you've reformed and seen the light. Maybe you won't see the inside of the gas chamber. Maybe you'll get twenty to life." He tried to look hurt. "Trying to help you out, buddy. That's all. We have your little drawing." He placed crime scene photos in a methodical grid on the table in front of me and laid a piece of paper with a familiar doodle in a plastic sleeve on top. The crowning blow.

I sat still and didn't blink.

He slapped me on the shoulder, my buddy, doing me a solid. "Admit it, man. You'll feel better. We'll all feel better, giving this poor woman's family some peace." He stood and leaned over the table. "Go on, take a look. Whoever drew this was a real artiste, don't you think?" He tapped the drawing with a manicured fingernail. "This is yours, right? I'm betting those are your neighbor's tits. Seems you might have been watching her and her tits. Same ones you sliced off her when you killed her."

I twitched, once, slightly. I had to, because in my mind I'd already leapt up and dug both thumbs into his eye sockets.

Blissfully unaware, my tormenter continued. "Then we have this beauty." He dangled a plastic evidence bag with a knife in it, a KA-BAR. A most particular and familiar KA-BAR. "Do you deny this baby's your knife?" He showed me the knife missing from my kitchen drawer. "Around here we have a term for that. We call it the murder weapon."

I'm a dead man.

Chapter Fifty-Eight

Kailey

"Captain, I'm ready for duty." I placed the therapist's clearance papers on his desk.

"Good, you're needed, officer." He rose and shook my hand, sat down, and continued. "Tom needed to take a leave. His wife has advanced breast cancer."

"Oh, my god. They have young kids."

"Three." He nodded. "It's a tough time for them."

"I can take his caseload. I don't mind some overtime."

"I'll put you down for it." He shuffled papers on his desk, a sure sign we were through.

I didn't move.

"Something I can help you with, officer?"

"I'd like to know what's been happening with the Patricia Keystone case. It was the last case I worked when Momma died."

He thrummed fingers on his desk. "Not going to let that go, are you?"

I figured mute may be my best option.

He sighed. "Have the team read you in. I'll put you on rotation."

"Thanks, Captain. I appreciate it." I turned to leave, my hand on the doorknob.

Captain Samosa stopped me. "Kailey, one moment. Have a seat."

"Sir?" I sat.

He shuffled through a pile of papers on his desk before selecting one. "Ah, yes. You'd be perfect for this. Since you've been on leave we have been given a liaison from DEA. They have an agent working an undercover case in town. I'd like you to make contact. Find out what progress they've made and how they'd like us to assist them. It's the Feds, Kailey. I don't have to tell you what that means."

No, he didn't. Politics, turf wars, interference, jealousy, and all-around stonewalling ahead. "Sounds great. I'm sure we'll all get along fine."

He looked at me with an expression that said he suspected I was yanking his chain but couldn't quite be sure. "Yeah, well, her name is Harper Salazar. Her phone number and information are all on this page."

"The agent's a female?"

"Not sexist, are you Kailey?"

"What? Me? No."

He laughed. "I know. That's why I asked. I'd like you on this ASAP."

"Right away, Captain."

Chapter Fifty-Nine

Junior

The door to the interrogation room burst open and in stormed Carlos Sanchez. "May I ask what the hell is going on here?"

Officer Dempsey in mid-rant about my guilt, stopped and said wide-eyed, "Two old pals chattin'. What does it look like?"

"I believe, sir, this innocent man asked for a lawyer. I will be happy to re-acquaint you with the law if need be."

Dempsey didn't reply.

"No? Excellent." Sanchez placed his briefcase on the table. "If you would be so kind, may I speak with my client? Alone?"

Dempsey slowly gathered his photos and papers and closed the file shut. "We aren't finished, Mr. Alvarez." He left the room.

"Are you all right Junior?" Mr. Sanchez sat in the seat recently vacated by Officer Dempsey. His cologne wafted over to me. It smelled like hope.

"They got all this evidence on me. Serious shit. I don't know how. They have my knife and claim it's the knife that killed my neighbor. They have my fingerprints on the knife. They have a stupid drawing. I'm fried, dude, a dead man." I ran my hands through my hair. "I swear on my mother's eyes, I did not kill that woman. I admit when I do shit, and I have done some really stupid shit in my time. But not this. This," I waved my arms around the room, "I didn't do."

"You think someone is setting you up?"

"Seems that way."

"Who?"

"There's a long list, sir." I scratched my head. "I tend to piss people off."

Sanchez smiled when he pulled a tiny recorder and a tablet out of his briefcase. He clicked his pen and said, "I'd say we have some work to do."

Chapter Sixty

Kailey

I called the number the captain gave me. "Agent Harper, this is Officer Kailey Carmichael, Midland Police Department. Please call me. I've been told we need to meet and sort through things. You apparently have an op working in our area, and we want our departments to mesh as effectively as possible for all concerned."

Five minutes after I hung up, my cell rang. "This is Agent Salazar, Kailey. When and where would you like to get together? I'm free today."

"Works for me. Do you want a public or private meeting?"

"Private, if possible."

"How about Resthaven Cemetery? Let's meet at Adam Roarke's gravesite."

"A gravesite? Perfect. Adam Roarke?"

"Kind of a local celebrity of sorts. An actor and director, started out as a gang member at thirteen. Ask anyone there. They'll direct you."

"Sounds appropriate. How about twenty minutes? Who should I look for?"

"I'm blonde, wearing jeans and boots. I suggest you do the same. There are some gnarly fire ants at Resthaven," I said.

"Fire ants?"

"Stay away from open-toed shoes and you'll be fine."

"Thanks for the heads-up about the ants. I'm a skinny Puerto Rican with dark hair, dark eyes, and I've been told, a bit of an attitude."

"See you there." I liked her already.

Chapter Sixty-One

Junior

I asked my attorney, "Want a list of all the people I've pissed off in Midland or since I hit jail?"

"Every single person you can think of. We covered a lot of territory the last time we spoke at my house. I have gone over what you said and made copies." He slid a stack of papers over to me. "Perhaps this will help jog your memory."

Sanchez sat quietly for several minutes and let me read.

I looked up when I finished and he said, "Junior, I reviewed your record. It is indeed an impressive list of, let us say, ill-advised escapades and they form a definite a pattern. In most you are either drunk or high or both. No tendency toward major crimes that I can see."

I nodded. "That's me. I thought this college thing might be my ticket, give me a chance to see the other side." I chuckled. "Biggest scam of all, right? Universe doesn't seem to want me out in the real world." I shifted in my seat.

The lawyer narrowed his eyes. "Junior, it has been my experience that we get the world we make for ourselves. You want out of the cycle you have been in all your life? I suggest we start now."

I must have stared at him like he sprouted wings.

"You are an intelligent young man, and I am willing to help you all I can. But we must be partners in this. In our immediate matter, the police have amassed a lot of evidence against you. It occurs to me, too much. Clearly, someone is out to bury you. So far, they are getting away with it. Your job is figuring out who that someone is. Who the hell did you piss off smart enough to accomplish this?"

Chapter Sixty-Two

Kailey

"It's a beautiful evening, Momma. You'd love it. You and I should be sitting out on the porch swing with a glass of lemonade." I leaned over and brushed dust off her headstone. "Love you, Momma." I stepped away from her grave and headed for a meet with Harper Salazar, DEA agent.

Adam Roarke's gravesite had one of the few benches, and the large oak tree planted behind it offered shade even on this hot day. Time to see what DEA is doing in the beating heart of our little oil community.

Midland expands and contracts with the whims of the world's need for oil, and when the boom happened it brought all sorts of trash with it. I didn't have to guess what brought DEA here. Within minutes I heard a car. I sat and watched. This spot came with a great view of the parking lot, and I saw a red BMW convertible pull up. If that's her, DEA is paying a lot better than Midland Police. She emerged wearing a white button-down blouse, starched jeans, and designer boots. Her hair swung in a ponytail tied with a white bow. A pair of aviator sunglasses completed her look. Who the hell dresses like that in Texas?

"Kailey?"

"Harper?" I rose and shook her hand. "Thanks for the meet."

"No problem. Glad to help out our brothers and sisters in law enforcement."

"Been in Midland long?" I asked and sat back down.

"A few months. You?" She remained standing in front of me. Her mirrored sunglasses kept moving, checking out the area.

"Forever." I said. "Born here. Tried to leave right after high school, but Midland pulled me back." I leaned back on the bench and propped my boots on a rock in front of me. "Where are you from?" Let her stand if she wants; it won't intimidate me.

"Boston, originally. Family moved us to Dallas about ten years ago. This is my first assignment outside of there."

I thought I noticed a weird accent. Bah-ston and Texas combined.

"I sort of have a reputation," she said. "A pretty good one. This assignment's important. In fact, I'm undercover. You and I meeting is not the smartest idea. Let's make this count."

Wow, is she wound tight. Fine. Axe the small talk. "My captain wants me to get our department up to speed on your investigation and offer to help any way we can."

"I've got it covered."

I waited. She stood. She finally gave up and sat next to me.

"Don't really need any help." Since she didn't rise to my gentle West Texas inquiry, I adopted a firmer approach. "You could help us and read me in on exactly what your department is doing in our town."

"Fine." Her leg bounced. "Big picture? We're investigating a drug ring with cartel ties. They run drugs from Mexico through to Canada, and we are pretty sure your town is a major link on their highway."

"And?" Momma didn't raise no dumb blonde.

"I'm here to infiltrate," she shrugged. "If I find the connection, we move in and take them out."

"You the only agent here?"

"Need-to-know basis, officer. Sorry. I can tell you I have several people sitting surveillance on a couple of key suspects. But we're in the early stages of our investigation. Our agents are still working on their methods of transport, the players involved, the timetables."

"So, you pretty much know zip."

She frowned. "What we do have is a pool going for whoever cracks the case first; fifty bucks buy-in." She brushed a leaf off the bench. "I intend for it to be me." Still no eye contact.

"Let's start with who you're checking out," I said. "This is my town. I grew up here. I know most of its bad players."

Nothing.

"Fine. I'll start. Drugs in Midland are old news, ever since we hit oil in the Permian Basin. We don't have the manpower to completely shut it down. I will say the gangs keep to themselves, mostly. Take care of their own business. Until recently. Someone did a drive-by on a gangbanger birthday party. Killed a college boy. Kind of woke everyone up. Naturally, no one saw or heard anything."

Finally she turned to me and took off her shades. "What gang?" She stared at me hard. "Wouldn't be Los Demonios, would it?"

"Los Demonios? That's who you're investigating?" Every cop in Midland knew that gang, and I knew plenty. Maybe if I share a little, she'll do the same. "We're investigating the murder of a civilian, an older woman, in one of our housing projects. I'm worried it could be them. She wasn't involved in drugs, far from it. But bangers come and go all around those apartments. Maybe she pissed off one of them. Thing is, her death looked nothing like a random accident. Whoever killed her made that very clear."

"What apartment complex?" She focused on me like seeing me for the first time.

"Chaparral. It's to the east, near the—"

"I know exactly where that is." She glanced at her phone again. "We have eyes on several complexes in town. Chaparral is one." She stood, and I joined her. "I'll be in contact, okay? Soon as I get something that might help you."

"Harper, we need to know what you're doing. Chaparral means something to you. Tell me why." So far she'd told me nothing. "I want to stay out of your way, and I certainly don't want you in mine."

She smiled at me and turned to leave.

I offered one last parting shot to her retreating back. "This is a small town. Actually I have one of the fringe gang members in a class I teach. Would you be looking at a Junior Alvarez, by chance?"

She froze. "Shit."

"I take it you know Junior."

"I might." She put her shades back on and sat down. "I might have an interest in Mr. Alvarez." She crossed her arms and stared straight ahead.

Whoa. Seems I struck a nerve. Interesting.

Chapter Sixty-Three

Junior

"When I moved to Midland I didn't know anyone. I saw a bunch of vatos in the park near where I live. Long story short, I got to know them. Most are long-time gangbangers and hard core. Miguel is in charge, and he's a smart M.F. Fingers in all sorts of businesses. Says he has plans for me."

"What is his full name?"

"Miguel Castillo. The gang is known as Los Demonios."

"I have heard of it. Continue." Mr. Sanchez, elbow on the table, tapped his temple with his finger.

I looked at the ceiling willing myself to recall past events. "Several months ago, when I didn't answer Miguel's calls or texts, he sent a bunch of assholes to my apartment."

Sanchez waited a beat and said, "Tell me more about the encounter. Specifics please."

"While I worked at the computer lab in school, they broke into my place and trashed it. When I got there one dude had his dick out and his paws all over my neighbor, Patricia. I clocked him and sent them all packing. I got her to promise not to report it. Did the asshole a solid. He left royally pissed and didn't see it that way."

"What is his name?"

"Freddie Medina. Has a huge tattoo on his forehead that says Fuck You. Not the smartest dude."

"That individual has been through our offices before. One of my junior attorneys handled his case. I will make a note to check his files."

"That's the one time I know of where Freddie and Patricia met. I embarrassed his ass. Interrupted his fun. He bugged out mad at her and me."

The lawyer glanced at his watch. Thin, gold, nice. "I am due in court soon. They are going to book you, Junior. That is how it is done. Remain quiet, comply with their requests. I will see what I can do to get you out on bail. Do not count on it, however. You are a flight risk and unfortunately, have no convincing ties to Midland." He closed his briefcase and clicked it shut. "Sorry, son. Stay with me. We will work extremely hard to see justice is not blind to you."

"Thank you, sir. That's more than anyone has ever done for me. Please thank Grace for me and tell her not to visit me in here."

"Sorry, Junior. I love my daughter, but that is like waving a red flag in front of a bull. She is her own woman these days. I have learned not to tell Grace what to do, merely to make suggestions. You must know, in her you have made a friend for life. You are stuck with us Junior, like it or not. I happen to believe she made the right choice. We will get you out of this mess. Trust me."

We shook hands, and he left.

A guard came in immediately and led me out of the interrogation room in handcuffs back to a holding cell.

He shoved me inside. I pushed my hands through the bars, and he un-cuffed me. Behind me, a blond guy reeking of puke and booze lay snoring on the concrete bench. A fresh pink lump rose on his forehead and patches of bare scalp oozed red where clumps of hair had been yanked from his head. Poor bastard must have pissed someone off. I sat as far away from him as I could. Next door I heard a woman clanging the cell door and slamming against the padded walls.

The cold concrete on my back brought me back to the first time I sat in a cell, incarcerated at twelve years old. Scared shitless then, I remember my whole body shuddered with fear and relief. I'd killed a woman in self-defense and the jury found me innocent, barely. They set me free, but a woman ended up dead, child abuser though she was and the system became my parents.

If they unsealed my juvie jacket, I'd see the inside of a gas chamber for sure. I closed that file in my mind. No good going there. I'd been let loose back then and the woman's death ruled justified. Yeah, and pigs can fly given the right motivation.

A portly deputy came to the cell carrying a threadbare towel. "Junior Alvarez?"

"Yes." I stood.

After a shower, they issued me a robe and plastic slippers and led me to a desk in the middle of the intake area. A gray-haired nurse who won't see eighty again, pointed to a chair in front of her desk. She stood slowly and creaked over to me carrying a thermometer. I opened my mouth, and she gently placed it under my tongue. It hung there while she hooked me up to a blood pressure cuff and clipped a plastic thingie on my finger. She wrote all my vital statistics into her computer. Put it all away.

"Mr. Alvarez, I have four pages of questions about your health. Shall we begin?"

"Yes, ma'am."

"Do you have any allergies?"

"No."

"Are you on any medications?"

"No, ma'am."

"Have you sustained any injuries that need to be attended to today?"

"No, ma'am."

"Ever have any broken bones?"

"Nope."

"Get all your childhood vaccinations?"

"Yes, ma'am. In juvie."

"Do you have or have you had diabetes, heart disease, nervous conditions?"

"None of those."

The questions kept coming. Some duplicates of ones I answered earlier. She asked if I knew today's date and our president's name. "Abraham Lincoln?" I said. She scowled and clicked away at her computer keys for several seconds. "Deputy Rodgers, take the prisoner to be photographed and pick up his uniform. Thank you, Mr. Alvarez. The deputy will show you the way."

Photographed, fingerprinted, and my information updated in the database, they led me to an area with shelves of uniforms, all different colors, individually in plastic bags. I've been in enough jails to know that each color meant something. Brown or blue meant low-level threat. Medical is green. Orange is mental health. Yellow is for snitches and people in protective custody, and Red is for the big one. Extra violent, murderer, and lockdown risk. Don't want to think what stripes mean. Those guys are mean mothers.

I got issued blue scrubs. Apparently I'm a low-level threat. In a weird way I felt insulted. I gave back my robe. Midland Jail has the latest duds for inmates. Hell, we look like doctors on TV.

I followed the guard to my pod. Wonder who my celly will be? Sunlight poured through the bars on the windows. I counted about one deputy to sixty inmates. They'd painted the pod pastel blue. How soothing. I'd blend right in. The cell door clanged open, and I entered to find, standing in the cell expectantly, none other than Chigger. I thought he lived in Mexico by now.

"Dude, I heard you were on your way." A feral smirk creased Chigger's puss. "Welcome, homeboy."

Chapter Sixty-Four

Kailey

I climbed the stairs to Heather's lab. Fluorescents in the ceiling hummed. She bent over a microscope but raised up when I knocked.

"Kailey! You're back."

"Yep. Raring to go. What's been happening since my banishment?" I walked over, and we hugged. "You look great."

"I'm happy to see you. You've been missed. Shinto has been a wreck without you. Just a sec, I need to get this email sent."

I wandered over to a spinning centrifuge. "Did you get all the Patricia Keystone evidence cataloged?"

"Couple of weeks ago. Shinto and Allen did a bang-up job." She tapped the Send key and smiled. "How can I help?"

"I'd love to see the results."

Heather stroked a few more keys and said, "All yours. Check your inbox."

"Can you summarize for me?"

"Didn't Shinto tell you? They found a ton of evidence, all pointed to one guy. They arrested him. Slam-dunk case."

"I love when that happens. Who'd they arrest?"

She screwed up her face. "I'm sure Shinto or Allen will fill you in. Heck, wait, hold on." She shuffled through a stack of file folders, peeling back tabs with her forefinger until she found one near the middle. She flipped open the folder to the cover sheet stapled to the front. "Says here the guy's name is Junior Alvarez. Put the bracelets on him in mid-pose at a drawing class. Apparently he's some sort of model."

"Thanks, Heather. You're the best lab rat I know."

I left, with my stomach in a twist, though I had no good reason why. Junior? A ton of evidence?

That didn't track at all with my image of the guy in my class at Midland.

What the hell do they have on you, Junior?

Chapter Sixty-Five

Junior

The door to our cell clanged shut. "I got the bottom bunk, Junior, bum knee." Chigger patted his left leg.

The power games begin. "Screw that, Chigger. You're on the top bunk." I stepped in close, towering over him. He backed up and bumped against the sink bolted to the cinderblock wall.

"Worth a shot, man." He snapped his fingers nervously. "I'm guessin' Freddie did his number on you like he promised, eh?"

I sat on the bottom bunk. "What do you mean? Talk to me."

"You know he's had a hard on for you ever since you started hangin' with us, right?"

"I know he's an asshole. Otherwise I don't care about him one way or the other."

"Should've taken notice, bro."

"Talk."

He sat next to me. "What's it worth to you?"

"How about not punching your lights out for starters? If the information is specific and there's proof, I'll even protect your sorry ass in here. Maybe even get my attorney to help you with your case."

Chigger jumped to his feet. "You are a dead man in here, boy. All I gotta do is say the word." He preened like a bantam. "How about I protect you?"

I leaned back against the wall, staring him down, ready to kick him in the balls.

He puffed out his chest. "Do me a solid and get your attorney to work with me, maybe I'll cut you a break."

I pushed off the wall, and Chigger shrank backward. I waited a beat. "Done," I said, and stuck out my hand. "What are you in for?"

Chigger relaxed and we fist bumped.

"This is what I get for doing a favor for a friend. After the robberies, I went Mexico, then I made one last run for Miguel. He likes that Mexican coke. Said his regular supplier ran into problems moving product. So he tripled my fee, and I took the bait." He spread his arms. "Here I sit like the fish I am."

"Tough break, man."

"The toughest part? I shot a cop back in the day. Before you met me."

"In Midland?" I said.

He nodded. "Pendejos haven't connected the dots yet. It's only a matter of time. I gotta get out of here. If they give me bail on the drug charges, I'm beatin' feet faster than frijoles through a Tijuana tourist. Back to my honey in Baja. I run that town, man."

"Yeah, you're a giant, Chigger."

"Seriously. You oughta come down sometime. I could have you covered in chicas and blow. No more Miguel or friggin' Midland ever again."

"I hear ya. Now, tell me more about Freddie."

Chapter Sixty-Six

Kailey and Shinto

I found Shinto working a speed bag in the police gym. "Shinto." I came up behind her.

She whirled around and grabbed me in her sweaty bear hug, gloved hands crossed behind my neck. "SHE'S BACK."

I gritted my teeth. "Um, I left Heather's lab . . ."

"Yes?"

"Whose shitty deductive prowess fingered Junior Alvarez for the Patricia Keystone murder?"

"We've got the evidence." Shinto cocked her head. "It's overwhelming, Kailey."

"Did you ever think maybe a little too overwhelming?"

"What's your deal with Alvarez? You still sweet on that loser?"

"Think, Shinto. Remember what was done to that poor woman? Some sick fuck tortured her, raped her. He sliced off her breasts, Shinto. I intend for him to burn in hell. No way Junior Alvarez did that."

"You psychic now?"

"You met him. Tell me you think that young man in our class is so twisted he stabbed her twenty-seven times."

"Allen seems pretty convinced." Shinto pulled at the Velcro ties on her gloves.

"Allen couldn't find the murderer in a Nancy Drew novel. With apologies to Nancy."

"We have the evidence. The captain chewed on our ass. The mayor chewed on his. Allen wrote his report, and I signed it."

"You signed a fairy tale."

"My stomach's been sick ever since I watched Allen question Alvarez." She kneaded her midsection as if to confirm it. "But what are you going to do?"

"We're going to go over it again and again until we find the evil son of a bitch who really savaged that poor woman. I want to watch them strap his ass to a gurney and shove the needle in. Wish they could gas him, zap him, shoot him, and hang him. I would really prefer a nice, botched hanging to tell you the truth."

Shinto grinned. "I have missed you, girl."

"Same here. Believe me. First thing on my agenda, I'm going to talk to Alvarez."

"He's lawyered up."

"Don't care. He knows things he's not telling. I'd bet my badge on it."

"Cool your jets. I've got a better idea. You get the pizza, I'll get the beer. We'll huddle at my house and comb through the files and photos separately. A little girl-on-girl action. So to speak."

"I could use some food." My two granola bars from this morning had long since disappeared.

Shinto clapped her hands. "Awesome. It's settled. We question everything. Make our notes and compare them. Then, when we're ready, we'll both go see him. Your boy's not going anywhere."

"He's not my boy, plus I think I should see Junior alone. I don't want to get you in hot water with your boy, Allen."

Shinto ignored my little dig. "Still drink that Lone Star swill?"

"Longnecks only," I said. "You still choke down anchovies on your pizza?"

"The fishier the better."

Before I made it to my car my phone pinged. "Officer Carmichael at your service."

"Kailey?"

"Harper?"

Harper huffed. "Now that we have our names clear, we need to meet. ASAP."

"Sorry, I'm in the middle of something." I snapped my fingers. "Hey, you like pizza with anchovies?"

"Why?"

"Another officer and I are going over the Junior Alvarez case. You interested?"

"That's actually why I'm calling."

"Meet us at twenty-six oh one Boyd in about an hour."

"Deal." Click and a dial tone.

"Good-bye to you too, Harper. Me, too. Can't wait. So glad you called." The dial tone had nothing to say.

Forty minutes later and balancing the pizza box in one hand so as not to tip and stick cheese on the box top, I rang Shinto's bell. Nothing. Naturally.

I stuck my head in the door and yelled, "Shinto, we're going to have a visitor." I hurried in ready to devour several pieces of the delicious pie. All the way there with the pizza smelling up my car, I'd developed a serious craving. Even for anchovies. Almost grabbed a slice on the way. Temptation, you evil, stomach-growling, bitch.

When I entered, I saw Shinto sitting cross-legged on the couch in a thin white t-shirt and gray gym shorts with the police emblem on both. She had files on either side of her and one open in her lap.

"Ooh, that smells heavenly." She stretched out her arms and wiggled her fingers. "Come to mama, baby."

"Heather?"

"Gone to stay at her apartment for a few days."

"I thought you two were going to move in—"

"We are. She needs more time is all."

"More for us," I handed her the box. "I'll get paper plates and napkins,"

She slid it carefully onto the coffee table and rose to help. "Who's the visitor?"

We both walked to the kitchen. I helped myself to a Lone Star from the refrigerator while she got the napkins and plates. I leaned against the counter and took a gulp. "DEA. Agent Harper Salazar."

"Why is she coming here?"

I shrugged. The doorbell rang. "She said she had some information that might help our case. More important, Captain told me we need to liaison with her."

"Oh, my," Shinto said. "Liaison."

"Shut up." I headed for the front door.

"She's a Fed, Kailey. She'll want quid pro quo." Shinto sneered.

I flung open the door and there stood DEA Agent Harper Salazar dressed in a sundress that had to have come off a runway in Milan.

"I brought dessert." She shoved a box into my hands and scooted past me and up to Shinto who dangled three Lone Stars between her fingers. Harper took one and said, "Hi, I'm Harper."

"Shinto."

"What an unusual name," Harper said. "I like it."

"Yours isn't all that normal either," Shinto countered. "Not really a man, are you?"

Harper winked. "I'm undercover and real good with makeup."

"I think I might like her," Shinto said.

"Pizza?" I offered Harper a plate and napkin while Shinto opened the box.

After we polished off the pie and a six pack of beer, we eyed the box that Harper brought.

She opened it with a flourish. "I made cupcakes."

Shinto snatched one, took a bite and licked the remnants of cream cheese frosting off her upper lip. "Oh my god. There are cupcakes and there are CUPCAKES." She finished another one and looked over what remained. "Where'd you learn to cook? Culinary Institute of America?"

"As a matter of fact, I did." She smiled. "Like 'em?"

"If tongues could have orgasms—"

"Shinto," I cautioned.

"Fine." Shinto bit into a chocolate cake with cream frosting and a sprinkle of coffee beans.

"Junior Alvarez especially liked that one you're biting into."

Shinto stopped chewing and her mouth hung open. "How did Junior Alvarez get a hold of one of your cupcakes?"

"Long story," Harper said. "He and I had a sort of encounter. He knows me as Elizabeth, the name I use while I'm undercover. A little spoiled, somewhat timid, rich girl who likes bad boys."

"Don't we all?" I said. "Now, girl, tell us what's going on. You tossed a rattlesnake in the middle of one investigation. Maybe two. We need to talk about that."

Harper nodded. "Thought that might get your attention."

"Where do we start?"

"How about we get back to the business of murder?" Shinto said. "Sprinkle in a little gang action for spice."

"Works for me." I leaned forward and snagged a key lime concoction with a green twist of lime embedded in the frosting. "Harper, you are looking at the big picture. Your cocaine highway from Mexico to Canada. Fill us in on that, and we'll fill you in on our tiny speck of a city here in West Texas. I got a feeling things are going to come together somewhere along the way."

"You told me about your goings-on at the Chaparral Apartments." Harper dabbed daintily at her mouth with a napkin. "I told you we kept that place under surveillance for a while, so I pulled some of our footage and saw something interesting about an hour before the murder. This guy, clearly not a resident, we'd seen him before, loitering around, generally acting suspicious. He must have walked by the apartment a dozen times. Then we lost him behind some bushes." She bent over and pulled a tablet from her Louis Vuitton purse. "Check it out." She tapped a few buttons and swiveled the tablet so we could all see.

"Government issue you that iPad?" Shinto asked. "I'm hitting Requisition up for one in the morning."

"Optimist," I said.

"Time and date stamp are on twenty-four-hour military time," Harper said. "Our cameras are motion activated, so you'll notice some jumps. Here is a printout of the relevant dates and times. My team reviewed the footage and captured all the times Mr. Suspicious was seen hanging around the apartment complex. I also noted all the times Junior Alvarez came and went. You want those too?"

"That would help." I saw Suspicious Guy onscreen for the first time. Much shorter and lots stockier than Junior. Tiny details, but important. "Harper, this is really good stuff. Now, what can we do for you?"

"I do want something from you both."

Shinto gave me her I-told-you-so-look I knew so well.

"Before I begin," Harper said, "I'll confess I have checked you guys out. I mean, a deep dive into you both. I know how tight your friendship is and how far it goes back. Shinto, I talked to your superiors in the Army and dug all the way back to your kindergarten teacher."

Shinto sputtered and stood. "That woman was a cunt."

Harper closed the tablet and folded her hands. "Let me explain."

Shinto sat down and said through clenched teeth, "I suggest you do."

Harper turned to me. "Kailey, I did the same with you. I talked to your superior in Dallas who fell all over himself bragging about you. I am very sorry about your daughter. One night we are going to have a sit down, and you are going to tell me all about Derek."

I shrugged.

"Ooh, yes. Let's talk about Derek." Shinto said.

Harper continued, "I've gotten permission from my superiors and yours to read you into my 'big picture.' Only thing is you will both need to report to me for the duration of the investigation."

Shinto sat back and crossed her arms.

I tapped my foot. Rapidly.

"Report to you," Shinto said.

"If you have a problem with that, you should talk with your captain. In fact, call him. He's expecting to hear from us."

Captain Samosa answered on the first ring. "Put me on speaker," he said. "I don't want to repeat myself."

"Yes, sir." I may have sounded surlier than I needed to be.

"Got a bee up your ass, Carmichael?"

"No sir. Officers Carmichael and Elliot, reporting with DEA agent Harper Salazar as requested."

"She filled you all in on our arrangement?"

Neither Shinto nor I spoke up.

"Officers?" he said.

"Captain, I have open cases." Shinto glared at the phone.

"Everyone has open cases, Shinto. Your partner Officer Dempsey has," he cleared his throat, "volunteered to help while you are out on assignment. I want your undivided attention on this case. If Allen needs assistance, which I am sure he won't, I'll assign someone. Questions?"

Again Shinto and I remained silent.

"Good. This conversation is over." We both heard the dial tone.

"What the shit?" Shinto glared at Harper.

Harper smiled tightly. "I'll ask one more time. Are we going to have a problem? Shinto?"

Shinto fumed and tossed the remains of the cupcake she'd been eating into the box.

I wanted to get us back on track. "I take it Junior likes your cupcakes?"

Harper brightened. "He also likes brunettes with money problems. I've been working him undercover, almost recruited him, when this arrest happened. Bad timing doesn't even come close." She grinned primly. "He's a potentially great contact. Been in the system since twelve or so. Bent but not too broken. Born to a crack-addicted mother and an addict father. Got streetwise way too early and remarkably survived it all with a touch of conscience." She stood and paced. "There's a glimmer of heart in that man, and I swear I'm beginning to see it."

Shinto chimed in. "Gee. Sounds like you really got to know our poor Junior Alvarez well." She said it all wide-eyed and innocent. I felt sure Harper would take the bait. To her credit, she ignored it.

"Junior's arrest screwed up my timeline and set me back. If we can get him out of jail I know he can be an asset." She stopped pacing and locked her gaze with Shinto's. "Any idea what idiot decided to arrest him?"

"What do you mean, Junior can be an asset?" I queried.

"While undercover as Elizabeth Parks, I've been working at the bank with Yolanda Garcia. She's the Los Demonios gang mama and Miguel Castillo's main squeeze. We've been hanging out together. One day she introduced me to Junior at the gang's party house. Junior was . . . interesting. She coughed. "We hit it off. I pulled his sheet, got a sense of his early years. No way he murdered that woman. I about convinced him I needed a job with his gang to make some extra cash when *bam*. He gets nabbed for a crime he didn't commit. Our first order of business is to get him out of jail and working for us."

Shinto looked at me. "That ought to make you happy, Kailey."

"What does that mean?" Harper looked from Shinto to me and back to Shinto.

"Nothing. I've thought Junior was innocent all along and it pisses Shinto off that I was right."

"No. I'm all about truth and justice and all that American way crap."

"See what I mean?" I said.

"Ladies, ladies—and I use the term loosely. We have a lot of work to do in a very short time."

"You're right," Shinto said. "Gotta say, you sure do know how to drop a bomb." She jumped up. "We have beer. Any more of those cupcakes left? Let's figure out how to get Harper's boyfriend out of jail."

Chapter Sixty-Seven

Junior

Chigger stroked his chin. "Freddie has always been Miguel's favorite. Until you happened along."

"C'mon Chigger, this ain't kindergarten." I chewed a piece of mystery meat and watched the circus around us in the cafeteria. I felt them sizing me up, the only really fresh meat in the cafeteria. Bring it on assholes.

Chigger nodded to a group strutting by checking us out. "Want me to tell you the story or not, dude?" He nodded to a friend. "Hey, Big Baby, how you doing, man?"

A lumbering, tattooed vato the size of a refrigerator shoved another guy out of the way and sat down next to Chigger, his tray a study in prison food architecture. He focused his beady browns on me and snarled. "Who the fuck are you?"

The dance continues.

Chigger elbowed Big Baby and said, "He's cool, Baby. This is Junior. Junior and I are tight, man."

Baby stared me down a few more seconds and then attacked the pile on his metal plate. The boy could eat. Watching him drove the hunger right out of me. I scooted back in my plastic chair and said, "Think I'll get some air." I picked up my tray, dumped all the food in the trash, and headed out of the cafeteria. Wonder if this place has a library.

Chapter Sixty-Eight

Kailey and Shinto

I stretched and felt a vertebrae shift. "Guys, it's late. What do you say we call it a night? Besides, Shinto drank all the beer."

She stuck her tongue out at me.

"What are we going to do with any of this anyway?" I raked hair out of my eyes. "We can't jeopardize your whole operation to get Junior out of jail."

Harper yawned. "First, I'll call my superiors, inform them what I've got, and see if they can't pull strings to get Junior out of this mess. Hell, I'll ask them to classify him as my informant, if I have to. I want to get Junior's take on our video. He lives there, for god's sake. May even be able to ID our mystery man."

"Indeed," I said. "Good thinking. Whatever we can do to figure out who that guy in the video is. Then again, we'll still have to connect him to the murder. At this moment all we have is him lurking around the apartment."

Harper got up, stretched, and scooped up papers. "Let's sleep on it. Meet up tomorrow around eleven? I hear La Bodega is decent. By then I should have some answers."

Shinto stopped collecting beer bottles for a beat. "Lady, you are a quick study. La Bodega makes the best migas in Texas. They will so kick your hangover in the ass. I'll check with some of my contacts to see if I can ID the asshole too. See you guys there."

"Funny thing," Harper said. "Never had a hangover in my life,"

Shinto squinted at her. "Of course you haven't."

Chapter Sixty-Nine

Junior

I got back to our cell and caught Chigger taking a dump. "Dude. Mercy flush. Jesus."

"Thought you'd never make it back," he said, plucking TP sheets from the holder on the wall. "Where you been?"

"Library."

"They got one of those here?" Chigger flushed and peeled his bony ass off the stainless-steel throne. "We need to finish our Get Out of Jail Free talk, bro."

"I'm listening."

"You need to know. Freddie's been bragging how he shafted you. Said he fucked that old lady you were sweet on. Then wasted her. Sliced her up bad. Stabbed her a million times and cut her tits off. Guy is one twisted motherfucker."

I clasped both my hands together and gripped hard to keep them off the little weasel's neck.

"Here's the best part," Chigger continued. "Says he stole your knife. Ripped you off one night when you were out. Then made sure she saw it up close. Called it your special knife for whores. She cried for you. 'Course you didn't come." Chigger chuckled. "He tossed your knife in the Dumpster behind your building for the cops to find." Chigger looked off into the distance and smiled. "Twisted asshole sure paints a picture, you know?"

I painted quite a different picture in my head, a finger painting in blood. Fuck You's face, his blood, and my hands tearing open his throat.

I hit the floor and began cranking out pushups. It was all I could do to stay sane. It probably also kept Chigger alive. I didn't give a shit. I kept at it until the guards rousted us for chow.

Chigger never said a peep after that and made a point of sitting the next table over from me at dinner.

When the whistle blew, I dumped another full tray of food in the trash and headed back to my cell.

Two hours later I heard, "Alvarez, Junior Alvarez, Number D723497." The guard's voice boomed down the row of cells.

I hit my feet before the key turned in the cell door. Outside, through my barred window, the sun lit the dark early morning sky with a tinge of purple. Chigger snored in his bunk. I stood at attention. The guard said, "You are being released. Grab your belongings. We're headed for processing."

I didn't question my good fortune. I needed to get my hands on a knife and find me one Fuck You asshole.

I signed for my items: wallet with eleven dollars still in it, house keys, thirty-seven cents in change, dead cell phone, and a wrinkled pile of clothes. I changed out of my prison uniform and got ushered into an interview room.

"Hey, what the fuck is this?"

The guard grinned. "Strings," he said and shut the door.

I heard the key turn in the lock.

I knew it had to be too good to be true. Roll with it, dude. I sat down and clasped hands and waited. Let's see what strings the system has in store for me.

The lock clinked again, the door opened, and Officer Kailey Carmichael, in full uniform, strode into the room. All business. All cop.

"Good morning, Junior."

"Professor?"

"For the umpteenth time, Junior. I'm not a professor."

"You're my strings," I said.

"Your what?"

"Not important. Am I being released or what?" I tried damn hard to be polite. Until I got out of here, I had to play the game.

"Junior, you are being released. Provisionally."

"Let me guess, you're my provision."

"Exactly." She stepped out into the hall and swung the door wide. "You like it here? Want to stay? Play cards with your buddies?"

I stood and walked out.

"I assume you know where the exit is," she said.

I said nothing. The catcalls and wolf whistles coming from the holding cells spoke for me. Female visitors always got that treatment no matter what they looked like and this woman, law enforcement or not, looked mighty fine in her tight cop pants and jacket.

She stayed silent until we burst out into the cool morning air.

"Car's at the curb. The blue one."

"Naturally, it's blue."

She chuckled at my comment.

Once at the car, she unlocked the doors and transformed from official cop to everywoman. The uniform coat came off. Official black shoes switched out for sneakers. Pulled back hair fluffed and hung loose.

"Nice," I said.

"Trust me, it's not for you. It's for where we're going. Get in."

When we were settled, she cranked the ignition and yanked the car into gear. "We got you out because we have some work to do."

"We? Who's we?"

"People who want to find the real person who murdered that poor woman."

"I know who killed Patricia. Don't you worry about that."

"Let me guess. You're going to go score a gun and blow his brains out?"

"I don't need a gun."

She eyed me up and down like she read my mind. That wasn't happening. I can barely read my own.

"How about some breakfast?" she said. "We'll eat, and I'll explain the situation. You hungry?"

I thought of the dinner I tossed in the trash the night before. "I could eat."

We pulled into a dump of a restaurant, La Condesa painted over top a cheesy mural on the outside wall.

"Your favorite special place?"

"I hope you like Mexican," she said.

"I've lived in Texas all my life."

"Then you'll like this."

We sat under the TV in the corner. The smell of chili, frying meat, and hot corn tortillas made my stomach sit up and growl. The menus on the table were greasy and food spattered. My kind of place.

She ordered the Machaca a la Mexicana, two eggs with machaca and pico de gallo, beans and potatoes. I ordered Juanito's Breakfast, two corn tortillas with two eggs topped with asadero cheese, salsa Española, chopped bacon, beans, and potatoes.

The woman certainly knows her comida. Our plates came, awash in red sauce and melted cheese. I inhaled like it might be my last breath. Sweet Jesus. I made a note to request La Condesa for my death row meal.

We ate in silence.

She wiped her plate with the last warm tortilla, shoved it into her mouth, and talked around it. "Now to business."

I finished at the same time and swallowed the last of my sweet tea. I sat back and enjoyed ten seconds of pure bliss before Chigger's revelations came back to me. A wash of stomach acid immediately started in on my breakfast.

"You're on everybody's radar. You get that?" she said.

I decided no comment may be my best strategy.

"You're my responsibility. My ass is on the line for you."

"I didn't ask you to do that."

"No. I'm telling you that's how it is. Our arrangement will run like grease through a goose. If you screw this up, I'll take you back to

County myself. For the record, *your* record will suck big time if I do. You understand?"

"I'll understand better when you explain what our arrangement actually is." I can't take much more of this cat-and-mouse crap. I need to get out of her grasp and find Freddie.

"Let's go. I'll explain when we get there."

I can't wait.

She drove like she had a bee up her ass. Her car rattled and vibrated when she took it over fifty. Piece of shit. You'd think a cop could afford better. I scratched my ear and glanced over at her. She looked to be about my age and pretty in a tough-cop way. Bet many a young man got a boner when she handcuffed him. I smiled at the thought. She snapped her head my way and squinted. Not possible. She's a mind reader too?

We pulled up to a yellow brick house with black shutters in a neighborhood I'd never been to before. A large tree threw shade on the hot Midland day. Green grass, big, floppy tropic-like plants under the tree. Nice place.

We got out and marched up to the door. I hung back, ready to knock, but my cop walked right in, no knock, no doorbell. I figured it must be her place and followed, until she yelled, "We're here."

Her boyfriend's house? Always wondered if cops dated cops.

Out walks hard-ass Detective Elliot.

"Shinto," my cop says, "you remember Junior?"

I froze.

"How could I ever forget?" Elliot grunted and pointed to a dark brown leather couch.

I'll be damned. Carmichael and Shinto Elliot, a pair of dykes? Then, another woman comes out in a robe, toweling off stringy brown hair. What the—? A threesome?

"Junior, Heather. Heather, Junior." Officer Elliot went to the new woman, tugged, and cinched the lady's robe tight.

I got tired of standing and walked the place, checking out the shelves, trying to look interested.

"Jesus, Junior, light someplace. Please?" Officer Carmichael said.

"No problem, officer," I said. "Always happy to help."

"You can start by calling me Kailey. That's Shinto. The drowned rat is Heather."

I sat on the couch next to my new friend Kailey and nodded in everyone's general direction.

"Why don't we cue up the video, Shinto?" Kailey said.

Shinto stopped messing with Heather's robe and made a face like she'd bitten into something sour. "Go big or go home," she said.

My prickly new friend disappeared into another room and came out with a laptop. She opened it on the coffee table in front of me and clicked the mousepad.

"Looks like you guys are going to get into something here," Heather said. "I'll leave y'all to it." She disappeared back down the hallway in the direction she came from.

"Here, big guy," Shinto swiveled the computer in my direction. "Take a gander."

The picture flickered grainy, like a video from a cheap security camera.

"This is from a security camera," Kailey said.

I smiled and said nothing. When I scooted closer to see better, I recognized the outside of my apartment building. "What the hell is this?"

"Keep watching," Shinto said.

A man scurried from the bushes on the corner of the property swiveling his head right and left like the cowardly piece of shit he was. I'd recognize Freddie's slouchy walk anywhere.

"Know him?" Shinto said.

"Never seen him before," I said.

But I will see him soon. Very soon.

"There are a couple more clips. See if you can make him out." Kailey got up to stand behind me. I felt her hands on the back of the couch.

I watched the skulking, murderous fucker track pretty much the same route in each video except the last one.

The last one differed, because Freddie disappeared up the stairs into my apartment.

"Son of a bitch," I muttered under my breath.

Kailey came around from behind the couch and slapped the laptop shut. "Tell me his name."

"How about John Doe? Give me a break, officer. This ain't exactly HBO quality."

"And I knew better liars in second grade," she said. "Who is he?"

I put on my gee-I'd-love-to-help look. Kailey sat down beside me with a grin that could freeze hot coffee in its mug.

"Junior," she said, "we are establishing trust here, today. Between you, Shinto, and me. Without trust, we can't rely on one another. If we can't rely on you, we don't need you." She sat back and crossed her arms. "Tomorrow morning you get to go back to cold oatmeal and rotten bananas for breakfast. Sound good?"

Not how I'd envisioned my day going. Not after a plate of the best food I'd eaten in years.

"Fine." Kailey stood. "You were right, Shinto. I should have listened to you. Junior's living in his own little fantasy world. Up. Let's go."

"Wait a second. Hold on," I said. "You don't trust me, right?"

"Brilliant," Shinto said. "Your boy's a genius, Kailey."

"Well, I don't trust you guys either, okay? So, there's something."

"What are you saying?" Kailey said.

"Mutual distrust. Let's build on that."

"Are you fucking high?" Shinto said. "I told you, girl. He's playing us. Enjoy your ride back home in that piece of crap car of hers."

I couldn't help myself. I laughed. Something about the sight of Miss Badass Cop driving that shit box of a car got me going. "Now that, we can agree on. That is the worst set of wheels. I felt ashamed to be seen in it and I just came from fucking jail."

That got Shinto laughing with me. And we couldn't stop.

"Smells, too," she said. "Notice that stink it has?"

"Like a burnt onion dog-shit sandwich?" I said.

"Exactly." Shinto howled, and I joined her.

"Okay, okay. Don't rag on my car. I'm going to get it fixed."

"Bwa, ha, ha." Shinto clutched her stomach.

Pretty soon Kailey couldn't hold out and laughed right along with us.

After we all caught our breath, Shinto wiped tears from her eyes, and Kailey went to the kitchen. She came back with a box of tissues, and a friggin' lightbulb clicked on in my head. What the hell, right? I've done stupider shit in my life than trust a couple of cops. At least these had a sense of humor.

"Okay, okay. Thing is, I might have a glimmer of a sort of an idea about who that guy on the video maybe could be."

"I like how positive you are, Junior," Shinto said. "Damn inspiring."

"Here's the thing, Junior," Kailey said. "We already know who that guy is. All we want from you is confirmation."

"Yeah," Shinto said. "It's like a test."

I nodded, collecting my thoughts. Either they were bullshitting or they weren't. Did it matter in the long run? Whether they knew Fuck You starred in their video or not wouldn't stop me from gutting the bastard.

"Freddie Medina," I said. "He has a real attractive tattoo on his forehead."

"Does that slime even have a mother?" Shinto said. "Bet she's proud of her little boy. Look ma, at my new tattoo! I'm impressed he spelled fuck right. Gotta give him that."

"We call him Fuck You because it's fun to say," Kailey said. "We've got him running with Los Demonios and Miguel Castillo."

"Why do you guys need me?" I said. "You got all that, what am I doing here?"

"You're going to help us put him where he belongs," Kailey said.

"I know exactly where he belongs," I said, "but I'll bet you every cupcake in that box over there we have a different opinion about where *exactly* is. By the way, I haven't eaten in at least an hour. I could use some dessert."

Shinto inclined her head at the box. "Knock yourself out. Keep your big mitts off the chocolate with coffee beans. That one's mine."

Holy shit.

I took a real close look at the cupcake box and the tasty morsels left in it. I'd seen those same cupcakes before. The chocolate with coffee beans was my favorite, too. I decided that the day Elizabeth offered me one.

Well, this changes things. This changes things a lot.

An hour later, back in my speck in the desert, the apartment felt like a release after jail. Didn't think the ladies would ever let me go. They peppered me with questions, and I dodged them up to the second Kailey dropped me off.

I plugged in my cell and sat on the bed to scroll through my missed messages. Elizabeth called a few times, Miguel seven times, and one random telemarketer. I couldn't listen to any of them right then. I had to focus and prioritize. My leg bounced in time to my thoughts. I needed wheels and answers, in that order. I dialed Elizabeth's number, and she answered on the first ring.

"Hi, stranger. How are you?"

"Jones-ing for cupcakes at the moment. How are you, Elizabeth?"

"I'm flattered you remembered. I might be able to whip up a new batch. Any requests?"

"You made a chocolate with coffee beans I really liked."

Silence.

"You there?"

She cleared her throat. "Running over my ingredients on hand. Might have to stop by the store later."

"Which brings me to the next reason for my call. I need a favor."

"Name it."

"I need a ride. Maybe on the way to your store?"

"You're on. What time?" she said.

"Need to shower lock-up stink off me."

More silence.

"Junior. What did you do?"

"Nothing they could hold me for. Not for long, anyway. But I got a feeling my life is going to get complicated soon. I need to prepare."

"How can I help?"

"Pick me up in say, an hour?"

"See you then, lover."

I hung up and replayed the call in my head. No question, my little cupcake has layers she's not showing me. How much does Elizabeth know about me? What's her connection to Kailey and Shinto? Who the hell is she, really?

Time to stir the pot, add some jalapeños, chili powder and a ton of tomatoes for my friend, Patricia.

I turned my shower to scald and waited for the steam to build. Jail showers never get hot enough. After my time at County and dealing with my new cop buddies, I felt the need to come clean. Squeaky. Clean.

Chapter Seventy

Kailey and Shinto

I picked up on the first ring, and Shinto's sarcasm oozed from the receiver. "That went well. Did you deposit our baby in his crib?"

"I did. Have you heard from our DEA boss?"

"Harper is MIA. Do you mind filling her in?" Shinto said. "Me and my girl are headed out for a movie with friends."

"Must be nice to have a life. Will your considerably better half be in the lab tomorrow? I have an idea I want to run by her."

"She will. Gotta go. See ya."

The phone went silent, and I put in my fifth call to Harper.

This time I waited for the auto message to finish and left a voicemail. "I didn't have a problem getting our subject out. We interviewed him. He identified Freddie Medina. I took him to his apartment. I'll be at the Midland Police Lab tomorrow following up on an idea. Call me."

At six a.m., bag of bagels and a box of coffees in hand, I pushed through the doors of Heather's lab and rounded the corner to her desk. "Good morning, Heather. I brought a bribe." I deposited the coffee and goodies beside her keyboard.

"Good morning, Kailey. I'm happy to see you, too. Why no, I'm not busy at all." Heather raised the Styrofoam cup up in a mock salute.

"Sorry. My manners go down the tubes when I'm in focus mode." I sat on the edge of her desk, took a healthy swig of my double espresso and closed my eyes, waiting on the heavenly caffeine jolt to come.

"What can I do you for?"

"Still have the evidence from the Patricia Keystone case handy?"

"You betcha." Heather peered into the bagel bag and pulled out a salt-encrusted delight.

I took the plunge. "Last night I watched Forensic Files and —."

Heather stopped with the bagel halfway to her mouth. "For the love of God, Kailey. Please tell me you're not interrupting my day to discuss TV science."

"Seriously, Heather."

"Sorry, Kailey." She bit into the bagel. "Come talk to me when you have something real to discuss."

I ignored her verbal slap. "Do we still have the knife recovered from the trash container in back of her apartment?"

"Yes." She scrolled through her email, ignoring me. Not a good sign.

I rushed ahead. "You identified it as belonging to Junior Alvarez."

"Chain of evidence from the scene did that for me." She opened an email and read.

"Did you take the knife apart and check for blood trapped under the handle? Maybe blood other than the vic's?"

She stopped chewing and drummed her fingers on the desk. "Forensic Files?"

I pretended not to hear and rummaged in the bag for my own bagel.

"Okay, you caught me. No," Heather said. "Allen insisted the knife belonged to Junior Alvarez." She pushed away from her desk. "Dammit. That makes me mad." She stood. "Follow me."

We made our way to the evidence room where Heather strode purposefully down a row of gray metal shelves. "Bingo." She reached for a cardboard container on the top shelf. The label on the end had Patricia Keystone and a case number scrawled in felt-tip marker. She lugged it to a table set against the far wall and lifted the lid. "What have we here?"

She reached inside and pulled out a plastic bag of crime scene photos. The top one on the stack a close-up of a boot print in a puddle of smashed tomato. "Check it out." She held it up. "Idiot stepped on a tomato at the scene. Tomato's in the freezer. Cast of the print is in here somewhere." She rummaged about. "But—" She removed a hunting knife, also in a plastic bag. "This beauty is what we came for. Let's see how much you retained from your crash course in the science of forensics."

Back in the lab she handed me a box of latex gloves after pulling out a pair for herself. "Suit up, Kailey. Let's see if I need to put Forensic Files on my Must-See TV list.

"First time through, if I remember right, we got a pretty good fingerprint. According to our records, definitely Junior Alvarez's." She plucked the knife from the bag. "Let's play your hunch, disassemble this bad boy, see if we can do your Forensic Files proud."

She peered closely at the pommel end and carried the knife over to a wall of cabinets. She searched the cabinets and came back to the work table with a selection of hasps, a drill, and a set of bits.

"When we get the end off, the rest should slide free, especially the handle washers and the finger guard. The tang is our pot of gold. If there's any blood hiding in this thing, it'll be on the inside of the finger guard and on the tang."

"How the hell you know all this shit, Heather?"

"A father and two brothers. All hunters. All knife freaks. I've reconditioned more knives than I have pairs of shoes."

She clamped the knife into a vise and matched drill bits to the rivet size. While she screwed a bit into place she said, "You can be my sous chef. Rustle us up some swabs and tubes. If we get lucky, we'll want to be crystal clear about what we find on this thing and where."

Heather worked, and I filmed the whole process on my iPhone.

"Good idea, assistant," she said. "Let's show 'em how it's done."

When the knife and all its pieces and parts lay disassembled on the table, Heather looked over at me and grinned. "Score one for late-night TV."

"We got blood?"

"Tons," Heather said. "Enough for several DNA samples. We'll run the lot. See if we, or Junior, get lucky."

"How fast?"

"Jeez, you don't want much, do you Kailey? Definitive DNA will take more than a month."

I groaned.

"Dallas is backed up," Heather said. "I can get us a preliminary taste here in a few hours. Depends how quickly the computers find a match. It won't be admissible, but it'll give us a pretty good predictor for your investigation."

"Oh, my god. Heather, I could kiss you."

"Please don't. Shinto would have both our asses."

Chapter Seventy-One

Junior

I paced, waiting for Elizabeth, planning my approach to get at the truth.

Her red BMW pulled to the curb and honked. I jumped in and smelled hot leather upholstery and peppermint Altoids.

The idling car didn't move.

She leaned forward without talking, switched off the ignition, and sat tapping her thumbs on the steering wheel. Her red fingernails and lipstick matched the car perfectly. If she meant to distract me, she was doing a good job. The car closed in on me and got hotter by the second without the AC blasting.

"Junior, what is this all about?"

"I miss your cupcakes."

"Bullshit, what's really going on?"

"Fact, it reminded me how much I miss your cupcakes when I got kidnapped and taken to Officer Elliot's house by Officer Carmichael."

She stopped tapping and stared out the windshield. When she turned to me she bit down on her top lip. "We need to talk," she said. "But not here."

"Let's go inside my apartment."

"No."

She cranked the ignition and revved the engine. "I've got a better idea."

She squealed away from the curb like Dale Earnhardt, careening around corners until we skidded to a stop in front of her apartment.

She opened the door and got out, retrieved her purse without saying a word, and headed to the front door. I followed. She unlocked it, tossed her keys in the bowl, and pointed to the dining room. We sat across from each other, and she put her purse on the table between us.

"Yes?" I said. "I don't smell any cupcakes."

"Get your mind off your appetites, Junior."

"Hard to do with you looking like that."

She opened her purse and dumped out its contents. A nine-millimeter Glock in its holster, an expandable baton, handcuffs, and a small leather wallet stood out in a sea of feminine crap.

"Tell me what you see."

"Kinky sex toys."

She picked up the wallet and tossed it to me. "Open it."

A gold badge topped by an eagle with Drug Enforcement Administration Special Agent Harper Salazar in blue jumped out at me. Her picture opposite it showed a stern, all business Elizabeth. The shiny gold DEA on the ID left no doubt about it.

"Last I heard impersonating a Fed is a felony, Elizabeth." Not great, but the best I could come up with while I processed the information.

"Read the name on the badge."

"So you want to lock me up too, Officer Salazar? Get in line." I stood. "Have a nice day, Harper."

I headed for the door and heard the slide on the Glock rack once. It stopped me.

"We aren't through here," she whispered. "Please sit down."

I remained standing, but turned around.

"I'm on the job, Junior. Undercover."

"Congratulations."

She tapped the gun barrel on the table absently. "I guess you might say things got a little out of hand with us."

"Tell you one thing, honey, you're good at your job."

She looked me straight in the eye and said, "I don't regret what we did. Do you?"

"You're the one with the gun. I'll say whatever you want me to."

"Oh, for Christ's sake." She set the gun on the table. "It wasn't all about the job, Junior."

"You sure fooled me. Here I thought my mojo was killing it."

"Your mojo did fine. Until you went and got yourself arrested for a crime you didn't do. I needed Kailey's and Shinto's help to get you out of jail."

"You Fed dudes must have a lot of juice."

"Enough. I want you to know, Junior, I never meant to let it go this far. You are a good guy. Plus, I can't lie, the sex was fantastic."

"Something about a woman in uniform with a gun gets me hot."

"No uniform, Junior. I'm undercover, remember?"

"I remember undercovers."

"Be serious."

"I am. Serious as a murder charge."

"I'm working on that."

"Can we work on something else in the meantime?" I went to her and planted a kiss on those bright red lips. She pressed into me, and I picked her up. She wrapped her legs around me as I made my way to her bedroom, kicked the door open, and threw her on the bed.

She bounced right back up and came at me, pulling at my clothes. Our mouths joined once again. I wanted to devour the woman. My hunger grew more desperate when she grabbed fistfuls of my shirt and yanked it over my head. I reached for the buttons on her silk blouse.

"Uh-uh." She pressed her palms against my chest. "It's a Dior. I'll get this, lover."

She unbuttoned while I stepped out of my shoes and pulled down my pants. Her silk blouse fell away and she wriggled out of her tight skirt. Her red thong and bra glowed fiery against her creamy mocha skin. The lacy cups of her bra swelled full when she bent over to unbuckle the straps on her stilettos. I touched her arm. "Leave 'em on."

I stood and pulled her up, pushing her none too gently against the wall. I covered her mouth with mine and stretched her hands above her head. My cock bumped against her flat stomach. She moaned and snaked her tongue into my mouth.

"Baby, I need you." I grunted. I gripped her hands in one fist while my other hand wrapped itself in her thong and ripped.

"Fuck me, Junior," she whispered in my ear. "Hard." She jumped and wrapped her legs around my waist again. I felt her hunger, hot and wet. I dropped my hands to her ass and dug my fingers in, pulling her to me as I thrust forward. I slid deep into her, and she groaned into my mouth, matching each of my thrusts with one of her own. Our mutual desires found their rhythm, pushing hard then harder, fast then faster.

We staggered to the bed, still joined. She fell back, and I lay down on top of her. The drive became unbearable and release would come only if I pounded harder and deeper. I did and I did and I did.

Afterward we lay sweating and breathing fast, bed covers tangled around us.

Her body shuddered against mine, and I raised up on an elbow to look my lover in the face. Only then did I notice the tears.

"Hey. Hey, now. Elizabeth . . . Harper? Or?"

"Call me by my real name, Junior. Please, I'm Harper."

"What's wrong? Did I hurt you?"

"No, no." She sniffed and turned her head to the side. "It's me. I'm such an idiot."

"I doubt that very much."

"This is unexpected. You. Me. Acting like this. I'm a damn professional, and see what I've got myself twisted up in?"

She rolled out of bed and plucked a tissue from the bed stand. She stood unselfconsciously naked, blowing her nose.

I thought it might have been the sexiest thing I'd ever witnessed.

Two showers later and a change of clothes for her, we sipped cold Lone Stars out on her tiny condo patio. Nothing like an icy beer after steaming hot sex, all of which was great, but I hadn't gotten a single answer to any of my questions. Might as well go right at it.

"Tell me one thing. Harper."

"Just one?"

"What are we doing here? The two of us?"

"Geez, Junior, it's usually the woman that leads with that."

"I don't mean—"

"I know what you mean." She dangled her beer bottle between two fingers. "For one thing, I need your help." She took a sip. "For another, I care about you, and I'm worried for you."

"I don't understand."

"You're hanging with some very bad people."

"Los Demonios."

"They're cartel, Junior. Your buddies Miguel, Freddie, Chigger, Dog, Yolanda." She drained her bottle and set it on the cement next to her chair. "I've had them all under surveillance for weeks. I'm here to bring them down."

Shit. "You really do your homework." A week before, I thought all she did was bake cupcakes.

"You think it coincidence your cellmate at County turned out to be Chigger?"

"You?"

"Me. Chigger and I . . . let's say the boy isn't the sharpest machete in the field. He tells me what I need to know, but he's still in lockup. I need eyes and ears inside the gang."

I caught her drift. "Sorry, sweet thing. You know what I think of you. I hope you do, but I'm no snitch."

"I'm not asking you to rat out your buddies."

"Then what? By the way they're not my buddies."

"I need some arm candy. Take me around the gang, let me hang out. I'll do all the heavy lifting. You stand around looking pretty."

"Can I think about it?"

"Take your time. I'll need your answer in oh," she consulted her iPhone, "four and a half minutes. Give or take."

"What happens in four minutes?"

"You're taking me to a barbecue. At Miguel's. I'm sure they sent you an invitation."

"I've been a little preoccupied. Jail and all."

"Think of the entrance we'll make. Badass felon and the hot chick with a hard-on for bad boys, crashing a cartel party for a few cold cervezas and barbecued ribs."

"I am kind of hungry."

"Then it's settled," she said.

Chapter Seventy-Two

Kailey

Heather swabbed every newly revealed surface of the knife; the tang edges, faces, inside the guard. Each surface got its own swab, and she placed that swab in a separate vial tagged with date, time, and a number. "Now comes the hard part," she said as she fitted them in a specially designed Styrofoam box destined for the lab in Dallas.

"What's that?"

"The wait."

"Where are you sending them?"

Heather tapped the label on the box. "Institute of Forensic Sciences, Medical Examiner's Office and Crime Investigation Lab in Dallas. Why?"

"I may know someone I can call there for us. Maybe push our samples to the front of the line."

"You want to solve this case before Christmas? Do it. But I wouldn't get my hopes up. Those guys in Dallas think the world revolves around—"

"Hey, Derek. It's me." I put my cellphone on speaker.

Heather leaned against the lab bench, watching me with raised eyebrows and a bemused smile.

"Took you long enough to call me." Even through the tiny speaker his voice sounded pissed.

I tried to sound upbeat. It wasn't hard. The sound of his voice made my heart beat fast. "How you liking life doing forensics in the Big D? I saw they posted you there after our forensics stretch."

"How the hell—?"

"Your Facebook page, darlin'." I smiled. I couldn't help it.

"I put that up for you," he said. "Hoped you'd see it."

"Could have called and told me," I said. "The direct route always works best."

"Wasn't sure . . . the way we left things . . . if you'd want to hear from me . . . I don't know." He mumbled something unintelligible. "I didn't call you. My bad."

Silence.

"Anyway, to answer your question, Dallas beats prowling the crime-ridden streets of Nacogdoches any day."

"Thought you said your home was a pretty quiet place."

"Too quiet. I like it here fine. Enough about me. How's your mom? Bet she loves having her big-deal daughter home again."

"Um, I friggin' hate Facebook, so you wouldn't know. My momma passed last month."

"Oh, Christ, Kailey girl, I am damn sorry to hear that. I know you and she were close. I have to ask. It's a stupid question, I know 'cause everyone asks it . . . anything I can do?"

"Actually, that's kind of why I'm calling."

"Anything. Name it."

"I'm sending you a case."

More silence. Throat clearing. "Not exactly what I meant."

"You said, name it. So . . ."

"I'm still new here, Kitten."

"Come on, people love you everywhere you go."

"People?"

My turn to be silent. "You don't want to open that up again, do you Derek?"

"I never closed it, girl. Don't suppose I ever will."

"Can you help me or not? It's a murder case. Messy one. I need to nail the son of a bitch, or a good man's going to pay for it."

"Don't think I like the sound of that 'good man' business."

"Jealous?"

"Should I be?"

I laughed to make a joke out of it. "You're the only man for me, babe."

"You said that once before. A couple times."

"Can I send you this or not? Derek, if you're not going to help me, I can go another way."

"Send it. Put my name on it. I'll see what I can do."

Click.

Heather looked at me with her head cocked.

"He hung up," I said.

"I'm shocked. At the way you sweet-talked him and all? Christ, Kailey."

"Put his name on the label before you send it," I said, and headed for the door.

"Kailey? KAILEY!"

"What? I get us the in we need and—"

"His name?"

"Oh, yeah. Sorry. Sergeant. Derek . . . uh . . . shit wait a second." I scrolled through my cell contacts. "McCormick."

"You're sure?"

"Shut up. We weren't big on last names."

"But big on other stuff?"

"He'll help us. Derek is, um, he's that kind of guy."

Chapter Seventy-Three

Junior

Harper and I pulled up to Miguel's house.

Harper pulled down the vanity mirror, touched up her lipstick and smacked her lips once, twice. "Look okay?" she said.

"Crap, woman. I'm only human. You didn't get enough back at your place?"

She laughed and blew me a kiss. "Hold on, I need to share this moment with my crew. Don't say anything stupid, I'm wired." She dipped her chin and spoke to her cleavage.

"We're on our way to the barbecue. Everyone in position? Start the recorders. Am I coming through?" She nodded and touched a finger to her right ear. "I'll check in by midnight. If you don't hear from me by two, come in with major prejudice. Harper out."

"Ready?" she said.

"As I'll ever be."

She opened her door and stepped out. I followed. The sound of Los Lobos's "La Bamba" fought to be heard over the loud background murmur and occasional shrieks of a crowd having a fucking good time. The smell of smoky-sweet barbecue and reefer carried on the warm, Midland night air. The scent of night-blooming jasmine met us on our way to the front door. Somewhere a dog barked.

I peered sideways at the woman next to me. Couldn't friggin' believe she was with me. She wore painted-on white pants and a see-through blouse that looked more like underwear than a shirt. Her bra, hot pink with sequins, matched her large dangly earrings. Her stilettos were fuck-me high.

Harper pirouetted without a wobble on those heels. "Like it?"

"Holy shit. Where you hiding your badge, much less your gun?"

"If I told you, I'd have to kill you."

"Why'd you have to be so damn sexy? Like a woman in heat, not one recently laid, and laid well, I might add."

She kissed me on the cheek. "That's what I'm counting on, lover." She grabbed my hand and tugged my arm tight around her waist. She pressed into me, and I could feel she was wired, mentally and physically.

Better watch what I say.

"Junior, whatever happens, you need to know how much you mean to me. Watch yourself. I don't want you to get hurt."

"Then you shouldn't have dressed like that. I'm going to be fighting vatos off you all night."

"You sweet talker, you. Whatever happens in there, I'm yours and you're mine." She stretched up and bit my earlobe. "Remember that and don't worry," she whispered, "I've got your back."

I kissed her on the top of her head and twisted the doorknob. "Ditto." I wanted to say more. Find the right words. For some stupid reason my throat got tight and I couldn't speak.

Soon we were in the party, and speaking was out of the question. Shouting became the communication of choice. Along with pushing, pulling, guiding, shoving, waving over heads and smiling like you could actually hear what the asshole in front of you said.

I made my way through the crush of bodies, holding tight to Harper's hand. The best antidote for new-to-the-party syndrome is always cerveza. I fished two Negro Modelos out of a cooler filled to the brim with water, floating chunks of ice, and bottles of beer. Thank god someone tied a church key to the cooler handle.

Our first job was surveillance. I staked out a piece of wall off to the side, and we claimed it for our own. Me, drinking my beer like I'd never taste another one. Her, standing there like a piece of meat in a den of lions. I served up my best barge-in-on-me-and-you're-dead looks. They did the trick for exactly fifteen seconds. A drunk cholo staggered up, eyed Harper up and down, and offered her a hit off a joint. She took it and lit the end of it up like a stoner pro. She exhaled and passed it to me, eliciting a frown from her newfound friend. I pretended to hit the thing, then passed it off to a woman three people beyond us. Cholo boy muttered something in Spanish and followed his weed.

"Watch yourself, honey," I said. "These people practically invented pot. I guarantee that's stronger shit than you're used to."

"You don't know what I'm used to, Junior. I'm good. Look around, tell me what you see."

I got back on point and scoped Miguel's group of party animals. I recognized most of his main gang, they and their dates made up about a third of the crowd. The rest I judged to be hardcore cartel by the tattoos, shitty haircuts, clothes that thumbed a nose at the Midland heat, and a general uncivilized manner. Like they'd mustered straight out of a prison yard in Mexico City to this barbecue in little old Midland, Texas, for their first brush with the outside world.

"Nice group of folks," I said.

Another vato strutted up in that limp leg style they all favor and leered at Harper and licked his lips. "Hola, chica. You look lonely standing there all by yourself. You need a real man, eh? Not this pendejo standing here like he's all that."

I took a step forward. Harper stopped me with a hand to my chest. She smiled at me and bent toward the cholo. He leaned in expectantly, smiling. She whispered, "You see any real hombres in here, you let me know. Comprende? Now largate. Go away."

He pretended to see someone across the room and slunk off.

"Hungry?" I said. "Measuring dicks always works up an appetite."

"Come on, Mr. Man." She laughed. "Let's get you some carne asada, ribs, a fucking hamburger, anything to sink your teeth into besides the local wildlife."

"Hola, amigo!" The voice came from behind us as we made our way out to the patio and the smoking grill. "Junior. Over here, hombre."

We stopped and let Miguel and Yolanda make their way through the crowd toward us. Miguel wore a pearl-studded shirt worthy of the most stylish caballero. Yolanda matched him with an outfit only a hair more subdued than Harper's. She looked hot enough to catch fire, and I carefully kept my eyes fixed on Miguel for their entire approach.

"I like your outfit," Yolanda said.

"Thanks," I said.

"Not talking to you, asshole." She winked at Harper. "You look like someone Claydesta Bank would never put on its payroll. That's a compliment, by the way." She extended her hand to Harper. "Welcome to our little party, Elizabeth."

"You have a lot of friends," Harper said.

Miguel took over the conversation. "This? Nah, this is mostly business. Got to keep up appearances. Drink, smoke, eat." He spread his arms wide. "This is our golf course. It's how our business gets done."

I made a point of checking out the crowd. "I see most of the guys here. Dog, Nacho, Eduardo. Don't see everyone."

"You mean Freddie?" Miguel stared at me with a noncommittal smile. "Oh, he's around. Like a dog you keep feeding. Couldn't get rid of him if I tried."

"Get rid of who?" Fuck You crept up behind Miguel and clapped him on the shoulder. "What'd I miss?"

"I don't know," I said. "Your balls?"

"They let you out, I see," Freddie said. "Someone should alert the local female population."

I stepped forward, and Fuck You did the same. My hands squeezed my beer bottle while I imagined them squeezing something else a bit scrawnier.

Miguel laughed. "Hey, hombres, relax, man. It's a party, eh? We eat, have some laughs. You two got some serious work to do. Repair bridges, eh? Be friends. You gonna work together; it'll be better for me, Yolanda, everyone. Trust me."

Harper stepped between us and whistled. "Who does your tats, Freddie? I'll be sure and never look him up."

Yolanda snorted and Miguel outright guffawed.

Freddie leaned forward, smiling like a rattlesnake would if it could.

"You might want to watch yourself, señorita. I hear chicas who hang around this guy end up with their tits cut off."

That did it. I glanced at Harper who simply winked at me. I went to pinch Fuck You's head off but he'd vanished, melted into the crowd behind him.

"Where'd he go?" I said. "Where'd the chicken shit run off to?"

"I told you," Miguel said. "He'll be around all night. Can't get rid of him. Forget him. Lighten up. You didn't bring this fine woman here to get into a fight with Freddie Medina. Have some fun. Have some food, wine, beer, whatever. It's a party, man."

The next few hours passed in a blur of three kinds of beer, cartel-grade smoke, and anything that would fit on a barbecue grate. I gave up trying to identify what I ate, my attention split between Harper and a constant search for Fuck You.

Asshole kept to the shadows. I'd see him talking to a few people, head his way, and he'd disappear again. Never stayed in one place long enough. Never stayed in the light. Who knew the fucker was half chicken shit, half ghost?

Harper did her thing. Mixing it up, moving around the rooms with Yolanda. I figured her for making IDs, recording names and faces for later. Giving the boys on the other end of her wire something to write down. Feds live and die by their paperwork.

I pulled out my phone, pretending to make a call. I needed to check the time. Harper had said two-o'clock to her gang. Sure enough, ten minutes to two, Apple time. Time to find my woman.

I found her out on the patio leaning against a column, a crowd of people behind her laughing and talking. Not paying attention. She looked more than a little drunk. Not good.

I hurried to her and heard Fuck You's voice.

"Misplace someone, asshole?" His voice came from the crowd, and he stepped out, away from it, and right up behind her. "I don't know, man." His voice dripped with concern. "She doesn't look too good, hombre."

I rushed forward and grabbed Harper as she slumped forward.

"Junior." She turned her face to mine and worked to form words. "He . . . my back . . . Freddie . . . call . . ."

She collapsed, and I hugged her to me.

My hands slid down her back. I felt something slick, and I brought a hand around. In the flickering party-lights the blood shone dark, almost black.

"Oops," Freddie announced to the crowd. "Bitch can't hold her liquor."

Harper's legs folded beneath her, and I whispered into her chest, "Get in here on the double, fuckers. Call an ambulance."

I laid her gently onto the concrete while people in the crowd shouted encouragement.

"Get her another beer, asshole."

"You're gonna get lucky tonight."

"Get her to the bathroom before she pukes her guts out."

Her breathing came labored and ragged. I kissed her forehead and stood up.

Freddie sported a smear of blood on his shirtfront and, more importantly, a knife in his hand. He wiped the blade on his jeans and left a dark smear.

"Lose another one, fucker?" he said. "You do got a way with women." He tossed the blade from hand to hand, acting confident. He'd been in enough street fights to rely on his skills and experience. The knife gave him courage the beer and smoke couldn't. Courage enough to sneak up on a woman and slide a knife into her back.

"Been looking for me? Should have looked harder. Maybe your girlfriend would still be alive. The old woman fought harder than this cunt." He darted forward, knife held low, ready to slash upward. It's what they all do. Like they learned it in knife school.

Big mistake.

I backed up and pulled off my shirt, wrapping it around my left arm. I took my time. I'd been to the same school. Graduated with honors.

"Come on, cobarde, coward," I said. "You're pretty good against old women and anyone else you can stab in the back. After I gut you I'm going to make you eat that pig sticker."

Unlike other parties where women would be wailing and men dialing 911, all these fine folks formed a circle around us and picked sides. Very few bid on the gringo.

Freddie circled to his right. As a right-hander it probably felt natural for him. Good. He made his first blunder. I circled left, against the grain, forced him to make his move early. He took a halfhearted swipe at me, and I stayed close enough so his knife tip grazed my shirt but missed my skin.

The apparent damage he'd inflicted emboldened him, and he went for the same move again, stepping in closer this time to draw serious blood.

I pinned his knife arm. My left forearm against his outside bicep, my right hooked inside his arm. I pushed with my left, yanked hard with my right, and popped his elbow backwards out of its socket. It sounded like popping apart a chicken leg.

He screamed and dropped the knife.

The crowd went quiet.

I bent and retrieved the weapon. It felt familiar. Like mine, but a bit worse for wear. Regular Marine-issue KA-BAR. In this shape, twenty bucks at any Army/Navy store. I doubted he bought his.

"My arm, my arm," he wailed. "He broke my fucking arm. Miguel. MIGUEL, GET HIM! SHOOT HIM!"

Miguel watched from the edge of the crowd and didn't make a move. Not that I cared. If Miguel wanted to die too, I'd be happy to oblige.

Freddie backed away, holding his arm. His squeals turned to howls.

"MIGUEL, YOU ASSHOLE, FINISH HIM." Freddie fetched up against the same column Harper had leaned against.

I stepped in close.

He pawed at me with his good arm. Fingers clawed, trying to make a fight of it.

I swatted his arm away like I would an obnoxious bug. With my other hand, the knife hand, I buried the carbon steel up to the hilt in his gut and whispered in his ear, "Uh-oh."

Air whooshed out like I'd punctured a beach ball.

"This is for Patricia," I hissed. I pulled out the knife and thrust it in a couple more times. Fast and hard, like they taught me in prison. Each shove felt better than the one before.

Fuck You's mouth gaped like a fish, and when I pulled the KA-BAR free the last time, I reversed my grip on the hilt. It dripped slick with blood, and I squeezed it tight in my fist.

His collapsing legs tried to take him to the ground, but I thrust my forearm against his throat and pressed back against the column, holding him up.

"Not yet, fucker." I leaned in close, made sure his eyes focused on mine. "This is for Harper."

I jammed the blade into his open mouth. This time I took it slow. I pushed and pushed until blood fountained from his lips, and I left the knife there while he gagged and slumped forward.

I shoved him away like a sack of garbage, and he collapsed.

I hurried over to Harper and cradled her head, whispering, blubbering like a baby. "You're going to be okay, honey. You're going to be okay."

She blinked once, looked at me with tears in her eyes, and sighed, closing them for the last time.

"FREEZE! EVERYBODY FREEZE"

Chapter Seventy-Four

Junior

The five guys in the holding cell with me kept to themselves. The bolder ones made a point to glance off slowly when I caught them staring. But glance off they did. No one bothered me. Probably had something to do with the blood caking on my shirt and the red stain that reached up to my right elbow.

"What'd you do this time, Alvarez? Hm?"

I recognized the cop outside the cell. Allen something.

"You got a couple folks fooled around here. Not me. You're bad news, and I'm going to make it my business—"

"ALVAREZ, FRONT AND CENTER."

A clipboard-toting cop walked up rattling a keyring. He slipped the clipboard under one arm and picked through the keys until he settled on one he liked. "S'cuse me, officer," he said to Allen and stepped in to unlock the cell door.

"What are you doing? Where you taking this piece of shit?" Allen asked.

"Where all pieces of shit go before they're released."

"Oh, come on. This must be some kind of mistake."

The guard waved his clipboard. "It's all right here, beside the coffee stain. See?" He jabbed a finger at the top paper. "Says 'Alvarez is to be released and escorted to interrogation immediately.' The order's signed by Officer Carmichael."

Allen pushed by him and yanked open the cell door. "Fine. I'll take him."

The guard shook his head dubiously. "I dunno. I'm the one s'posed to transport prisoners while in the facility."

"I'm doing you a solid." Allen leaned close to read the man's name tag. "Officer Preston. You'd be wise to accept it as such."

"Knock yourself out. Sign here," he mimicked Allen's name tag move, "Officer Dempsey, and he's all yours."

Allen scrawled something on the man's pad and tossed him the pen. "You heard the man, Alvarez. You and me are taking a walk."

He stepped wide to let me out of the cell. "Oh, shit, I almost forgot," he said. "Hold up."

He whipped a pair of cuffs off a clip on his belt. "Hands in back. You know the drill."

"Officer Dempsey, I don't think this man requires—"

"But I do think, Preston. You do your job, walk up and down jangling your keys and look important. I'll do mine."

He squeezed the cuffs tight around my wrists. "Too tight? I hope."

I stared at him. No comment. Let him play his Dirty Harry games.

He shoved me forward toward the exit door. "Geez, Alvarez. You smell like a dead animal." He sniffed loudly. "Yeah. Definitely something died."

I flashed on Harper's face, her eyes closing. I stopped and flexed my fingers. Contemplated snapping his neck.

"Oops. Sore spot, Alvarez? I should think you'd be used to shit dying around you."

It took all I had to stay rooted in place.

"Let's go, let's go." Allen shoved me.

I didn't budge.

I turned toward him, and he reached for the holster at his side. The empty holster. He'd stashed his pistol at the entrance where all guns are confiscated before officers are allowed into the lockup facility.

He hesitated, and I felt my face crack wide with a smile. First time I felt like smiling in forever. It must have looked horrible, from the way he paled and backed up a step.

"We going to have a problem here, Alvarez?"

"Take me to your leader officer." The contempt I put into the last word tasted good in my mouth.

We made it to the outside of Interrogation Room Six without further incident. I saw movement behind the frosted glass in the door. He knocked, and we pushed through into one of the larger rooms in the facility, large enough for an actual conference table ringed with chairs.

Captain Samosa sat at one end, Officers Kailey Carmichael and Shinto Elliot, a couple men I didn't recognize, a beefy white guy and a tall black guy in their DEA-issue gray suits sat in the chairs along the side. My lawyer, Carlos Sanchez, took the other end facing the captain. A tiny handheld tape recorder sat dead center on the table.

"Hi, there, professor." I turned and showed my cuffed hands to Kailey, and she smiled at me with sad eyes.

"Professor?" the captain said.

"It's nothing," Kailey said. "Our little joke."

"In the meantime, I'd like to thank you all for coming," I said.

"Sit down, asshole," Allen snarled behind me.

I kicked a chair aside to get into it.

My lawyer rose from his chair and walked around the conference table, thumbs hooked in his suspenders. Everything casual except his eyes. He stopped beside me before I could sit. "You doing all right, son?" he asked.

I nodded.

"Officer." He directed those blazing eyes at Allen. "I suggest you remove those handcuffs from my client immediately. Every second you waste," he consulted his watch, "I will add a thousand dollars to the lawsuit we will summarily bring against you and this department."

The captain rose and spread his hands to calm the waters. "Gentlemen and ladies." He nodded to Kailey and Shinto. "Let's all keep our heads and have no more talk of lawsuits or any other nasty business. We are all on the same side, here."

"What side would that be sir?" Sanchez asked.

"Why, justice, of course," the captain said. "Officer Dempsey, remove the cuffs from our, um, guest, and let's get this mess straightened out. It's taco night at home, and I hate to miss my Mary's tacos."

Allen produced a key and unlocked my handcuffs and stepped back. He couldn't bring himself to remove them completely and left one cuff dangling. I brought my arms around and finished the deed for him. He reached for his cuffs, and I tossed them on the table.

"These gentlemen here are from the Drug Enforcement Agency," the captain said, "and have asked that we remand Mr. Alvarez into their custody."

Sanchez barely touched his seat before rising again. He peered at the captain first, then the Federal agents, each in turn. "That. Is. What we in the legal profession refer to as, it is in Latin, so let me translate, BULLSHIT."

Carlos Sanchez the calm, collected, lawyer changed in an eye blink. He shoved his chair backwards and stalked the room, a lion after prey. "This man, my client, is a goddamn hero. You have heard the tapes. I have heard the tapes. I presume everyone at your precious DE goddamn A has heard the tapes. You take my client into custody tonight, and I swear by Justice Thomas of the Supreme Court I will sue the federal government after we are through with the Midland Police."

The white DEA guy snorted. "Can't sue the federal government. Everyone knows that."

"Happens every day of the week, Perry Mason," Sanchez fired back.

"Can't sue and win, I meant to say," the Fed said. "We're the DEA. We have more lawyers on the payroll than this place has cops."

"Then I suggest you go find the smartest in the bunch and run down the facts for him. He will send you back here with your ass in your hands. Want to save your career and your ass? Let my client go. Now. Tonight."

The black DEA agent spoke up, clearly the higher ranking one of the pair. "Unfortunately, it's protocol. We have heard those tapes you refer to and it certainly sounds as if your client did all he could to assist Agent Harper Salazar. However a decorated federal agent lost her life in the performance of her duty. We need to cross every T and dot all the I's before we can even think of closing our investigation."

My lawyer smiled like a predator and sat down, opened his jacket, and removed a fountain pen. He unscrewed the cap. "Do you have a pen? If not, I am quite sure the Midland PD can produce all you need. We will sit right here and cross every T and dot every I together, after which my client Junior Alvarez walks out of here a free man, and you two fine gentlemen get to keep your jobs. We will even allow you to push Record." He nodded at the tape recorder in the middle of the table. "To forestall any unfortunate misunderstandings of what might be said here."

Sanchez looked my way for the first time since I'd arrived and winked. "How are you doing?"

"I've been better."

"I am truly sorry about your friend, agent Salazar."

I nodded. "Thanks." I didn't trust myself to respond with anything much longer.

"These folks have a job to do." My lawyer reverted back to his full-on counselor mode. Reasonable, polite even. "We want to help them do their jobs the best we can, so we can get you the hell out of here as fast as we can. Yes?"

I nodded once more.

"Good. Here is what I suggest, if it meets with the approval of all assembled here. I propose we play the tape of the incident through from beginning to end." Sanchez placed his briefcase on the table and unsnapped the clasps. He removed a twin to the tape recorder on the table. "I took the liberty of having my staff copy the tape for us. My client will narrate as best as he can the events that are occurring at that point on the tape." He peered at the captain. "May we have some water in here, please?"

The captain pointed at Allen. "You. Go get us some water from the kitchen. Cold ones. From the back. Get enough for everyone to get parched twice over."

"But Cap—"

"Now, officer." He smiled. "I know we'll all appreciate your sacrifice."

My lawyer took control of the room once again. "Thank you, sir." He cracked his knuckles and paced as he talked. "I want to point out that while we have all heard the tape on this machine, Junior has not. He was there. He lived it, for the most part. But this will be the first time he hears it. I know you will all agree there are portions on this that are difficult to listen to and none of us were there. I ask your forbearance in regard to my client. If at any time he exhibits distress or otherwise indicates he would prefer not to continue, this little session ends. No questions."

All the other players glanced at one another. The lead Fed squirmed in his seat and seemed about to speak up. The captain spoke first. "Mr. Sanchez, I am sure we can all appreciate the unusual set of circumstances we face here. Why don't we push ahead and do what we can to everyone's satisfaction?" He glared at the Feds as he finished up.

The lead DEA spoke. "You realize, it is hard to predict the future, even for the DEA." He smiled at his little joke. No one reciprocated. "But if Mr. Alvarez is willing to proceed, the, um, government would be most grateful."

Allen returned with his arms full of water bottles. He approached to deposit them on the table and somehow tripped on my shoe. The bottles slid across the table, and people snatched at them before they slid off onto the floor.

I saw Shinto Elliot rise halfway out of her chair. Officer Carmichael grabbed her arm.

Allen turned to me, his face red. "You did that on purpose."

I raised my eyebrows and tried to look hurt. "Thank you for your . . . service?" I said.

"That's enough of that." The captain glowered my way. "We are doing our best to accommodate you, Mr. Alvarez. Are we not officers?"

Shinto stared at me stone-faced. Kailey actually smiled at me.

"I hope we can expect the same from you," the Captain continued.

"Yes, sir, of course, sir." I smiled sweetly at Allen, who backed away and pulled up a section of wall to lean against. His red face showed up as a wonderful contrast to the industrial light green of the painted cinder block.

My lawyer opened a water bottle and swigged. "If there are no objections, we would like to begin. Junior, are you ready for this?"

I nodded.

"If it gets too rough, you signal me, and I will end it. Yes?"

"I'm good. Let's go."

"Paint the picture for us, to the best of your recollection. Where you are at the time, what you see, who you're seeing."

Sanchez leaned over and pushed Play.

The sound on the tape wasn't too bad for coming out of a one-inch speaker. After a while the quality made no difference. Hearing Harper's voice put me right back at Miguel's. I forgot she'd wired up for our mission. Hearing our conversation in the car and on the front porch might have made a lesser man squirm. If they expected squirming from me, they were gonna be sorely disappointed. I felt happy to hear her again. What I said on their damn tape made zero difference to me.

"Junior, whatever happens You need to know how much you mean to me. Watch yourself. I don't want you to get hurt."

"Then you shouldn't have dressed like that. I'm going to be fighting vatos off you all night."

"You sweet talker, you. Whatever happens in there, I'm yours and you're mine."

I rubbed my earlobe at the memory of her nipping it. I unscrewed the cap on a water bottle and took a drink. I cleared my throat. "We're on the porch, getting ready to go in," I said.

"Remember that. And don't worry," she whispered, "I've got your back."

We heard the door open, and the sound level of a party at full blast boomed from the tiny recorder. I replayed the scene in my head, smelled the smells, saw the people bopping to the music and milling about. I heard the clink of bottles and tasted the first swallow of that ice-cold Negro Modelo.

"Getting a couple beers, here. Looking over the crowd. I think this is where a cholo walks up with a joint and—"

"Watch yourself, honey," I said. "These people practically invented pot. I guarantee that's stronger shit than you're used to."

"You don't know what I'm used to, Junior. I'm good. Look around, tell me what you see."

"It sounds like she hit it, but I grabbed it before she could. That's what's happening. She would never have—"

"Don't worry about that, Junior," Kailey said. "We all know Harper was good at her job." Officer Kailey Carmichael, backing me up. Thanks, professor.

"What are you seeing here, Junior?" beefy DEA said.

"Los Demonios. Most of them. A bunch of cartel."

"How did you know they were cartel?" asked the captain.

"How they look, act. Like their shit don't stink and how you ought to be happy they let you smell it."

"Nice group of folks."

"Hola, chica. You look lonely standing there all by yourself. You need a real man, eh? Not this pendejo standing here like he's all that."

"Vato Number Two," I said. "Bad news." I grinned at the memory. "She handled him fine."

The tape picked up her whisper like she'd said it for our ears.

"You see any real hombres in here, you let me know. Comprende? Now, largate. Go away."

"Hungry? Measuring dicks always works up an appetite."

Someone at the table chuckled.

"Come on, Mr. Man. Let's get you some carne asada, ribs, a fucking hamburger, anything to sink your teeth into besides the local wildlife."

"Hola, amigo! Junior. Over here, hombre."

"That's Miguel and his woman, Yolanda."

"I like your outfit."

"Thanks."

"I wasn't talking to you, asshole. Welcome to our little party, Elizabeth."

"Elizabeth is the name Harper used when I met her. Her undercover name."

"I see most of the guys are here. Dog, Nacho, Eduardo. Don't see everyone."

"You mean Freddie?"

"That's Miguel again."

"Oh, he's around. Like a dog you keep feeding. Couldn't get rid of him if you tried."

"Get rid of who? What'd I miss?"

"I don't know. Your balls?"

"They let you out, I see. Someone should alert the local female population."

I heard Allen behind me chuckle and cover it with a cough. I resisted the urge to whirl around and rip his throat out.

"That piece of shit talking is Freddie Medina. Or Fuck You, as most of his asshole friends and enemies call him. Not to his face."

"Hey, hombres, relax man. It's a party, eh? We eat, have some laughs. You two got some serious work to do. Repair bridges, eh? Be friends. You gonna work together, it'll be better for me, Yolanda, everyone. Trust me."

"That's Miguel, always the businessman." I allowed myself a laugh. "He's smart, focused, dangerous as hell. Good thing you scooped him up when you did."

Carlos Sanchez reached over and stopped the tape. "It appears no one told you."

"Told me what?"

"Miguel Castillo and his woman Yolanda slipped through the DEA's net."

Number Two DEA cracked his knuckles. "We snagged twenty-three known cartel affiliates, several Los Demonios, and three trash cans packed with drugs in the raid. It counts as a win. A big win."

"Thought you Feds were supposed to be good," I said. I leaned over and restarted the tape. "You net all the baitfish, let the shark swim off untouched, and lose an agent worth five of you. Big win. Stellar work."

"Who does your tats, Freddie? I'll be sure and never look him up."

We heard Yolanda and Miguel laughing on the tape. I remembered Freddie's face and the sneer.

"You might want to watch yourself, señorita. I hear chicas who hang around this guy end up with their tits cut off."

I squeezed my water bottle and geysered a stream of water onto the table.

Sanchez stopped the tape.

"You okay, Junior?"

I didn't answer for a few seconds.

Officer Carmichael spoke up. "This is where Freddie admitted he murdered Patricia Keystone. No one else knew her, uh, breasts had been removed."

I nodded and then said, "I'm fine. Really." I leaned over and pushed Play. "This next part is where Harper and I became separated. I concentrated on Fuck You. She went off to do her agent thing."

We heard snippets of her conversations with several people I could not identify. I'd left her by then. Let her go off unprotected while I searched for Freddie. When I found her again, I was too late. Fuck You found her first.

"Hola, chica. Remember me?"

I heard the whisper. I pictured the face that went with it.

I heard him giggle. *"Say hello to my little friend."*

Her gasp made everyone in the room sit forward in their chairs.

I stared at the recorder, willing it to change the script. But it couldn't.

Unh . . . Junior . . .

"Junior? Lo siento. Sorry, chica. Your boyfriend is out there looking for me and guess what. It's me who finds you!"

We heard her moan.

"One more for Junior." We heard him grunt.

I didn't hear much more of the tape. Tried to block out the gasps and grunts as she made her way, I assume, to the column where I found her standing.

Freddie then came back into the picture. *"Misplace someone, asshole? . . . I don't know, man . . . She doesn't look too good, hombre."*

I saw the whole thing played over again. Her white face, her standing up against the column, desperate not to fall. The collapse. The way she struggled to form her last words.

"Junior . . . he . . . Freddie . . . my back . . . call . . ."

Once again, I felt the weight of her in my arms. The wet on her back. Saw the blood on my hands.

"Oops . . . Bitch can't hold her liquor."

"Get in here on the double, fuckers. Call an ambulance."

"That last was me, talking to you assholes." I looked each DEA agent in the eye. "She's on the pavement. I held her to make her comfortable as I could. She bled out, and I couldn't stop it. No one in the crowd gave a shit."

"Get her another beer, asshole."

"You're gonna get lucky tonight."

"Get her to the bathroom before she pukes her guts out."

"Lose another one, fucker? . . . You do got a way with women."

"That's Freddie Medina. The next sounds you hear will be me killing him. You want to arrest me for that? For ending that scum's life? Fine with me."

Someone at the table sniffed, Kailey. She used both hands to wipe her eyes.

A couple of the men refused to look at me.

The captain cleared his throat. "Stop the tape," he said. "We're done here." He pointed at Sanchez. "You take Junior home. Get him cleaned up. Paperwork will be out front for you in the morning. As far as Midland PD goes, Junior Alvarez is exonerated of all charges." He focused on me. "I don't mind saying, every one of us in this room owes you a debt, Junior. And our apologies." He looked hard at Allen. "Everyone."

Carlos Sanchez nodded and gathered his papers and the recorder. "We certainly appreciate that, Captain. Thank you. There is one more thing, if I may."

"Yes?" The captain made it halfway to the door and his wife's tacos.

"I am assuming the previous charges concerning the death of one Patricia Keystone will be dropped as well? As a show of good will, perhaps you could vacate Junior's probation for his prior insignificant infraction for us as well."

The captain stared at my lawyer like he might be some unknown species of vermin and then he grinned. "Why the hell not, counselor? I'm in a forgiving mood. Besides, I'm hungry. You've got it. Now don't ask me for another goddamn thing, or I'll rescind everything I said. Goodnight."

Chapter Seventy-Five

Junior

I felt cold dew soak through my pants. Sitting on a hill with a good view of the funeral, but far enough away to be out of the formalities, I'd been sitting for hours. First to show up, I'd be the last to leave. Naturally, they held Harper's funeral in Dallas. Oakland Cemetery looked more like a park with huge, droopy old oaks and streams and waterfalls. Kids ought to be throwing Frisbees in the grass and families having picnics. Instead, large statues intersected bronze plaques that lay embedded in the ground and occasional pop-up vases full of flowers dotted the landscape.

I sat and watched. Heard the wail of bagpipes lead in a parade of mourners. Law enforcement in rank and file. Family and friends milling in behind. Official-looking church folks directed traffic with appropriately solemn faces. The crowd swelled big enough the preacher spoke into a microphone. The words echoed over the green lawns, coming in waves to me, riding on the breeze.

When he finished, several folks, probably family, walked to the open grave, bent down, and grabbed fistfuls of dirt to drop inside it. Law enforcement officers stood at attention and snapped a salute while three riflemen in back fired seven times; the old twenty-one-gun salute.

Took forever for the crowd of uniforms to thin out. Midland PD had shown up in force, decked out in full dress blues. Dallas PD dwarfed their number. Feds from the DEA and probably a couple other agencies wore their best dark suits, sunglasses in place. But leave they did. Soon the only ones left were a grounds crew, two men in overalls with shovels, and one uniform. Midland PD, by the cut of it.

I stood and stretched, pulling my pants free from my damp ass. I took my time, willing the straggler to get the hell out of there, but he never budged. Fine. The walk from my vantage point should have taken three minutes. I took ten. No luck.

The cop had his back to me as I approached. I got within a few feet, and he spoke. With a female voice. "Took you long enough."

"Officer Kailey Carmichael. Should have known it was you."

"How you doing, Junior?"

"I'm not one for crowds. Especially at funerals. Especially cop funerals. Too many cops all in one place."

She chuckled. "I hear you. Did you catch it all from your little hill?"

"Thought I hid myself pretty good."

"You did. But I knew you'd be here. No way you were going to miss her funeral."

"Seemed like a nice one from up there."

"Should have seen it from down here. Several in my crew asked about you."

Silence.

Kailey took her cap off and wiped a forearm across her forehead. "Yeah, well, I think they did a real nice job. We always do when it's one of our own." She kicked at a piece of turf. "Got any plans?"

I looked at her. Tried to figure out the agenda behind the question. "You mean, don't leave town. Stay close. That sort of thing?"

She shook her head. "We're not all assholes, Junior. No. I really want to know. You seemed to be getting your life straight before . . . when . . ."

"When everything went to shit and two amazing women that seemed to give a crap about me got themselves killed."

She narrowed her eyes and stared hard at me. "It wasn't your fault, Junior. None of it."

"Easy to say."

"Not so easy. I've been where you're at."

"Doubt that."

"My husband murdered my sweet little girl, two years old, one of God's angels on earth. To get back at me for leaving him. I didn't get a chance to gut the bastard like you did. He chickened and shot himself before I got the chance."

"Jesus. I'm sorry."

"My mom died two months ago. The only other person in my life who gave a shit whether I lived or died. So yeah, I think I qualify. In fact, you may have a little catching up to do."

I laughed. On a day when I might have killed someone for cracking a smile, I actually laughed out loud. "If you don't mind, I'll let you keep the lead on that one."

We shared a chuckle and stood silent together. Neither one knowing what the hell to say.

I broke the silence and turned her question around on her. "You got any plans?"

She nodded solemnly. "Shinto and I are going to start in our tiny corner of Midland, Texas, and put every motherfucker who harms a child and/or a woman behind bars or in the ground. Whichever comes first."

"I like your style, Professor," I said.

"You ought to. I learned it from you."

"Harper would like that. And while we're on the subject of plans, I got some unfinished business of my own I want to clean up."

"I thought we took care of all your loose ends."

"Your DEA boys missed one. We're standing here because Miguel's mad dog stuck a knife in Harper's back. I owe her to make that right."

"Miguel's in Mexico, Junior. Surrounded by his cartel buddies. We have no jurisdiction in Mexico."

"I don't need jurisdiction. All I need is to get close to him."

"Let's make a deal."

"I haven't had great luck making deals with cops. No offense."

"Come back to Midland with me. We'll get you settled. I have a good friend in Dallas law enforcement we can use to go after Miguel. Together."

"I don't think so."

"Cartel's not going anywhere, Junior. Miguel's not going to disappear. Unless his partners in crime do the deed for us."

"That's what I'm worried about."

"Revenge isn't much of a plan, Junior. You've got a chance at a real life, with real goals, making a real difference. Don't screw that up."

"I'll think about it."

"Think harder." She stepped up to me and threw her arms around me and hugged me. Tight. Took me a second to return the hug. She pushed away from me and looked me in the eyes. "There're other people who care about you, Junior. If you give them the chance." She turned to leave. "See you back home."

"Hey, Professor," I called. "That rat hole restaurant of yours was—?"

"La Condesa?"

"Still in business?"

"Twenty-seven years and counting."

"Maybe we can order up some nachos and beer sometime."

She put her hat back on and squared it. "I'd like that. Oh." she snapped her fingers. "I almost forgot. Next semester starts in a month, and I'm getting the hang of this teaching thing. I'll expect you in your regular seat."

The End

ABOUT THE AUTHOR

Frances Hight is a third Generation California native who has lived in Oklahoma and Texas before finally settling in Florida. She is a multiple award-winning mystery/thriller writer with ties to critique groups in San Francisco and Orlando. She loves cooking and takes cooking classes when she travels posting photos of her successes and even tasty failures on social media.

Made in the USA
Columbia, SC
31 May 2021